PRISONER

ANNIKA MARTIN & SKYE WARREN

He seethes with raw power the first time I see him—pure menace and rippling muscles in shackles. He's dangerous. He's wild. He's the most beautiful thing I've ever seen.

So I hide behind my prim glasses and my book like I always do, because I have secrets too. Then he shows up in the prison writing class I have to teach, and he blows me away with his honesty. He tells me secrets in his stories, and it's getting harder to hide mine. I shiver when he gets too close, with only the cuffs and the bars and the guards holding him back. At night I can't stop thinking about him in his cell.

But that's the thing about an animal in a cage—you never know when he'll bite. He might use you to escape. He might even pull you into a forest and hold a hand over your mouth so you can't call for the cops. He might make you come so hard, you can't think.

And you might crave him more than your next breath.

PRAISE FOR PRISONER

CHAPTER ONE

~ABIGAIL~

HEAVY BARS CLOSE behind me with a clang. I feel the sound in my bones. A series of mechanical clicks hint at an elaborate security mechanism beneath the black iron plating. I knew this would happen—had anticipated and dreaded it—but my breathing quickens with the knowledge that I am well and truly trapped.

"Can I help you?"

I whirl to face the administrative window where a heavyset woman in a security guard uniform stares at her screen.

"Hi," I say, pasting on a smile. "My name is Abigail Winslow, and I'm here to—"

"Two forms of identification."

"Oh, well, I already filled out the paperwork at the front desk. And showed them my IDs."

"This isn't the front desk, Ms. Winslow. This is the east-wing desk, and I need to see two forms of identification."

"Right." I dig through my bag for my driver's license

and passport.

She accepts them without looking up, then hands me a clipboard with a stack of papers just like the ones I already filled out.

I've been dreading this day for weeks, wishing I'd been assigned any other project but this one. You'd think I was being sent here for a crime. My professor—the one who'd forced me into this—warned me that prisoners were not always receptive to outsiders. Apparently nobody here is.

I complete each form, arrange the pages neatly on the clipboard, and bring them back up to the window. The guard accepts them and gives back my IDs…still without looking at me.

My hands clench and unclench, clench and unclench while the guard eyes my paperwork.

Seconds pass. Or are they minutes? The damp chill of the place seeps in through my cardigan and leaves me shivering.

Leaning forward, I read the name tag of the guard. "Ms. Breck. Do you know what the next steps are?"

"You can have a seat. I have work to do now, and then I'll escort you back."

"Oh, okay." I glance at the bars I just came through, then the open hallway opposite. "Actually, if you just point me in the direction of the library, I'm sure I can—"

Thunk. The woman's hand hits the desk. I jump.

Her dark eyes are faintly accusing, and I wish we could go back to no eye contact. How did I manage to make an enemy in two minutes?

"Ms. Winslow," she says, her voice patronizing.

"You can call me Abby," I whisper.

A slight smile. Not a nice one. "Ms. Winslow, what do you think we do here?"

The question is clearly rhetorical. I press my lips together to keep from making things worse.

"The Kingman Correctional Facility houses over five thousand convicted criminals. My job is to keep it that way. Do we understand each other?"

Heat floods my cheeks. The last thing I want to do is make her job harder. "Right. Of course." I shamble back, landing hard on the metal folding chair. It wobbles a little before the rubber feet stop my slide.

I understand the woman's point. She has to keep the prisoners in and everyone else out, and keep people like me safe.

I reach down and pull a book from my bag. I never leave home without one, even when I go to classes or run errands. Even when I was young and my mother used to take me on her rounds.

Especially then.

I would hide in the backseat with my nose in the book, pretending I didn't see the shady people who came to her window when we stopped.

A little green light above the barred doors flashes on and there's an ominous buzz. Somebody's coming through, and I doubt it will be a library volunteer. I slide down.

Pretend to be invisible.

It's no use. I peer over the top edge as a prisoner saunters through the door, and my pulse slams in my throat double time.

He's flanked by two guards—escorted by them, I guess you'd say. But they seem more like an entourage than anything. Power vibrates around him like a threat.

Read, read, read. Don't look.

The prisoner is half a foot taller than the guards, but he seems to tower over them by more than that. Maybe it's his broad shoulders or just something about the way he stands, or his imperiously high cheekbones. The dark stubble across his cheeks looks so rough and unforgiving I can feel it against my palm; it contrasts wildly with the plushness of his lips. His short brown hair is mussed. There's one scar through his eyebrow that somehow adds to his perfection.

The little group approaches the window. I can barely breathe.

"ID number 85359," one of the guards says, and I understand that he's referring to the prisoner. That's who he is. Not John Smith or William Brown or whatever his name is. He's been reduced to a number. The woman at the desk runs through a series of questions. It's a procedure for checking him out of solitary.

The prisoner faces sideways, spine straight, the corner of his mouth tilted up as if he's slightly amused. Then it clicks, what else is so different about him: no visible tattoos. Tough guys like this, they're always inked up—it's a kind of armor, a kind of *fuck you.* This guy has none of it, though he's far from pristine; white scars mar the rough skin of his hands and especially his forearms, a latticework of pain and violence, a flag proclaiming the kind of underworld he came from.

The feel of brutality that hangs about him is compelling and...somehow beautiful.

I drink him in from behind my book—it's my mask, my protective shield. But then the strangest thing happens: he cocks his head. It's just a slight shift, but I feel his attention on me deep in my belly. I've been discovered. Caught by searchlights. Exposed.

My heart beats frantically.

I want him to look away. He fills up too much space. It's as if he breathes enough oxygen for twelve men, leaving no air for me at all. Maybe if we were in the library and he needed help finding a book or looking something up, then I wouldn't mind the weight of his attention.

No. Not even there. He's too much.

Two sets of bars on the gate. Handcuffs. Two guards.

What do they think he would do if there were only one set of bars, one guard?

My blood races as the guards draw him away from the window and toward the inner door, toward where I sit. His heat pierces the chill around me as he nears. His deep brown eyes never once meet mine, but I have the sense of him looming over me as he passes, like a tree with a massive canopy. He continues on, two hundred pounds of masculine danger wrapped in all that beauty.

Even in chains, he seems vibrant, wild and free, a force of nature—it makes me feel like I'm the one in prison. Safe. Small. Carefully locked down.

How would it feel to be that free?

"Ms. Winslow. *Ms. Winslow.*"

I jump, surprised to hear that the woman has been calling my name. "I'm sorry," I say as a strange sensation tickles the back of my neck.

The woman stands and begins pulling on her jacket. "I'll take you to the library now."

"Oh, that's great."

That shivery sensation gets stronger. Against my better judgment, I look down the hallway where the guards and the prisoner are walking off as one—a column of orange flanked by two thinner, shorter posts.

The prisoner glances over his shoulder. His mocking brown gaze searches me out, pins me with a subtle threat. Though it isn't his eyes that scare me. It's his lips—those beautiful, generous lips forming words that make my blood race.

Ms. Winslow.

No sound comes out, but I feel as though he's whispered my name right into my ear. Then he turns and strolls off.

Chapter Two

~Grayson~

I COLLAPSE ONTO the hard cement floor, cool against the sweat and burn of my arms and shoulders. Teke's up on the top bunk, scribbling in a notebook. He's been buried in that thing the whole hour I've been doing push-ups. What the hell is he writing? It's weird, him writing, and when you're locked up, you notice anything weird.

I yank out my earbuds and turn off my iPod, and the heavy bass is replaced by the tormented cries and mindless noise that goes on 24-7 in this place.

He catches me looking. "What?"

"You Stephen King up there or what?"

"Maybe."

I grunt like I don't care, but now I need to know. I sit up and mop my face with a threadbare washcloth. Teke never offers information for free. Putting me in here with him, it's just another punishment. Teke is dangerous, yeah. But not to me.

Guys inside, they're like dogs. They smell what you

are the moment they meet you. Decide right off whether they can fuck with you. I work a kink out of my neck, hoping he offers more.

"Telling my story." He flips a page. "It's therapeutic, man, don't you know?" His tone drips with sarcasm.

Now I really do look at him, because when you're inside, you don't reveal personal shit. That's how you survive. "The fuck?"

"My years as a poor misunderstood brown boy. For English class."

English class. That explains it. Teke's been working hard to better himself through education, or at least pretending to. I can't blame him. He gets time knocked off for educational achievements, and he has parole coming up. A family on the outside. A mother who still thinks he's innocent.

Nothing I do will cut my sentence or make my time easier. When you get convicted of killing a cop, you're done.

They put guys like Teke in prisons close to their family system so they can keep up their relationships with a hope to go straight.

It's the opposite with me. They put me hundreds of miles away from my crew. They took my phone and letter-writing privileges. No contact with the outside world.

Makes it hard to escape. But not impossible. Nothing stops me and my crew. Killing a cop is one of the only bad things I haven't done.

Teke keeps scribbling. "Just some tragic shit from high school."

"You're putting true shit in there?"

"Ms. Winslow knows when you make it up."

Ms. Winslow. My body stills as I flash back to her sitting there in that metal folding chair. The way she looked at me over her book.

That look was a bolt through my gut.

She had these fine features, like a doll or something, and her brown hair was up in a bun like some fucking librarian. Hiding behind her book. The kind of woman nobody sees, but I saw her. I saw the way she shifted. Saw myself twisting that long brown hair around my fist as I fucked her face.

I see you looking at me, I thought at her. *You take a good long look, baby.*

I've been told I'm beautiful. By women. By men. I hate it every time.

"Nothing close to the bone," Teke adds.

"You couldn't pay me enough to dance like a trained monkey for some teacher," I say. More than that, I would never tell anybody about my past. They wouldn't believe it if I did.

Teke eyes me. I'm pushing his buttons, but I can't stop because Ms. Winslow is at the other end of it. What is it about her?

"Telling some fucking sob story." I move to one-armed push-ups. Five sets of one hundred push-ups, and then I'll move on to jump squats.

Teke goes back to his notebook.

I burn through my set, but I can't get Ms. Winslow out of my mind, peering over the top of her book with those searching brown eyes, scared, maybe a little bit excited. And then that flare in her gaze when I tasted her name on my lips. *Ms. Winslow.*

My pulse kicks up. How would it feel to push her? To undo her? To break her fucking glasses? Because I got the sense she might like her glasses broken.

Yeah, the distance between prim and primitive is not so very motherfucking far. I wonder if Ms. Winslow knows about that.

I finish my set and collapse.

The more I think about it, the less I like the idea of Teke and the other guys telling Ms. Winslow personal stories.

"Stupid high school stories," he explains, maybe taking my silence for judgment of him.

I grunt.

"I don't give a crap," Teke continues, not that I asked. "Let all those fuckers on the Internet read it. See what I care."

My gaze rivets onto him. "What fuckers on the Internet?" None of us have access to the Internet.

"Our stories. They're going in this journal she's putting together. *The Kingman Journal.*"

"To go on the Internet?"

Teke shrugs. "Who's going to read it?"

I pat my forehead with the cloth, trying not to look like every cell in my brain is buzzing. She's putting the stories online…for the outside world to read. It's exactly the break I need.

"Maybe I'd like to write my memoirs," I say.

"What? You?"

I shrug. "Why the fuck not?"

"Too late. Class is full."

"Maybe there's room for one more."

Teke gives me a disgusted look because he knows I'll find a way in.

I put in my earbuds and crank the music, mind spinning.

I wait a day to try to get permission to sign up for the class, until Dixon is on duty. I go up to him at lunch. The newest guards on this wing, they'll say no to anything because they're scared assholes who don't want to look soft. The old-time guards want to break your balls. But a guy like Dixon, he's been around enough that he's done establishing his cred, but he hasn't put in enough years to erase the hope that people can better themselves.

He eyes me under his tan cap. "You suddenly want to take a class? You up to something?"

I shrug.

"An English class. *You* want to take an English class."

"What? I read. You've seen me reading." I know he has.

He twists his lips and pulls out his iPad. Every guard has one now. He turns it so I can't see and slides his thumb across the screen a few times. Maybe he feels protective of poor Ms. Winslow. Maybe he sees what I see—a woman so carefully put together, she's just begging to be messed with. But that's the last thing on my mind. I'm planning to be a star student.

"Guidelines say twelve to sixteen." He looks up. "I'm seeing sixteen. And it's already started."

"You can't stick another in? Maybe ask her…" Because guidelines are made to broken. Like rules. Like people.

He looks back down. "What about modern lit? That one's not full."

"I'm more interested in contemporary memoir," I say. That's Ms. Winslow's sixty-four-dollar name for the class. *Contemporary memoir.*

"I don't know," he says.

I wait. If he asks her, she'll say yes, and we both know it.

When you're inside, everything has a certain value,

and if you want it, you have to trade for it or fight for it. Cigarettes, protection, information, fresh air. If this guard was a fellow prisoner, I could strong-arm him a different way. But he's a guard, and so we bargain.

"Fifty bucks…"

"Guidelines say sixteen students," he says.

Damn. "A hundred." It's all I have.

He shakes his head. No.

This is dangerous. He knows I want it bad. He smells it—the guards have a sixth sense like that. But I have to get in. Teachers like Ms. Winslow don't last long; I'm betting *The Kingman Journal* won't make it past the first issue. And I need to put a little something in that issue.

I pull my iPod out and slap it onto his desk. My music. It took me months to save for the thing. Even more to buy a few good songs from the shit selection they have at the canteen. No Internet, remember? Well, that's about to change.

Dixon pulls out the jack and takes the iPod, leaving me with the earbuds. And just like that, I'm in.

CHAPTER THREE

~ABIGAIL~

THE ENGLISH DEPARTMENT hallway smells like dust and aging paper. I breathe it in, and my heart rate slows. This is a far cry from the cold, gray prison.

On the first day of class, I'd stood at the front of the room, hands clasped together, knuckles white, as sixteen men in orange jumpsuits filed in. I know what they saw—a prim, buttoned-up schoolgirl. They could sense my uneasiness. I gave out the syllabus, fumbling my speech, stiff and unnatural. The only good thing about the class was that the man from the east entrance hallway wasn't in there.

Ms. Winslow.

I couldn't get out of there fast enough, and I can't go back. I just can't.

I head toward my advisor's office, determined. Desperate. I need her to let me out of this project. One of my classmates is doing a memoir project with high schoolers. Others are working with veterans, nurses, the elderly. It's not fair that I got the prison inmates. Not when it drags up every bad memory I have. Not when I think I might belong there more than anyone knows.

No one can ever know.

I take my seat outside my advisor's office in Kendrick Hall. Scuff marks from thousands of students cover the faded hardwood floors, and the walls are still a vibrant mahogany, untouched by the years except for the gouges in the molding where people have etched initials and dates.

This building is like an ancient oak; we can leave marks, but the tree was here long before us and it will remain long after. I close my eyes. I've fought hard as hell to get here. I've made it two years—I'm a college sophomore now. I can't let this stop me. My whole life, the darkness has threatened to swallow me up, but I won't let it.

The door opens, and I stand. The woman who greets me is beautiful—glamorous, even—with bow-shaped lips and low-lidded eyes that makeup can't replicate. Her hair is blonde, bordering on gray, arranged in a wispy chignon.

"Abigail," she says with a smile. "Please come in."

"You could have called through the door." As usual she ignores the small note of worry in my voice. Politeness is a big deal for her. I understand that—it's a big deal for me too. Sometimes I think it's the only difference between the slums I come from and where I am now.

She winds her way through the cluttered office with ease. It would be impossible to tell she was blind if I didn't already know. It probably helps that she's worked at the same university, in the same office, for twenty years. She invited me into her office after my first day in her class, and I've been beyond grateful for the special interest she's taken in me.

Until our project started. Prison? No.

"So," she begins, settling into her seat, "did you blow them away with your eloquence and poise, the way you blow me away?"

I laugh unsteadily. "Not really. Not at all." I hate the idea of disappointing her. So few people have ever cared about me. But I hate the idea of that prison even worse. "It's not working. Isn't there any way I can change projects? The prison. It's too dark."

Like the way I am inside, but I can't tell her that.

"All the more reason to teach the class, Abigail." Her voice is faintly reproving. "What's really bothering you?"

She's not going to let me out; I can already tell. Panic bubbles up in me and pours out as words, desperate words. "I can't be effective in there. I'm wasting project funding. I'm wasting prison resources. They don't take me seriously—"

"You get them to take you seriously by taking them seriously," she says. "If you treat them like people, they will respond as people."

My mind flashes to the man in the hallway, the one who whispered my name. I think about telling Esther about him, but what would I say? *There was a man who made my heart beat twice as fast, who made me feel hot and cold at the same time.*

"It's not safe," I say.

Concern washes over her features. "Did you feel like you were in danger?" she asks.

I wish I could lie to her. "Not exactly danger…"

"Guards stayed with you?"

"Always," I admit.

"And the men? They behaved?"

"I guess. Aside from a few class comments. One suggested I got lost on my way to the little girl's room. Another suggested some alternate uses for my pointer."

A smile plays upon Esther's lips. "At least they won't lack for creativity. I do remember that," she says, and suddenly I'm the one remembering. Esther hasn't always been blind. And I already know she taught a class at the prison, back when she was an undergrad like me. "Did you feel as though you were in physical danger?"

"No." It's not the inmates I'm afraid of, not really. It's the whisper that says I might not be different from them.

"Then what's the danger, Abigail?"

I know what she's thinking—that I'm too timid, too

safe, in my writing and my life. *Be more open, be more willing. If it doesn't scare you, it's not worth writing about.* She's always pushing me to explore the shadows inside me. She doesn't understand.

"It's not right for me."

"I know you don't want to be there, but it's not only about you. Those men have committed to your class— you can't fail them now, and contrary to your own very faulty self-assessment, you have what it takes to be a wonderful teacher for them. I see it, even if it's hard for you to do the same."

I'm shaking my head, glad she can't see me.

She sighs. "Two more classes. Stick it out for two more sessions and if you still don't like it, we'll talk about changing your project."

"Really?"

She purses her lips.

"Thank you," I say.

"Those men may seem resistant to what you do. But a few of them need desperately to speak, to tell their stories. Some people need to tell their stories in order to be healed, to be whole, and you can give them a space in which to do that. You have a gift, Abby. You care deeply about stories, about people. That's what they need."

I think of the man in the hallway and wonder what story he might tell.

CHAPTER FOUR

~ABIGAIL~

I SET THE last memoir essay on top of the stack and take a deep breath. I may hate being here, in this room more like a prison cell than a library, but I have to admit the essays were some of the best things I'd ever read. Raw emotion tossed onto the page as if it weighed nothing.

My dad was in lockup for hitting my mom. I tried out for orchestra even though he said not to. He couldn't do nothing from jail. I didn't make the cut, though. It's probably for the best cause he got out early for good behavior.

Did Teke's father hit him too? Was that what had changed him from the hopeful musician to a hardened criminal? I press the heels of my palms to my eyes. *Get it together.*

A loud clang. They're coming. The library is small, but it takes them a long time to wind around the tall metal shelves in their orderly formation. I can hear them shuffling, the clink of metal cuffs a chilling accompaniment.

Our classroom is a space in the back of the resource center with sixteen chairs and desks arranged, like everything in this prison, in an unimaginative square—four up the side and four across. A desk and chair set reserved for me faces the area where the men are to sit, like an old-school classroom. The desk at the head of the class is a reminder that I'm in charge, even if I don't always feel it.

The furniture is bolted to the floor so it can't be used as weapons. No walls or doors separate us from the main area, but I don't mind. The guys spend enough of their day penned inside. In the library, with the scent of old paper and book glue wafting through the air, they can be in the open.

I greet each student as he rounds the nearest shelf. "Hello, Teke. Griff. Good morning, Jacob."

Some of them return the greeting. Others grunt or nod. A few ignore me completely, not meeting my eyes.

All the seats are full. I wait for Mr. Dixon to round the corner. He's the guard assigned to watch my class, and he always brings up the rear. *Never turn your back,* he explained the first day. I'd asked him then if he'd like to participate, since he had to sit in anyway. He blushed and told me he'd better focus on the task at hand. That was too bad. I bet he'd have stories to tell.

Except the man who turns the corner after all the students are seated isn't wearing a brown guard's uniform.

My breath catches. *Him.*

My gaze darts away, running for cover, before I can stop myself. *Chin up.* I may be young—younger than anyone else in the room—but I'm in charge. I'm the teacher, even if it's only a required project for my undergrad class. My pulse thumps unsteadily, and my hands become slick with sweat.

It's not his fault that his eyes are like dark diamonds, hard and deep. It's not his fault that he stands a whole head taller than Dixon, the guard, or that his neck is as thick as a tree trunk.

It's not his fault that he's terrifying—and strangely compelling too. So handsome it's hard not to look. Offensively handsome.

I force a smile. I can do this. "Hello, I'm Ms. Winslow."

Of course, he already knows my name. He mouthed it from across the hall.

No, I'm overthinking this. He's probably forgotten it by now. I'm nothing to him. I'm nobody. That theory seems to hold when he nods and says simply, "Ma'am."

"I'm sorry I didn't get a chance to tell you earlier," Dixon says. "There's one more student for you."

One more student I can deal with. But him? "He's already missed two classes."

Dixon looks uneasy. His gaze doesn't meet mine.

"Grayson's a smart one. Won't cause you any trouble, I'm sure."

Grayson. There's something almost regal about it. About him.

But Dixon is wrong—Grayson is already causing me trouble. The class is sitting idle while we figure this out. And I'll have to work with this guy one-on-one to get him caught up, and that feels so personal. Memoirs *are* personal, which is exactly why I don't want this guy in my class. Bad enough I have to be here; I don't need this strange awareness I have of him. *Attraction.*

I shake my head. "Maybe he can join a different class. There's not really a desk for him anyway."

That seems to stump Dixon, who touches his shirt pocket as if the answer to this problem might be in there. But it's not like he can bring in a new desk and chair and weld them to the floor.

"I'll stand," Grayson says in that low voice.

I raise an eyebrow. "Then how would you write?"

The corner of his lip turns up, a faint challenge that Dixon can't see. "One word at a time, same as all of them."

His comment makes me smile. I'm probably not supposed to. *No weakness.* But he's really kind of a bastard.

I hate that I like it.

"You'd have to do extra assignments to catch up."

Grayson nods, his expression somber. I can't believe he wants to be here, but then I remember what Esther said, about people who are desperate to tell their stories and sometimes they don't even know it. Who am I to turn him away?

"You can take my desk."

"Where will you sit?" Dixon protests, but it doesn't feel genuine.

My smile is wry. "I'll stand. I'm not the one who needs to be writing."

"Go on then," Dixon says, peering down at his iPod or his phone or whatever he's pulled from his pocket. He's not very attentive, but I haven't minded. I've never felt unsafe with the sixteen felons in my class. Until Grayson, who makes me nervous just by looking at me. My gaze falls to his forearm, scarred with white lines. The scarring looks almost deliberate, some kind of an X with strange detailing on the ends. Like a barbarian tattoo.

My gaze snaps up to meet his. He's seen me staring. He moves toward me with a mixture of distaste and fascination. I finger the top button on my shirt, feeling exposed, wishing I'd grabbed my cardigan from my desk, wishing I'd worn pants instead of a skirt, not that it would matter. I feel like Grayson can see right through my clothes, right through my defenses.

All prison aisles and passageways are roomy, wide

enough for at least three guys. Mr. Dixon told me it's that way on purpose—it makes it easier for the guards to cooperate when a man must be subdued, and it cuts down on prisoner conflicts in passing. But Grayson fills the space. He's huge, invasive. Alive on my skin.

I move to the side as he approaches, making myself small. "Have a seat," I say sharply. "We have a lot of work to do."

In a voice deep and velvety, he murmurs, "Yes, Ms. Winslow."

Shivers slide down my spine. I feel the way I did the first time he said my name, but it's stronger now that I can hear him. With just a few syllables he puts me off balance. What will he do with a whole essay?

I watch him saunter on toward the front, sooty brown hair cut short, big, muscular shoulders outlined where his jumpsuit pulls tight. His walk is slow and loose and cool. He moves like he owns the room.

Then he takes my seat in the front, settling in his muscular bulk, shifting slightly sideways, making himself comfortable in the shitty, too-small chair, a barbarian prince on a throne. How is he doing this?

And then he smiles at me.

God, that smile. It should be illegal.

I tear my eyes away, feeling flustered and a little angry, and address the class.

"I was so impressed with the pieces you turned in

this week. I felt like you guys really ran with the assignment. The art of memoir is bound up in the small things. A long-ago incident. The way the light catches on something." I go on with my prepared talk, clutching the papers they'd turned in via Dixon.

The first day of class I'd made the mistake of asking for the guys to recall meaningful incidents in their essays, and I'd gotten a lot of bullshit narratives—stuff about cars, hitting home runs, performing musically, even a tale of a ride on a yacht. Just that broke my heart. So for the second assignment, I'd asked for something small and meaningless. The only guideline: it has to be true. And I would know if it wasn't.

The results are moving—tales of everyday disappointments and small cruelties they professed not to care about. Protesting too much.

I go on, struggling to stay cool and composed—not easy with Grayson's gaze heavy on my body. I can see him in my periphery, occupying my desk, the one barrier I had.

And suddenly I realize that he knows it. He knows exactly what he took from me. Control is something he understands. I learned about it too, early on. I learned who to avoid on the street. I learned when to stand my ground. He sprawls there, an insolent lion, thrumming with relaxed power.

It's cool in the library. Goose bumps cover my skin,

and beneath my bra, my nipples turn hard. I want desperately to grab the cardigan off the back of my chair, but *he's* there.

I swallow and smile brightly. This is *my* class, and I'm in control. "Today I want to narrow the scope a little bit more," I say as if my heart's not pounding a billion times a second. "We're going to think about objects. I'm going to have you open your notebooks and list twenty random"—here I raise a cautionary finger—"*but specific* objects from where you last lived. For example, a fork. But you can't simply say *a fork*. You have to say something about it. For instance, where I live, we have this fork in our utensil drawer—my dorm roommates and I got it in a silverware grab bag at a flea market, and it's the best fork in the place. The other ones we have are from Target and they're flimsy, but this one, it's thick and substantial, way nicer to hold, so we always fight over who gets it, because it's just better—"

A few of the guys are chuckling. Others are exchanging glances and stifling laughter. My face heats when I realize what else my description sounded like.

"Hey!" Dixon barks out; then he goes back to his phone.

I make the mistake of shooting a glance up front, at Grayson. He's not laughing and tittering like the rest of the class. No, he's just sitting there, brown eyes glinting. I flash on how big he would be, how it would feel to hold him *there*. My cheeks heat to an epic burn.

And he quirks his lips.

Oh God.

I turn away, a deer caught in the headlights, determined not to lose control of the moment. "But without the dirty double meaning, please. No bananas…" If you can't beat 'em, join 'em, right? "No doughnuts, or…you know. Got it? I mean it." Then I just laugh. It's my nervousness and the craziness of it all. "Oh my God, I can't believe I said that."

This breaks the tension. Guys are snickering and smiling. A few make wisecracks—nothing too outrageous, because Dixon is on alert now, but it's as if we're all laughing together. As if we're being real with each other. Humans, not numbers. And suddenly, I feel good. I didn't want to be here, still don't, but since I have to, this isn't so bad. As long as I ignore the concrete walls closing in on me and the metal bars on the windows. And Grayson.

I'll give you twenty minutes." There's a shuffle of papers. At the end of the twenty minutes, I'll have them expand on the item they feel the most energy around. That will be the next assignment.

I look over at Grayson, who's been observing all of this with an expression that's unreadable, but I can't help but think that he's annoyed. As if I've done something he doesn't like, or maybe he prefers me flustered and out

PRISONER

of control. I set the papers aside on the media table, steel myself, and walk to him.

"Can I have my…" I point to my sweater on the back of the chair.

He twists his big body and grabs it off. My belly tightens deep down as I look at my soft sweater lying across his rough, corded hand. He's taken my refuge, my seat, my sense of control. He looks at me like he *sees* me. Oh, it's good he's chained up—it really is.

He holds it out to me on a finger, closer. "I don't bite," he says. "Much."

I snort and grab it. My finger brushes his and sparks enough electricity to jolt my heart out of my chest.

He sits back, watching me pull my sweater on. It feels strangely intimate, dressing while he watches, and makes me thankful for Dixon's presence, distracted as he is. And for the other guys, busily scribbling away, whispering when they think I'm not looking. I can't imagine what it would be like to be alone with this guy. He scares me in a way that's different than a dark-alley scare. An alley I'd know how to handle. Him? Not so much.

I grab my briefcase and set it on the corner of his desk, rooting around for the papers I passed out on the first day. My gaze isn't meeting his, but that's only because I can't find what I need. My voice comes out low so as not to disturb the rest of the class. "So you're

29

interested in creative writing?"

His voice is quiet. Rough. Slightly mocking. "Yes, I am, Ms. Winslow."

My cheeks heat again. If it weren't for the menace glittering in his eyes, he'd be beautiful.

"Here's the class schedule. You've missed two assignments, but it's no more than a few paragraphs of writing." I explain the assignments—the meaningful event and the non-meaningful event. "We'll be doing exercises for a few weeks and then choose one exercise to polish. Toward the end we'll create a journal to be published online and in print, full of our vignettes."

His lips quirk at the word *vignette.* I wonder suddenly what level of education he's had. Being that he's a latecomer, they didn't supply me with his background info like I got with the other guys. Does he ping on the word because he doesn't know it? Or maybe he does know, and he finds it pretentious.

Who cares? I'm the teacher here. I'm in charge. I set the briefcase on the desk like a wall between us.

CHAPTER FIVE

~GRAYSON~

S HE STANDS THERE behind her fortress of a briefcase. Books, briefcases, glasses—it all just makes me think about exposing her, stripping her, making her helpless. She'd hate it and love it—I know that for a fact. It's like I know her even though I never saw her before this week.

My mind goes to the glasses. How well can she see without them? I'm hoping not well at all, because it would be hot if I took them away. Hot for me and also for her.

And then there are blindfolds.

Snap out of it. I'm here to be the perfect student. I should be focusing on her silly assignment, listing objects.

She's digging in her briefcase for something. "…since you don't have one of your own."

She pulls out a clothbound notebook, worn on the edges. I watch her page through, dark brows furrowed. She has an old-fashioned look, features carved with a delicate instrument, perfectly polished, eyes big and soft.

I can imagine her in a black-and-white photo standing in front of some old-timey farm, pitchfork in hand, with that prim look. Prim in a way that gets me all kinds of hot.

Her lips are moist, or at least the top one is because she sucks it in when she's nervous, and I want more than anything to suck it in myself and maybe even bite it. And to take those glasses away. Every house I've ever robbed, every establishment, it's the same story—you identify the first line of defense and take it away. That's how you get control. For her, it's those glasses.

She's ripping pages out of her notebook, and now I feel shitty because it's obviously her writing book and she's clearing it for me to use. What's in there that she doesn't want me to see? She pushes it across the desk, open to the next blank page.

"You write in it upside down and from the back?" I ask.

"Yeah," she says. "I'd rather have my margins at the bottom instead of the top." She folds the pages and stuffs them into her case. "It's easier on the hand."

I nod. Modifying your tools. That's a pro thing to do. I find I like that. Admire it, even.

"Twenty objects. You understand?"

"Yes, Ms. Winslow," I say.

She blinks.

I need to stop saying her name like that. She turns

away, addressing the class. "How are we doing? Questions?" Her bid is met with silence. She walks up the side of the room in that pencil skirt and now that red cardigan, which felt soft as kitten fur. "As insignificant or boring as you want. It just has to be true. No fake stuff." Up she walks, and around the back. "The most boring bit of honesty is worth ten thousand times as much as the most glittering piece of fiction in this class."

I look at Teke in the back row, scribbling away, and I think about what he said—that she knows when you make stuff up. But will she really?

The idea of giving her anything real from my past feels like acid in my gut. Too high a price to pay. But I have to get in that online journal.

Stone's got alerts set up for certain terms; it's a way we identify places to hit. Whatever I write, if I weave in the right terms, he'll see it in her little magazine. He can't call me, but he knows I'm here, and it won't take him long to catch my message. The censors are good here—I can only sneak in a name, who to bribe, but that's all I'll need. Stone and the guys can take it from there.

But my instructions to the gang have to be hidden inside something devastating enough to create a smoke screen. I have to make up something good, because no way can I give her anything real.

Teke raises his hand, and she walks over to him. He

points to something on his paper, lips moving as he asks a question soft enough where I can't hear. Apparently she can't either, because she leans closer.

I grit my teeth. Every guy in here is checking her out. Even Dixon, who's married with three kids. He looks too. I mean, she could be eighty years old and they'd still be looking, because we're hard up. But she's not eighty. She's...what? Eighteen? Nineteen? Eyes so fucking hopeful. God, she's young.

But not too young. The curves beneath her stiff linen skirt give that much away. She's all woman.

Forcing my gaze away, I glare down at the blank sheet of paper. Twenty things. Ordinary things. *Real things.* This is gonna be easy. If I could fool the head of the Cincinnati Art Museum into letting me "appraise" the tsar exhibit, this girl doesn't stand a chance. I almost feel bad for her.

Another guy speaks up without raising his hand. "The last place I lived was the Jersey Penitentiary. There wasn't ten things in the whole place."

That draws a laugh.

"Twenty things," she says, not backing down. I like that about her, how she tries to be strict. It won't work on me, but the other men here, they respond to authority. She gets that.

An image of a baseball game forms in my mind. I didn't play much baseball—they took me away when I was five, but I remember tagging along with my older foster brothers. They gave me the position of point guard. They'd make me be point guard and wear the right-handed mitt, and I would stand next to the water bottles and keys and keep score and get the balls. Those were the happiest times I remember, out in the sunshine playing baseball with my older brothers. I barely knew what I was doing—I don't know shit about baseball except that part.

That was one of the things I would daydream about after they took me away. I start my list:

Water bottle next to a chain-link fence.
A piece of glass that is perfectly sharp on two corners, but with soft ridges on the other corner.
Flattened Taco Bell cup full of ants.
Right-handed mitt.
Mike's hat for first base.
My shoe for second base.
Scrubby dandelion in the dust.

Working my way around the playground, I fill out the list just as she claps her hands.

"Pencils down," she says like we're taking some big test. "Now we're going around the room, and each of you will share one thing from the list. You get to pick which thing. It can be the most important thing, or the least. Big or small. Anything you want." She nods toward

Teke. "Go ahead."

Teke's nervous. Sweating. It's weird to see him this way. He could crush her as soon as look at her. That's how fucked up prison is—it reverses the natural order of things.

"There was a pistol," he finally says. "A Beretta. But not just any gun. It got me through some tough times, you know. Kind of like it was lucky or something."

She beams at him, all proud that he came up with something meaningful. It makes my gut twist. If the gun had been lucky, he wouldn't be here.

Each of the guys has her full attention as they share their piece. It feels faintly like jealousy, watching her. I want her attention on me, but it never comes. We hear about a plaid couch. A hat. A key chain.

I pick up a pattern—she likes the personal stuff. The embarrassing stuff. She lights up on stuff you feel shitty about.

She never calls on me. Every guy here shares something except for me.

"Now I want you to pick one item, whatever you feel the most strongly about, and write a paragraph about it."

What. The. Fuck? I raise my hand.

She comes over, her eyebrow raised coolly. "Yes, Grayson."

Grayson. Is that supposed to mess me up, when she says my name low and throaty? Hell, it just makes me want to hear it again. But closer, quieter. Along with buttons flying, silk tearing. Petal-soft skin I can bite and mark.

"Why didn't you call on me?"

"This was your first class. I didn't want to put you on the spot."

I'd wanted to test my theory. Now I can't. "Are you going to read our paragraphs?"

She hesitates. "That's the idea. Feedback helps you improve and eventually prepare your work for publication."

I can't completely hide the smirk at that. *Publication.* Of our *vignettes.* She's so fucking overblown. Instead of being annoyed, though, I find it hot.

Her eyes narrow. "There's only fifteen minutes left, so you'd better get writing."

"Yes, Ms. Winslow."

Something flashes in her eyes before she turns away. And I write, because this is important. Getting her approval so I can send a message to my crew.

I think about my foster brothers and the kind of things they used to feel shitty about. I remember the Jordan Clinic incident—my brother felt shitty about that. It was right after he made the high school baseball team.

I decide to write his story like it's mine. I don't know much about baseball—I was five when I stopped playing any kind of games—but I'm going to try to fake it. That's typical childhood shit, right? I try to imagine what it would've been like.

It's the happiest day of my life when I make the high school baseball team. Me and the guys go out celebrating, and we get really wasted. We get wild and start throwing rocks at windows and tagging walls like we sometimes do. I guess they all deserved it except Jordan Clinic. Mr. Jordan, he was never anything other than nice to us kids, but we trashed his window and spray painted inside.

I really get into it, using the scene where he told me.

The next day, I took my uniform out of the box. And my mitt. As point guard, I got the right-handed mitt. I tell my little brother about what we did, pretending it's all a joke, but even he can see how shitty I feel about Jordan Clinic. How bad old man Jordan would feel when he saw what we did. I put on the uniform for him and show it off, but I just feel bad...

I can still see him in our room; I can still taste how guilty he felt.

It's a little heavy-handed, but I think she'll buy it. Senseless violence and guilt. How can you go wrong with that?

CHAPTER SIX

~ABIGAIL~

S TUDENTS FILL THE space around me, expanding through the hallway like a deep, rushing breath. In and out, like the school is meditating its way through a day of classes. In a few minutes they thin out, leaving the door to Esther's office in plain sight.

My appointment started fifteen minutes ago, and I've been standing here for much longer than that. I've done my two additional sessions at the prison like I said I would. I need her to let me out of the class. She'll be disappointed, but it's too much for me. *He's* too much for me.

I square my shoulders and knock.

"Come in, Abby," she calls right after my knock, her voice serene, expectant but not impatient.

I push inside and find her in front of her desk. Did she know I was standing just six feet away? From her gentle smile and squeeze of her hand on my shoulder, she did.

"I'm sorry I'm late," I say. "I don't know what got

into me."

"There's nothing to worry about."

That's it. No pressure. She settles herself behind her desk and waits for me to speak.

I start haltingly. "Well, they didn't mock me the last two class sessions like they did at first. That's one thing at least."

She nods encouragingly. "You connected with them."

"The first pieces of writing they turned in were…overblown. Their second set of assignments, you could feel the truth. That part was good." I think about the way we laughed together. Maybe there was a little connection. But I think they need someone older, someone who actually wants to be there. And I need to be anywhere but prison. "It's not a total failure, but…"

She waits.

"It's still not going to work. I haven't changed my mind. The class feels out of control." I'm the one who feels out of control.

"It sounds just the opposite," she says.

"I got a new student," I say. "The class was full."

"Ah," she says, a wealth of meaning in that one word.

"I said he could join the class, but there are too many students now, and everything's falling apart. It's not working. Bottom line." And that was the deal we made. I need her to not go back on it. I did my time; now I want out—just like the inmates have their sentence and then they're free.

"All right." There's no censure in her voice. I want there to be censure. "He's disruptive?"

"Not really. Even though he's sitting in my chair. He took over my chair." I stifle a smile. He really is kind of brazen.

"And your class? Has he taken that over too?"

"Not really." *Not the class. More like my mind. Even my body.* He keeps popping into my thoughts in a sexual way, and I'm not really a sexual person. Don't have time for that sort of thing, anyway. "The prisoner... Grayson...he's a good student. He's magnetic, persuasive, and clearly very intelligent. A bullshitter, though. But even his bullshit is...haunting."

"How so?"

"With the other students, their stories were boastful. Lifestyles of the rich and famous." I pause, thinking about his telling detail—the baseball point guard. There's no such position. And he's right handed—he wouldn't wear a right-handed mitt. "Grayson talked about baseball in his piece, and even though he obviously grew up in America and everything, he got it all wrong. From what he said, you'd think he never played it. That's how they used to bust Russian spies, you know? Because what American boy doesn't know baseball?" As Esther nods, I go on. "It's eerie. Even the poorest American boy knows the sport. Even kids in juvie. It's one of those lies that reveal too much."

"He has a story," she offers.

"I guess. But somebody else can help him better than I can. Anybody else."

"Is that your job? To help him?"

"No," I say, feeling petulant. I know what's coming.

"No, your job is to give him a safe space within which to tell his story. That's the gift of the class."

She doesn't get it—I don't have a space large enough for Grayson. He feels endless and frightening, full of secrets and strange magnetism. Like a black hole where, if I go near the edge, I might fall in and never find my way out.

She leans forward, brow furrowed with concern. "He didn't…touch you, did he?"

A little zap of surprise jolts me. "He never touched me."

Even if a glance felt more intimate than a touch.

"Okay," she says. "If you want to switch up projects, I'll look at your joining Callie at the senior center."

She's trying to hide her disappointment, but I can feel it, and I'm suddenly pissed at myself. I'm better than this. Stronger than this. Last class time, I'd made that nice connection with the guys, and what if one of them really needs to tell his story? What if Grayson does? Nobody threatened me. Nobody touched me.

Nobody ever can.

I sit up straighter. "Never mind. I'll stay."

Her expression clears. "You're sure?"

"I've gotten this far. I'll finish it out." There are just a few more weeks. I'll ignore Grayson and focus on the journal. I'll get it done and get on with my degree, with my life, and forget I ever met a prison inmate named Grayson.

✧   ✧   ✧

I SIT AT my post in front of sixteen desks and chairs that will soon be filled with my students, including Grayson, who will take my chair and desk, as he did the last time. No, he won't just take it—he'll own it. He'll watch me while he does it, enjoying every second.

We're doing private conferences today. The conference with Grayson will be hardest. I shuffle through their papers, marked in red but hopefully not too much. My heart pounds.

The men are to read silently under Dixon's watch—I've photocopied an essay by James Baldwin I thought they would enjoy, and I'll pull them out one by one to discuss how their final projects might evolve from the seeds they've sown during the exercises. We'll conference at the small table at the far side of the resource area. Not exactly private but removed enough to have a quiet conversation. I'm hoping to get through them fast so I can duck into the little office and hide out with a book.

The clock hits 1:59, and I go to stand at the edge of the space. I've worn a suit jacket today. Armor. I hadn't needed it until Grayson.

I greet them by name as they file in. Jordan. LeShawn. Roman. Teke. They take their usual seats.

Grayson's always at the end of the line. At first I thought it was because he likes it that way, the bad kid sitting in the back of the bus. Now it occurs to me that it lets Dixon keep a closer watch on him. Like Grayson is dangerous, or some kind of escape artist or something, so big and brutish and insolent.

He comes around the corner, fixing me with an amused gaze. I look down at his thick wrists, chained loosely together, and at his muscular forearms and the white scars etching his skin. Raised scars, and it's definitely a design. Did he do that? Or did somebody else? My heart pounds as I imagine what it would feel like if I touched it—smooth? Rough? Hard? He seems hard all over, but of course there would be soft parts of him too.

My cheeks heat.

"Hello, Ms. Winslow," he whispers as he passes by, and the intimacy of it steals my breath. Like he guessed my thoughts...and some dark part of me finds that exciting.

I swallow it down.

"Hello, Grayson," I say, grateful that he's under guard. He's too big, too beautiful, too dangerous, too everything. He steals the show. He fills the room. He leaves a wake of pure energy in my belly as he continues to the front.

I hand out the essays, and I relate the plan for the day, the way my professors sometimes do. "We'll be conferring on which the exercises to develop and polish. I'll choose a few to be published in the journal— anonymously, and only if you want to be included." I've said this before, but I want to make sure they understand. "You'll get class credit for doing the work. Being published in the journal is just an extra, okay?"

The sessions go by quickly. Griffin'll be doing a piece on a collection of beer mugs he was given by an elderly neighbor. I encourage Teke to get deeper into the experience of the day his dad got out of prison. A few of them talk about becoming fathers. It makes me feel a little bad about the way I thought about dumping this project.

Grayson's last. He takes his chair, casually crossing his ankles like tree trunks between us, settling his hands onto his thighs. His heat fills the space. How does the prison even hold him?

I smile nervously and cast my eyes to the other side of the space, where Dixon halfheartedly watches over the guys. Still, it makes me feel better, knowing he's there.

He'd protect me if anything happened. Wouldn't he?

I look back to find Grayson's sharp eyes twinkling, lashes dark and thick, all that knowing allure. My breath speeds up, and my hand flies to my glasses as if to adjust them even though they're perfectly straight. Sometimes I just need to do that.

"Let's see." I shuffle the papers, finding his. For a second my gaze strays over to the corded muscles of his forearms, brushed with a smattering of hair. The strange design, like a white tattoo. But it's not a tattoo. It's a scar. Even chained together, his hands are muscular, massive, capable.

I picture him standing in front of me and touching the bottom of my chin, lifting my face to look up at him, running a finger down my neck. I imagine his thick finger resting against the tender divot at the base of my neck.

"I'm excited about the journal," he says, startling me.

I straighten. He sounds genuine, as though he really is excited about it. God, what am I doing? "I'm glad," I say.

He nods. "I like the idea of different voices filling the bandwidth. It's what the fucking Internet is for, right?"

I nod eagerly until I realize he's just feeding me my own sentiments, crudely rephrased. I slide over his papers. "The journal is memoir. Not fiction."

He cocks his head. Regards me warily.

"And what you've given me…"

His eyes darken. His voice is husky. "You calling me a liar, Ms. Winslow?"

My mouth goes dry. "I don't think it's a real story. Or at least, it's not your story."

He looks at me long and strong, and my pulse goes into overdrive. I can't read him, but it doesn't take a genius to know he's not happy with me. Again I look down at his hands.

He finally speaks. "You don't think it's real?"

I swallow and place my hands in my lap. "I don't."

His massive chest rises and falls with his every breath. I wonder what he did. I wonder what happened to him. How can he not know baseball? Why does he have the scar design? What makes him seem so different from other guys?

"You know why I'm in here?" he asks suddenly.

I shake my head. "That's not something they tell us." I get the feeling he knows that, and that the question was designed to taunt. I glance again at Dixon, who's out there talking with the guys in front of the block of desks. When I look back, I find Grayson eyeing my hands, still in my lap. Or maybe he's just eyeing my lap.

The line running between us pulls tight. I'm in charge, but he has all the power. I shouldn't allow that. I shouldn't like that.

I remind myself that I know more than he does

about stories. I know that when you tell a fake story about yourself, it's because you're protecting the real story.

He seems excited about the journal. So I use it. "You'll get credit for doing the writing, but you can't get into the journal with anything fake."

His eyes glitter.

Chapter Seven

~Grayson~

THE CLASS IS about getting out of this place. I remind myself of that over the three weeks we spend on what Ms. Winslow calls drafting. But I get into it a little.

She's standing beside the desk when we shuffle into the library classroom. I think it makes her feel safe and in control. She greets all us guys by name, as if to prove that she remembers us. That we matter.

The sound of my name from her lips makes me tense, just like always. I never get tired of those pencil skirts. Does she know how the fabric hugs her? She couldn't look hotter in a goddamned bikini. I want to run my hands over her hips, tracing her shape through the fabric. Wouldn't even need to undress her. I could come just from that.

I walk over and take my place at her desk. Take her chair. Her space. She doesn't look at me, but I can tell she feels it—there's something that connects us, like underground electric lines. My gaze rests on the tan canvas bag she brings to class every day, full of books.

She heads to the side of the room. "Today we're going to journal with a prompt," she says, adjusting her glasses. It didn't take me long to figure out they're her protection, the way she pushes them up on her nose when she's nervous, shifts them while she thinks. "Close your eyes for a moment and imagine you're falling. Is there a parachute? Where are you falling from? What do you see on the ground? How does it feel?"

I close my eyes and imagine my hand sliding underneath her tight skirt, between her legs. Two fingers working the fabric of her panties over her clit. It's become an obsession of mine, all the ways I could make her come without really touching her.

Her sexy voice intrudes. "Do you feel scared? Exhilarated?"

Yeah, both of those. It's been that way my whole life, a feeling of falling. Sometimes I wake up at night with a jolt, arms raised to protect myself even though nothing's there. No one's been able to hurt me for a long time, and I keep it that way.

Though lately I've been waking up with a hard-on. I have to beat off just to get some rest.

So really, she's the one who's making me come without touching me.

"Don't take the first word that comes to your mind. I want you to really think into it, feel it. The right word is so important, you guys."

She walks up and down the side, eyes bright. She wants us to feel so much. She cares. It makes me want to shake her or something. Warn her about caring too much about people like us.

Because sometimes we start to care back. And that wouldn't be good for her.

"The right word makes all the difference," she continues, "and finding the right word has nothing to do with vocabulary. The right word is already inside you. You just have to dig in and find it. And I know you can. Don't settle for a vague word either. You're better than that. Go for the precise word. Dig deeply. Challenge yourselves."

She turns, strolls the other way, seventeen pairs of eyes following her ass. A strand of dark hair has fallen from her bun. I picture tucking it behind her ear, real gentle. That would be a challenge: being gentle.

"Go ahead and write, then," she says in her encouraging tone. She means it. So sweet my teeth ache. I want her to use that voice to say other things. *Go ahead and kiss me, then. Go ahead and lick me, then.*

Go ahead and fuck me.

Yes, Ms. Winslow.

This is getting to be a problem. I'm in class for one purpose—to escape. Nothing kills my hard-on faster than thinking about captivity. I can't stand walls. I don't even like ceilings. The bars... I'm fucking allergic to the bars.

I spent the first week in lockup in full-on panic. Shaking, throwing up. Yeah, it was a regular carnival ride. Then the public defender—he was a good guy, actually—started making noise about the situation, so they brought a psych in.

That was the worst.

They shot me full of so many drugs I couldn't see straight. Couldn't stop the nightmares from coming. The only thing I hate worse than lockup is being drugged, so I actually worked with the psych, doing his bullshit breathing techniques and saying this and that to myself. It works—most of the time.

It's not falling that scares me. At least there I'm out in the open. It's the cage waiting for me on the ground that fucks with my head.

I look up and find her watching me from the side of the room. "Question?" She pushes off the wall and moves toward me.

"I can't think of anything," I say.

"It looked to me like you had an idea."

"Not the kind that's fit to print," I say. "Especially not in a *vignette,* if you know what I mean."

I meant to put her off guard, like it was something X-rated, which partly it was, but she just looks at me, unblinking and unafraid. Again I have this feeling of knowing her even though I don't. I wonder if she feels like she knows me too.

"Can't you imagine falling?" she asks.

I don't need to imagine it. I know how it feels.

I look around, but everyone's busy writing. "You know that game little kids play where they stand in a circle and one falls and the others catch him? Not one motherfucker in here would ever play that game. Any one of us would rather get punched in the face. So you think we're going to be playing that game on paper?" I cross my legs. "No one here wants to think about falling. Giving up that kind of control."

"Including you? You won't play the game, not even on paper?"

I shrug. "You're saying you want the truth, so…"

"Are you refusing to do it?"

"I'm being honest here. Giving you something you say you want." Christ. She cares so much about guys being honest, she has me telling her something none of the other guys ever would. I feel like I'm in the mind-fuck hall of mirrors.

But then her eyes change. Smile eyes without the smile. She appreciates it. "I guess honesty about falling is a little bit like falling," she says finally.

I snort, because she's smart, and I like that. "Yeah."

"Trusting somebody to catch you," she adds, looking at the far wall, eyes full of thoughts. I get the feeling that she's talking about herself suddenly.

Something lights deep inside me, like a wire sparking in the darkness. I seize it. I don't know why; I just have to. "Will they?" I ask. "Will they catch you?"

Her gaze finds mine, and something flares in me. Because I would catch her. And the hottest thing is that I think she knows it. Maybe nobody has ever caught her, but I would. I would catch her. I would keep her. Make her mine. As soon as I get the thought of her as mine, I can't get rid of it. It fills me like a fire, and I need to tamp it down because this is a thousand miles off my plan.

She nods at my forearm. The crossed battle-axes. "Did that feel like falling?"

My mind goes back to us boys scratching away on each other in the basement. The pain felt like love and fury and freedom. "The opposite," I say. "Exactly the opposite."

She seems about to say something, and then she stops and swallows, and God, I want to kiss that neck, breathe her in.

"Does it have a meaning?"

I look up at her. "Yeah."

She gets from my tone that it's off limits, even to her, because she nods, then looks around, seeming to remember the rest of the class. She points to the notebook. "Just do your best." She walks off.

I stare after her, needing to follow. This thing between us is sizzling now.

The other guys are still busy writing.

I set my pen to the paper and do a few doodles. Then I raise my hand.

Dixon is busy fiddling with his phone, so I cough and stomp my foot. He finally looks up and sees my hand. He didn't know she left either, and anger flares inside me. He's supposed to be protecting her from assholes like me.

"What is it?" Dixon says, finally motivated enough to move.

"I have to piss," I say.

He shakes his head. "Wait until you get back to your cell."

"I'll go right here."

Some of the guys snicker.

If I piss myself in the library, they'll probably throw me in solitary again. But only after Dixon takes me to the infirmary to deal with bodily waste cleanup and files a bunch of paperwork. I've seen it happen like that with other guys. In short, he doesn't want me to follow through on the threat.

"I've got seventeen of you," he mutters, more to himself.

"There's a bathroom in the back office, right? So you'll be able to see me if I tried to escape." I make my voice casual. If you come right out and say it, people think you won't do it. Some reverse psychology bullshit. But he does have a straight line of sight to the office door. Calling for backup to handle a potty break will take forever and probably annoy the controller of the east wing too. That's prison politics for you.

"Okay," he finally says. "Go straight into the office. You'll go to solitary for a month if you touch Ms. Winslow. Two minutes."

He's lazy. He should never allow this, but I don't say that. I nod and walk over to the office.

I don't have to touch her.

There she is, sitting behind the librarian's desk…with a book in her hands. She's *reading?* She expects us to spill our guts out there, and she's in here reading the latest thriller or whatever the fuck. I want to be offended, but something about the way she's hunched over raises the hairs on my neck. She's hiding. Afraid. It's the world's nerdiest fight-or-flight reaction. I like it.

She looks up, then, startled, and slams her book shut.

"Sorry," I murmur. At her questioning look, I clarify, "For losing your spot."

She stands up. "It's okay. I've read it before. What…what are you doing here?"

Now that's the question. Because I should be out there working on the building blocks of my fucking escape plan.

I step closer and watch her eyes widen. I take another

step and another; I'm behind the desk. She backs up. The swivel chair spins out of the way. One more step for each of us and she's against the wall.

But I'm still not touching her. Her chest heaves. My gaze falls to her neck, where her pulse bangs away. I let her watch me watching it.

Is she worried? Even without the threat of Dixon, I wouldn't hurt her.

"What are you doing, Grayson?" Her voice wavers, a parody of the authoritative tone she uses on the class. "Return to your seat."

"I will. But first…" I'm close enough that my breath ruffles the hair at her temple. Her body's like a furnace in front of me, singeing my face, my chest, all the way down my body. Can she feel me too? As long as I don't touch her, I'm not breaking any rules.

One minute left.

I breathe in deep, storing the honeysuckle scent of her away to examine later, when I'm alone in my cell. "But first," I whisper, "you never answered my question. Will anyone catch you?"

"It's just an imagination exercise."

Liar, I think.

Her irises are a crackle of brown and gold through the lenses of her glasses, pupils wide and wild. She can fake control, but not up close. She keeps her gaze on mine, as though she thinks looking away will be a sign of weakness—she has no idea how hot it is. I've never met a woman like her, and let's just say I've met a lot of women.

She watches my face, trying to look confident. Her breath is shallow. A little panic. And there's something else that makes my blood sing. Arousal.

CHAPTER EIGHT

~ABIGAIL~

HE'S NOT EVEN touching me, but I feel pinned to the wall by the force of his presence.

The crazy thing is, I knew he would come, the same way I know a storm is coming from the swirl of danger and electricity in the air.

Dimly I think I should call out to the guard, but it's like one of those dreams where I can't call out. Or maybe I don't want to, because being around him is a forbidden pleasure. Like soaking up the sun when you should be inside doing homework.

Except the sun doesn't murder people.

He watches me steadily and I think again how his beauty is a kind of cruelty. The scar that cuts through his dark eyebrow points to the outer edge of his cheekbone, and I spot a tiny scar there—the end of the cut, as though somebody wanted to get his eye but didn't.

The chains clink softly as he raises his hands to my face—slowly, as if he doesn't want to break the trance he holds me in. My pulse races.

His movements are strong and steady. His pointer fingers alight on the outer edges of my glasses. Oh God, he wants to take my glasses off.

"Don't," I whisper.

"Don't what?" He takes hold of the corners of my glasses, watching me with that deep brown gaze.

"You can't take my glasses."

His mouth is just inches from mine, words warm on my nose. "I think I can."

My heart pounds—it's fear and something else. "No," I say. "Don't, Grayson." I try to suffuse my tone with warning. "You want me to call Dixon?" It's the last thing I want to do, though. Grayson would be thrown out of the class. Possibly into solitary.

"I don't think you'll call Dixon," he whispers.

My breath hitches as he begins to pull them off, as the ends slide along my temples, grazing the tender skin, leaving a trail of sensation that's sweet and dark.

He lowers them and looks into my eyes with nothing between us, making me feel him, feel his heat.

Now I'm the one falling, right into a black hole. I feel dizzy, breathless.

What the hell am I doing?

I snatch the glasses from his hands and put them back onto my face where they belong. "Step back, prisoner." I give him a shove, and he steps back, lips twisted in amusement.

"Yes, Ms. Winslow."

My blood races, hands tingling from the feel of his chest where I touched him. It scares me, how easily he invaded me, took me over.

I adjust my glasses, defining the boundary between us, trying to get some control back, because this is all wrong. "You want to have a piece in *The Kingman Journal*?"

He shrugs, but it's too late because I know he does.

I hit him in the one spot where he's vulnerable. "Then you'll write the truth about when you were a little kid. The truth."

Chapter Nine
~Grayson~

THE NEXT TIME in class, Ms. Winslow rearranges the seating to be in alphabetical order, starting in back. She acts like she's doing it to split up a few of the guys who've been talking, but we both know that's not why. She wants me out of her desk, out of her space. Being that my last name is Kane, that puts me in the middle back. Zieman gets her desk.

I'm good with the new arrangement. More than good, because my job here is to get a piece into the journal, get my message to Stone and the rest of my guys. As long as they see it, they'll come through. I can trust them like that, and they trust me enough to know that if I have a plan, it's solid.

You're either weak or strong, and I'm stronger than whatever is between me and Ms. Winslow. I have to be if I want to get out of this place.

So I sit in class and listen hard without making eye contact. I absorb her lessons without thinking about how her voice sounds. I try to use the shit she suggests, and I block out everything else, like the way her hands felt on me. The feeling of taking her glasses. The way she looked up at me. The way she felt like mine.

Ignoring her just makes it worse. I see her even when I don't look at her. I feel her move around class, feel her moods. Back in Franklin City, near our hideout, there are these signs that say: DANGER: BURIED ELECTRICAL LINES. That's how I feel in class. Buried electrical lines running between us, way the hell deep down.

Chapter Ten

~Abigail~

THEY SAY THERE are two types of fear—the kind that has you running far, far away, and the kind that shakes you so deeply that you can't look away.

For me, Grayson is the second kind of fear. I rearrange the seating to get some distance from him, because what happened in the back office was so, so wrong.

But sometimes at night I think about it with this horror and fascination swirling in the pit of my belly. The memory of it is a contraband jewel I absolutely shouldn't possess, but I can't help taking it out and looking at it.

The new seating seems to work; in fact, Grayson seems to want to ignore me as badly as I want to ignore him. No more knowing glances, no more wicked smiles. He applies himself to the work like it's a matter of life or death.

So I give my lessons from one week to another. I walk up and down the side of the room while they write.

If somebody were observing the class, they might

think I was the most aloof and professional teacher ever, and that Grayson is just a number to me.

They'd be wrong.

Grayson touches me deeply, over and over, kills me, really. Not with his hands or eyes, but with his words. His vignette is shocking. Raw. Heartbreaking. It's about a boy being held prisoner in a basement, though on the face of it, it's the story of a boy's pet rat, Manuel. Only this rat doesn't have a cage or a little water bottle or a wheel to run on. This rat lives in the walls. It's a rodent, the kind that should be killed with a trap, but it means everything to the boy. He coaxes it out and feeds it. There are other boys here. These boys seem to be trapped with no TV, no games. I don't understand what's going on or who is holding him. He doesn't have enough food to eat, but he breaks off little bits of pizza crust so that Manuel will come back.

The vignette runs back and forth between the rat and the boy and the time the rat doesn't come back for days. The boy marks the days on the wall with a nail, staking out the southeast corner where the rat comes and goes. His precise focus on dates and hours suggests that he has nothing else but that rat.

The boy doesn't get to go outside. That fact is never stated, but it's painfully clear.

The piece is subtle but powerful, and his honesty and bravery blows me away, because he dug into the darkest part of his life with quiet acceptance and a total lack of self-pity. My childhood had darkness too, but I am honest enough to admit there's self-pity. And not much acceptance, really.

There are no adults in this story. Only the boy, the rat, Manuel, and some of his friends who *ooh* and *aah* over the rat. Grayson describes the rat vividly, the gray fur and twitching nose, the crooked spot in his tail where it must've been broken once.

Kind of like the boy's arm got broken. That's how Grayson puts it in the story—his arm *got broken*. The passive language and the absence of explanation imply someone broke it on purpose. Who? The vignette doesn't tell.

There was this shock before the pain set in, he wrote. *That was the good part, because once the pain started, it never went away.* Grayson's writing voice is both insightful and matter-of-fact.

Who was keeping Grayson in that basement? What horrible things happened to him there, where a dirty, skittish rat was the best part of his day? It's moving in the way that it skirts the edges of the reality of it, implying it but never quite naming it.

I think about intrepid little Manuel, twitching his whiskers, looking for his pizza crusts. When he's missing for a few days, I know he's left for good. Sometimes I dream up this whole life for him playing outside, and it makes it easier.

I give him suggestions on cleaning up the language, but the piece is solid, and it has the ring of truth, though I'll admit to having my moments of doubting him after the baseball story.

One night I Google him, just because I have to know for sure that it's real—because I want to believe him. I've refrained from Googling the men in my class—it feels like an invasion of their privacy, and it still does as the page loads with hits for Grayson Kane.

Search listings promise sordid tales of a trial, but something darker draws my attention—a row of images.

There he is. Grayson. Not Grayson like I know him now, tall and wide and intimidating as heck. This Grayson is a little boy. I recognize his features in the young, solemn face.

On a milk carton.

He stares into the camera without a smile. His hair has been cut straight across his forehead, a bowl cut. His eyes are dark and solemn.

I click.

MISSING, it says on the milk carton above the image. It gives his height and date of birth and his weight. Seventy-five pounds. *A little boy.* Last seen near a white and blue ice cream truck.

If you have any information regarding this missing youth, please contact your local county sheriff's department.

A lot of missing child cases are custody disputes, but

the ice cream truck suggests he was taken. Kept. In a *basement.*

How long was he held before they found him? A day? Two days?

Long enough to make friends with a rat. Two weeks?

My stomach churns—but not with doubt like before. Now it's filled with anguish for the little boy I never knew. For the little boy I read about in a short memoir piece. There are so many gaps between the scared boy he was then and the scary man he is now.

I close the page. I've seen enough.

At some point Grayson was taken. *Held.* Those were his brown eyes staring out at me from the back of a milk carton.

✧   ✧   ✧

I'M EXCITED AND relieved when the box of professionally printed journals arrives at my dorm room. It's just two days before the launch party, and I was worrying the copies wouldn't come in time.

I pull one out and run my finger over the header. I stayed up so many nights getting it just right. The program grant even paid for a graphic designer to do the cover, and it's gorgeous. This project seems to mean something to the guys, and it means something to me now too.

I recall Esther's words about giving the men space to

tell their stories as I turn to Grayson's page. I wanted honesty from him. The kind of depth I knew he was capable of.

I got so much more.

It makes a brilliant centerpiece for the first issue. It almost hurts to publish it, putting out words so incredibly raw.

The Kingman Journal is already up online and the pageviews are rising. People are drawn to the realness of the pieces as much as I am. There are ten pieces in all, unless you want to count mine—part of the project was that the teacher participate and write a vignette of her own, so that the stories appear alongside each other. I just put in something old I already had—a piece about my first day at college. It's a sort of stupid piece, but the journal is for the guys, not for me.

Chapter Eleven

~Abigail~

THE CLASSROOM IS the same stark room it's always been, but it strikes me now, on the last day, that I'll miss it. We did something meaningful here, and I'm glad I didn't quit. A sort of wistfulness overtakes me as I stand in front and wait for the men to enter.

I curse myself for having worn my blue cashmere sweater—I know better than to wear something so formfitting, considering the way the men look at me. I don't know what got into me.

No. Actually I do. Grayson. Will this be the last time I see him? Of course it will.

I feel it when he enters—it's as if the atmosphere brightens and intensifies, and there's a lightness to his step that's new. Dixon walks beside him, talking to him in low tones, maybe scolding him, but Grayson doesn't seem affected. He smiles, and a miniscule indent appears on his cheekbone; most people would see it as a dimple, but I was up close with him that day in the library, and I know that corner of his cheekbone is where that tiny, ancient scar is. It's his skin pulling around it. A genuine smile—not mocking. He seems…happy.

Is it because of his memoir and *The Kingman Journal*? I think about what Esther said, how some people need to tell their stories to be healed, to be whole. It feels almost too prideful to think I might have played a role in that new happiness, the new hope.

From his chair, he catches my eye and nods. I flash on the milk carton, that boy looking out with his big brown eyes. But this isn't a day for sadness. He would never want my pity. I nod back.

I look at each of my students, nodding in turn. I know them now. Deep inside where it hurts the most, I know them. But even so, the sea of orange is intimidating. It always has been. Even with Dixon standing against the wall, like always.

Dixon, who looks strangely watchful. There's a sheen of sweat over his forehead. As if he's nervous. Why would he be nervous?

My stomach turns over. This feels wrong. But maybe I'm only upset because it's my last day. I don't know why it should upset me this much, unless Esther was right. I got too close to them. To Grayson, to all of them.

"Let's start," I whisper even though no one can hear me. Some of the men are going to be reading from their pieces today. I clear my throat and try again, but nothing comes out. My throat is swollen.

The room feels wavy with discontent, like a dark forest before a storm.

That's when the fight starts. Two guys have an exchange that ends with them yelling in each other's faces. I don't even have time to process what this means. The guard is going to fix it, right? Dixon will fix it.

But he doesn't. Something's wrong, very wrong.

Dixon moves closer to me as the two begin fighting with fists. *Smack.* Flesh against flesh. Dixon is standing in front of me, blocking me. I peer over his shoulder, and in a flash four more guys are up fighting too. Then the room erupts.

Suddenly Dixon's pulling me away, fast enough that everything turns into a blur. A gunshot rings out. Are they shooting the prisoners? I search for Grayson, but I don't see him.

"Come on!" Dixon says, pushing me between him and a door in the corner that I hadn't noticed before. He must have grabbed my bag from the desk before we left, because he shoves it in my arms now.

Panic beats in my chest. "What's going on? What are you doing?"

He's typing something into a little keypad. "Getting you out of here."

An alarm sounds—not the bell kind, but a low, ominous staccato. Another shot. It sounds like a bomb. The place is like a volcano bleeding orange.

Grayson's in there. Is he okay?

There's smoke coming from somewhere. The door opens, and Dixon pulls me through into a large concrete passageway lined with pipes and panels.

We rush down the hall. Clomping footsteps ahead, like a herd of elephants. Dixon pulls me against the wall as a dozen men in riot gear pass.

"Where you going, Manny?" one of them shouts to Dixon in a deep baritone.

"She doesn't belong here," he yells in answer.

Dixon propels me, practically shoving me along. Buzzers sound as we go through one door and then another. Why did the guys start fighting? Are they safe? Is Grayson? We end up at the front office, which is buzzing with activity. Two minutes later I have my purse and I'm out in the crisp, cool day.

Alarms blare, even outside. "Where's your car?" Dixon asks.

I point.

He jogs me down the long row of cars and over to where I parked. "You need to get off the grounds as quickly as possible. This is a very dangerous place right now. Someone'll call you later to take your statement."

"Wait. What did that guy call you? Manny?" I don't know why I'm fixating on this, but it feels important. Like life or death. "Is that your name?"

"Yeah. It's a nickname."

"What's your real name?"

"Manuel," he finally says. "But no one ever calls me that."

I point to my car. "Here I am," I say, pulling out my keys.

"Go." He turns and runs back toward the foreboding gray building.

I stand there, shaking even more now than when I was inside. *What the hell just happened?*

Manuel. His name is Manuel. A common enough name, but a strange coincidence. *Grayson's rat was named Manuel.*

And something else was strange about Dixon. He didn't bother to break up the fight; instead he got me out of harm's way. I want to be grateful for that, but all I keep thinking is how he didn't stop the fight. He didn't even seem surprised, and then there's the way he was nervous when class started.

As if he knew this would happen.

I'm in the visitor's lot, near my car. I look around at the cars still in the lot and there, up in the next row, is a beat-up green car. There's someone getting in. A big guy. Dark hair. He's standing next to the car, ignoring the alarm. But it's taking too long to get the key in…

He doesn't have a key. He's breaking into a car. The realization hits me and in the next second I think of why a prison alarm would go off. If an inmate escaped.

Was this part of a prison escape? Was this man a prisoner?

Of course!

And Dixon just helped them. It makes sense now, his actions. Did they threaten him? Is that how they got him to help? Then the man in the car turns to glance back at the prison, just for a second… and I recognize him. It's Grayson. Oh God, it's Grayson.

I whirl around and unlock my door, pulse racing, and slip in, closing the door quietly so he won't see me.

What are the odds he forces his way into my memoir class only to escape on the last day of class? It can't be a coincidence. I think about the way he wanted to get in my class, even after it started. The way he was desperate to have his piece in the journal. What if he'd sent a message with it?

My face heats with shame and anger as I think about how Grayson's vignette ripped out my heart.

Was it all made up? The whole boyhood captivity story? Manuel the Rat? I felt so sick about that little boy, scared and alone. And it was all a coded message. Now I know that Dixon's name is Manuel. That means something.

I was shaking with fear before, but now I'm shaking with anger as I imagine his smile. Like a fool, I thought I'd helped him. I thought I'd made a difference. I guess I did make a difference—just not one I would've wanted.

He used me. Played me.

I memorize the license plate and pull out my phone. I need to call somebody. No one knows why the riot broke out. No one knows that Grayson is about to escape in that specific car except for me.

I slide down low in my seat. Do I dial 9-1-1? The prison front office? I have to tell someone—Grayson could be dangerous. No, he *is* dangerous. He could be a rapist, a murderer. I really wish I'd seen his file like the other guys. What did he do to get locked up?

I scan the parking lot, wondering if I should run back to the office and tell them, wondering if there's still time.

I look over and we lock eyes.

He's spotted me.

Get out! Start up the car and go! I'm still holding my cellphone in one hand so I can call 9-1-1, but that isn't going to help me now. I hunt for my keys—where are they? Did I drop them on the way to my car? No! I unlocked my door. Did I stick them back in my bag? I do that when I'm distracted. I dig through my bag with shaking hands. Where are they?

When I look back up, he's standing there. Watching me with cold eyes.

Shit shit shit.

Frantically I return to my bag, throwing out receipts and fluffed-out, unused tampons. This whole thing's unreal, like I've stepped into a Salvador Dali portrait of a prison break.

I find my keys and shove them into the ignition.

Glass crashes in my ear. I swing my gaze around to a gun, held by a bloody fist stuck into my passenger window.

Grayson.

He reaches in and opens the door. "Drop the phone. Now."

I drop it in my lap as he slides in, right over the glass, and shuts the door.

He grabs my phone from my lap and examines it.

"No calls went through." My voice only shook a little.

"Good girl." He sets the phone against the dashboard and smashes it with the butt of the gun—three hard, violent whacks and the thing is in pieces. He tosses most of it out, and casual as can be, he buckles up. "Drive."

How dare he? How *dare* he expect me to help him? My lips press together, and everything in me revolts against him. He tricked me. He *used* me.

"I'm done helping you." I look away, scanning the area for guards, anyone.

He sighs as if I'm making his life difficult. I want to punch him.

Something hard presses against my ribs. Fear clenches my throat. I glance down, already knowing what I'll see. He's pressing the gun right into me. A shot at close range from a weapon that large? I'm no expert, but I know that means death. He's going to kill me. Tears spring to my eyes—tears of humiliation and horror.

"Maybe you didn't hear me," he growls in a tone that chills me to my toes. "I said *drive.*"

Chapter Twelve

~Grayson~

S HE'S SMART, I'LL give her that much. I knew from the moment she saw me that she'd figured out about the escape. And the memoir.

The angry expression in her eyes tells me she's feeling betrayed. Would she get all offended if a bear took a swipe at her? Because that's what this is: nature. I learned about the natural order of things early on in life. Things you do to survive. Lessons you never forget.

"You gonna drive, or do you want to end up like your phone?"

Her eyes widen with that shocked flare she sometimes gets, and she puts the car into gear and starts heading toward the gate. Nothing like a violent little demo to spur a woman to action.

"So it was all bullshit," she says. "Made up."

"What? You don't like Manuel the Rat suddenly? The poor little rat?"

Her soft, smudgy brown eyes shine with anger. The idea that my vignette might be fake has her angry, and that does something to me, even though it shouldn't. *Getting away*—that's what I should be caring about, not Ms. Winslow's precious feelings.

Sirens sound. Reinforcements. Cherries flash in the distance. As long as the brawl keeps going, they won't be able to do a decent count and they won't know I'm gone. My gaze darts to the speedometer. She's going thirty-five in a fifty-five mph zone. "You get this thing the fuck up to the speed limit, and you keep it exactly there," I growl. "Drive natural."

"Or what?"

I let my voice go cold. "You really want to find out? You think you know me?" She looks over at me, and I let her see all the hell inside me. "You don't know anything about me. Nothing."

She speeds up, eyes fixed on the road.

"Easy," I say as the cops come over the hill from the other way—a whole line of them. I have a buddy waiting to meet us at a place just over the county line.

Stone. Tough motherfucker and loyal to the end. He's been looking out for me since we were kids in that basement, and we'd do anything for each other.

Flashing red lights fill the rearview mirror, and my heart pounds. So far so good. More than good, because after all this time chained up and monitored and kept away from her, never able to touch her, she's under my complete control, mine to do what I want with. It's as dizzying as the sky overhead, wild and white with clouds.

"We're just out for a nice afternoon ride, you and me."

Her jaw is set hard. Yeah, she's good and pissed. And scared.

I glance ahead at the fields rolling on. The wide-openness is hard to get used to after two years of being confined. God, walking out of the joint today through the parking lot with all that sky above me was so overwhelming I could barely act normal, and then there were all the cars I had to pass by, all the places people could jump out from. I knew people weren't hiding behind cars, ready to jump out, but in prison you learn to avoid that kind of thing. Second sense. And then I spotted Abby, and everything evened out.

Abby became my anchor. She steadied me, somehow.

So I took her. There's something about driving away, something sweet about freedom with a pretty girl in the seat beside you. Even if that pretty girl hates you. Even if the guys in your crew would all tell you to kill her. Maybe I should.

"See, here's something for you to ponder," I say to her as the fields flash by. "You're smart, so you need to be thinking what you are to me right now. Do you know what you are to me, *Ms. Winslow?*"

Fear lights the fine, sharp features of her face. Her thoughts have gone dirty. Like I might rape her. The rims of her big, brown, frightened eyes are smudged with makeup. It's a good look for her. I wonder if Ms. Winslow understands that to the outside observer, fear and arousal look like very much the same thing.

Just a little something I picked up back in the days of basements and rats—that it's best not to show any fear when guys older and stronger than you are thinking about having a little fun, because when really sick motherfuckers see any kind of life there—fear, anger, happiness, anything—they want to fuck or beat it out of you. Then again, when you act dead, they want to get you lively, and that's never good, either.

Tidbits that didn't go into the vignette.

The rat's name wasn't Manuel, of course. The rat had no name, and he never came back, either. I told myself he found a better gig, and I really did believe it. I still believe he got away. But if I'm real honest, I know I need to believe it. I need to believe at least one of us came out of there okay, and it sure as hell wasn't me or Stone or any of us.

I spent a lot of time imagining the rat romping around outside in the grass.

Especially when they'd do the films, because they'd make you feel good in a way you didn't want to feel, but I'd be thinking about that stupid rat running around outside chasing moths in the grass.

And there's Ms. Winslow with that quiet, prim look

of hers and those brown eyes understanding something crucial about my time in that basement. It was nice for a while to have somebody else know. Sure, Stone and those guys knew the hard stuff, but I'd never told anybody about the sappy stuff and the way I'd imagine that rat running around outside like some cartoon character. I wonder sometimes what it would be like to tell all of it. How it was to hate somebody's touch until you crave it. How it was that night when my crew and I killed them all. But it's better for her if she thinks it's made-up.

I look over at her driving, concentrating so hard, like she does with everything. She's a perfectionist, my Ms. Winslow. She probably slaved over every little comma in that stupid journal.

It's then I think about touching her. Maybe just her neck or her cheek. I wonder if she'd jump. Or if she'd cry. Or hell, maybe she'd eat it up. There's one thing I do know: she'd feel it. Really feel it, because it would be different and new and all wrong, just like me going across that parking lot, feeling that huge, crazy-ass sky blazing above me. Out of my cage.

Her lips are pressed together, eyes firmly on the road, but not just for safety. She's also avoiding me, like I'm not here with a loaded gun pointed at her ribs.

How would her neck feel against my cheek? Does she smell like honeysuckle everywhere? What would her tits feel like in my palms underneath that kitten-fur sweater? She tries to obscure them with clothes, but you can tell they're nice. I'm thinking B-cup, maybe C, depending on what kind of bra she wears, a topic I've mused on pretty extensively, let's just say.

Yeah, I really, really want to touch her. It doesn't hurt that she's so hot, with those smudged-up eyes and pale skin and the way her pulse beats in her neck. I imagine her under me, skin to skin. How smooth she'd feel.

I run my thumb up the back of the Glock. A nice piece. Smooth and warm from the body of a guard who's currently out cold. Two long years without a woman's touch. I'd be mad with lust for any woman. I tell myself it's not about this woman with her books and glasses and prim hairdo, trying so hard to drive naturally even though she's shaking.

She doesn't have experience at this, and she sometimes makes jerky movements, but I don't yell at her for that. I don't want to hurt her for things she can't control.

I shift in my seat, shaking her out of my mind because I know how quickly things can go bad, and if she forces my hand, if it's a choice between her or my crew...

She needs to not matter.

First thing Stone and I need to do when we get up to Franklin City is find some women to fuck so I can get my head back on straight. Right before we all make

Governor Dorman sorry he was ever born.

I smile inside, imagining him hearing the news that I've busted out. Not like Dorman can go into hiding, being he's a governor and all. No, he'll be easy to find. Not easy to get to, with all that security, but we'll figure it out.

More cops. She's going fifty-five exactly.

"What you are is a liability, Ms. Winslow. You made the car, probably even memorized the fucking license plate. You were going to call the cops on me."

"No," she whispers.

Liar. She's too smart to do otherwise. "So I took your car instead. But that means... It means you aren't that useful anymore."

She's silent. I'm scaring her, but I need her to understand the thin ice she's on so she doesn't do something stupid.

"My point is, if you don't drive perfect, then maybe I should be driving. Right? Am I right?"

She stares at the road, lips pressed together, which plumps them out a little bit, and suddenly it's too much, and I reach up to her face. It's like an out-of-body experience, seeing myself do it, taking this liberty just because I can. She jumps as I graze her cheek with two knuckles. I draw them slowly down her silky skin, toward her chin, drinking up the feel of her, rich with electricity, rich with peace. She's mine, and I want her so bad, it's like a fever.

I pull my hand away. She's breathing fast, hands gripping the wheel.

Softly I say, "That was a question, baby. You need to answer my questions now just the way I've been answering yours these past weeks. And if you're good, I won't make you list off twenty motherfucking items in your house, okay?"

She looks over, anger in her eyes. I shift the Glock so it catches the light, reminding her who's in charge. To remind *me* she's expendable. The gun helps. It keeps us both focused.

She fixes her attention back on the road. "Fine. You're right," she says quickly. "If I don't drive perfectly, you should be driving."

"Very good, Ms. Winslow. But if I'm driving, how can I hold this gun on you? How do I know you might not jump out or do something crazy? Flag down cars or something. You see my dilemma?"

"Yes," she whispers. I can tell from her face she really has worked it out, but I spell it out anyway.

"Bottom line, you drive nice, that's one less reason for me to kill you." I watch the lump move inside her smooth throat. A gulp of fear. It's almost comical. "Gulp," I say.

Her eyes flash at me. "Fuck you," she says.

"Are you offering?" I ask, the feel of her skin still blazing on my knuckles.

She sniffs angrily, like that's an outrageous idea. I flex my hand. Her cheek felt warmer than I expected. Her belly would feel warm under that sweater. And she'd be jumpy with every touch. Oh, Ms. Winslow would be very, very jumpy, tensing with every slide of my finger, every kiss, every little invasion. That's how she'd be at first, anyway. I'd make her keep the glasses on the whole time. Unless I went ahead and broke them, like I was thinking earlier, to put her off balance. "Do you need those glasses to drive?" I ask.

She furrows her brows, trying to decide whether to lie or not.

"Never mind," I say.

"Where are we going?"

"We're going to meet my friend in a secluded area."

She gives me that look again. The flare of surprise— and a little bit of something else too.

"Why, Ms. Winslow, *please.* Mind out of the gutter." I smile and sit back. The smile is there to put her at ease. Stone'll want her dead. It's going to be a problem.

Another pair of cop cars heads over the hill. "You just drive nice, okay?"

"*Nicely,*" she snaps.

"What?"

"Drive *nicely,* that's how you say it. Not *drive nice.*"

Oh God. Nice*ly.* Correcting my grammar even at gunpoint. I'm so fucking hot for her, I think I might burst into flames.

CHAPTER THIRTEEN

~ABIGAIL~

THE CAR FEELS unwieldy in my hands, as if I'm suddenly driving around an elephant instead of my trusty old car. The steering wheel tugs and gives unexpectedly, and it's hard to keep the speed at exactly fifty-five. Any second now he's going to notice.

And then he's going to kill me.

Out here with Grayson, anything goes. That's what the crisp air and too-bright sun are telling me. *Anything goes.*

The patch on his guard uniform says Dixon. Guess Manuel gave it to him. *Or Grayson took it.*

"Is Dixon okay?"

Grayson chuckles. "He's okay. He's fifty grand okay."

A bribe, then. Dixon took a bribe to look the other way, to give up his uniform to help Grayson escape. It shouldn't surprise me, but it does. Dixon was supposed to be one of the good guys. "How did you know he would take it?"

"I wanted to get in your class, but it was full. He took my iPod and got me in."

My hands tighten on the wheel. "So?"

"If someone'll take a small bribe, they'll take a bigger one."

"That's disgusting."

"That's the world. I called in a few favors...made a few bribes...threatened a few people. Like you."

"They'll catch you. They'll hunt you down like an animal."

"I don't think so," he says, his voice more thoughtful than afraid. "I've been planning this since I got inside. No, I'd been planning it since before then, since I started doing shit that could get me arrested. And now that I'm out, I'm not going back anytime soon."

"You could just *not* do illegal things."

"That's no fun, sweetheart. And you look like you could use a little fun."

The woods get thicker as we drive, with fewer dirt-road turnoffs. The town where I live is a half-hour drive south of the prison, and we've been heading north forever. Nothing's north. I haven't seen a cop car for a long time. Did I miss my chance? Should I have crashed this car right in front of the cops so they'd have to stop? But for all I know, my little blue Honda would explode on impact. Or maybe the man beside me would shoot as soon as I turned the wheel. It takes a lot to invite death instead of postponing it.

Because that's all I'm doing here, by obeying him. Postponing death.

Suddenly he rests his palm on my shoulder. The pressure is light and affectionate, like the touch of a friend. Or a boyfriend. Heat builds under his palm with the thin fabric of my summer sweater acting as a conduit. I'm acutely aware of the satin bra strap that he's almost, *almost* touching…and I know he could do more.

He could move the strap aside. He could make me have sex with him, and there's nothing I could do to stop him. That's what the hand on my shoulder tells me.

"Turn right here," he says. I see the building up ahead.

It's a gas station! That's my chance to escape. He has to know it, but he's not acting concerned. Nothing ever concerns him. That's going to be his downfall—that confidence. If I can find a way to use it.

We get closer, and my heart sinks. The building looked white from a distance, but up close you can see the way paint has peeled into yellowish grime. It's an abandoned gas station.

"Right here."

I slow and pull in. The part where you'd pay at the pump has been ripped out, leaving only two metal beams in the middle. It looks like something out of an apocalyptic movie.

He may be a cocky bastard, but he's a prepared cocky bastard.

Off to the side is a car with a man standing next to it.

"Pull up next to him," Grayson says.

The man's stance is wide. Arms crossed. He doesn't flinch as I aim a little too close to him.

Grayson squeezes my shoulder, and I straighten out and stop a few yards away. My foot is on the brake. He's the one who reaches over to shift us into park. Then he turns off the car and puts the key in his pocket.

"Stay here," he says before leaving the car.

Does he think I'll obey? I sit very still, hands on the wheel, staring straight ahead. But inside I am clawing my way out of here. I am straining at the chains, just as surely as he did in prison. In this much, we are alike. Neither of us will remain in captivity if we can help it.

There's not much in the car. Damn myself for keeping it relatively clean. What am I going to do with a stack of student memoirs? Fold them into an origami gun? I have nothing.

Then I remember. *Pepper spray in the glove compartment.*

It's really so little. But what else do I have?

Get away. Use the pepper spray. Take his gun.

And then what? If I had a gun, could I pull the trigger? If I knew I'd end Grayson's life to save my own, would I do it?

Chapter Fourteen

~Grayson~

Stone's standing beside a car, feet crossed at the ankles, coolly taking everything in. He didn't even flinch when she was heading for him. The hard-ass.

I'm not going to let him be a hard-ass about this. I slam the door behind me and close the distance between us, grabbing him in a bear hug. After a second, he hugs me back.

"Fuck," he says gruffly.

I close my eyes, gripping onto him. Knowing he and the crew were all out there, pulling for me, ready to help, that got me through. He lets me go and studies my face. I wonder if I look different.

He nods toward the car. "What the fuck?"

"Nothing. My chauffer."

He pulls out a nine and hands it to me. "Do her and let's go. Hurry up."

My heart pounds. Something deep and visceral rejects the idea of a bullet in her brain. Of animals picking her apart. "She could still be useful."

"To the *cops*, maybe," he says. "She saw me, Grayson. There's no choice."

I glance back at Abby, sitting rigidly upright behind the wheel. Her glasses are on perfectly straight, but a strand of hair has escaped from her bun, and she's staring ahead with utter composure, a look that is so her, just so very her, it does something to me. And suddenly all I can think is that she's mine. It's not even a thought, it's a foghorn, blaring in my head: *mine*. "Here is messy. Bad place for a body."

"Put her in the dumpster," he continues. "No one'll find her for a while. Nobody will think anything if dogs come sniffing around…"

My pulse whooshes in my ears. "No."

"Fine. I'll do it." He takes his weapon back from me. "Go change. Got your clothes in the back of the car. Quick and painless, okay?" He chambers a bullet, weapon flashing in the sun. He catches me staring. "You like? Platinum-plated German number."

I watch myself close my fingers around his wrist, my corded hand tight on his shooting arm, matching scars on our skin. "I got it under control."

He stills and looks up at me, eyes like emeralds. Softly, he says, "Do you?"

"Yeah. I'll handle her," I growl.

He frowns. I wonder if he's thinking about how I let them trap me, frame me. My stomach twists as I remember the spray of the cop's brains on the pavement. The governor's men pointing at me like I did it. The gun I hadn't seen in forever, glinting on the ground. My gun, my prints. Masterful fucking frame-up job. We hadn't even seen it coming.

"Grayson," he says. "Don't be fucked up."

I grab the back of his head and pull him in, close enough to kiss, and look at him straight. "I said I got it."

The moment draws out, then I feel him soften. "Fine, I get it. I understand." He twists his arm out of my grip. "Two years. Okay. Fuck her and then kill her."

I let him go. "Safer anyway, going in separate cars." It's true, and we both know it. "We have to get out of here. I'll meet you back there." *At the Bradford*, I mean.

"They'll be looking for that thing." He nods at her little car.

"I'll change the plates. I got this."

He grins. "Good to have you back again, brother." He reaches into the car and pulls out a bundle. Clothes. I strip down to my boxers. He takes the guard uniform and stuffs it into a nearby barrel as I pull on the black T-shirt and a familiar pair of jeans.

"Fuck, yeah," I say. He even brought my old work boots. He hands me money, identification, plus a phone. He offers me a piece, but I have the Glock I got off the guard.

"Take 54 to I-98," he says.

"I know the way."

Franklin City is at least ten hours away from here. Most people are moving out of Franklin City these days—huge chunks of it are abandoned, crumbling, not just the neighborhood where the Bradford is, but beyond it, like a spreading disease. And then on the outer edges of it are the mansions, like parasites, feeding. That's where the governor lives.

Stone heads back to the Dodge. He assumes I'll kill her, and that makes me uncomfortable—because I don't lie to my guys. Especially not to Stone. We're brothers. Closer than brothers. What is it called when you walk through the same fire and wear the same scars?

I go back to the Honda as he tears out onto the two-lane highway. I set my hand on the hood and suck in the sweet smell of freedom, waiting until his car is the size of a penny. I lean down and look at Abby. Still trembling. Is that all she'd do if I touched her? Tremble?

It fills me with an uncomfortable mix of hate and lust.

The car door is light as tin; I get a bad feeling, like I forgot something important.

It's only when I'm seated and buckled up that I realize she's gone past trembling. She's in full-on earthquake mode.

She heard us talking.

Fucking old cars with their shit insulation. I reach for

her, but she's expecting that. She bolts from the car and runs on foot. My long-ass legs are folded into the floorboard and my shoulders are practically hunched, so it takes me a good sixty seconds to unbuckle, get out, and round the car, weapon in hand. By that time she's across the street and racing into the woods.

I cross the road and dive into the brush after her. She's going to be sorry she ran. I follow the sound of her crashing through the underbrush with Stone's voice in my head. *Shoot her. Get out of the area.*

But I can't—not yet.

That's when the sirens sound.

Fuck!

The car is just begging for someone to stop and check it out, parked in an abandoned station with both doors hanging open. They'll call it in. Find out it's hers.

I'm going to catch her. And when I do, I'm going to teach her what happens when you disobey.

There's a natural order to people: the strong and the weak. I've been the weaker one before. I know how much it hurts. But pain only makes you harder. Stronger.

Chapter Fifteen

~Abigail~

I RUN LIKE hell through the woods, pepper spray clutched in my hand. The underbrush feels like nails, digging at my arms and cheeks as I pass, but it's not the kind of thing you care about when an escaped prisoner is trying to kill you.

I crash over a bed of sticks and moldy leaves in my stupid high-heel boots, running like crazy toward the darkest part of the woods—we passed a lot of fields, and that's exactly where I don't want to end up. Grayson would have a clear shot in a field.

Here is messy. Bad place for a body, he'd said.

I know the next stop would be somewhere good to leave a dead body. Maybe a river.

I jump a fallen tree and stumble, smashing my shin into a rock so hard it feels like I cracked a bone. I hear the brush snapping behind me, and something else—a siren! I jump up and keep going, racing madly. They'll find my car. Will he forget about me and save himself? Maybe they'll come out here with dogs.

I run, forearms first, fighting the underbrush. *Stay alive.*

I can hear him back there. Which means he's close enough to hear me, and maybe close enough to see me in my bright blue sweater.

The siren is gone. Did it get turned off, or did the cop keep driving? I dart right, change direction, but I hear him again. I have no idea where I am, where the highway is, nothing. All I know is that I have to survive.

When I enter a particularly thick, dark stand of trees, I decide to play my last card. I slip behind the first trunk, trying to keep my breathing under control.

I hear him slow.

And then nothing. I wait, back flat against the nubby bark, shin screaming with pain, pulse whooshing in my ears. My sweaty fingers are wrapped around the canister of pepper spray that's so old I have no idea if it even works.

It's all I have left.

Silence. He's back there somewhere, just waiting. Watching. I picture his hulking muscular form.

I swallow, trying to remember where the last sound from him was. Two feet away? Twenty feet away? The waiting is getting excruciating. I look around for other weapons—maybe a rock to smash him with in case the pepper spray doesn't work.

Nothing.

A twig breaks nearby. I stiffen.

Then another. Soft footsteps.

Then his voice. "Ms. Winslowwww," he says softly. It's almost a whisper. I shouldn't be able to hear something that quiet, but the woods are strangely amplifying. It makes me wonder if he can hear my heart pounding.

My breath sounds hoarse in my ears; I will it under control.

Another soft crunch. It comes to me that I should throw something, to make a sound elsewhere and divert him, the way they do in the movies, but I'm afraid even to move. I curse my skirt with no pockets—no coins, no keys.

I think about throwing my glasses. I could probably make it through the woods without them, but I can't part with them. My glasses are my security, and I have so little now to protect me.

Another step. He's closer.

Silence.

Crunch.

Quietly as can be, I bend over, pick up a stone, and hurl it.

It hits a nearby tree.

I stiffen at the sound, a soft rustle. I don't hear anything else for a long while.

And suddenly he's in front of me. I hold up the spray

and pump the nozzle. It hits him right in the eyes.

"Fuck!" He grabs me by the shoulders, eyes shut tight, coughing. He can't see me, but he's got me anyway. Tears run down his cheeks. I try to jerk out of his arms, but he won't let go. I try to kick him in the balls, but I end up hitting his thigh. He swears and jerks me closer.

I feel my throat seize up like I can't breathe. My lungs clench, desperate for air.

I spray again, getting him in the shirt. Still with his eyes closed tightly, he presses me against the tree with his big body. I writhe and twist, but he's a big warm boulder, pinning me, pressing me with his body.

I'm coughing uncontrollably now, eyes watering. Tree bark juts into my back, and with him on me, I can barely breathe. He feels down my arm until he finds the spray and wrenches it out of my hand.

He's blinded, or at least he can't open his eyes. "Fuck!" he says again, tossing it.

I try to knee him, but all I can do is stomp his foot, writhing wildly, gasping for air.

"Damn it!" He twists me around, and my glasses fall off.

His eyes are still closed, but that hasn't diminished his ability to hang on to me and control me like a rag doll. He puts a leg in front of mine and pushes me forward. All I can do is fall, but he's got me. He's lowering me, face-first, to the forest floor. He presses his knee into my back, one hand fisted in my hair, the other around both of my wrists. Sticks and pine needles feel rough against my cheek as his weight crushes me.

"Calm down," he grates. "Give it up."

I'm coughing, wheezing. I had asthma as a kid, and that's what it feels like now as the pepper spray stings me all the way down. "Get off!" I gasp. "You're too heavy—I can't—get air."

"It's the spray," he says. "Breathe normal."

I gasp for air, panicking. "I can't!" Is this how I die? Suffocation?

"Pretend," he says, letting up his knee. He shifts so that he's straddling my back. He grips my wrists now, pressing them above my head, and I feel his boots locked over my thighs. His weight is off my back. "It's something every thug like me knows, how to not breathe in the fucking Mace. It's cop killer 101."

"You're not a cop killer." *Or is he?*

He snorts.

I choke and cough. I still can't breathe. *It's not working!* He's going to let me die.

"Relax," he says softly. "You're making it worse by panicking."

Hoarsely, I try to get air. The sounds scare me. I really can't breathe. I suck faster as the panic rises.

"Hey," he whispers. "Shhh." He brings his head near

mine, breath tickling the back of my neck. "Pepper spray is an inflammatory agent, okay? It swells your throat and sinuses, but it doesn't shut them."

I gasp.

He continues to speak in his calm, strangely soothing voice. Why is he soothing me? I can feel him rattling against my defenses with every word. "You're still getting air, okay? Focus on that, Ms. Winslow. That little passage of air you can still breathe through. Slow it down now, got it?"

I can't slow it down. It's like I don't know how to breathe anymore, and I'm shaking.

And suddenly he's stretching his big body over me, on top of me. His weight isn't entirely on me, or else I'd be squished; it's more of a dull weight, as though he's holding himself against me, warming me, pressing me to the forest floor. Into my ear he whispers, "Breathe with me."

I suck in a faint breath. "Get off me, you caveman!" Why is he even trying to help me?

"You're okay, baby," he says. "Match my breath."

I feel his chest expand against my shoulder blades. He's like a big, warm animal on me. I twist, but there's no moving. He presses down harder, and something about his weight soothes me. I hate that he's actually calming me, helping me. I don't want him to make me feel good—he's my enemy.

I wheeze lightly.

He breathes on, hot and slow against me. A bird calls in the distance. I can hear the hum of the highway, the drone of a helicopter. My eyes tear, and my limbs feel floppy and warm, and suddenly I'm doing it—I'm breathing. I take an almost regular breath.

"There you go," he whispers.

"Fuck you. I don't want your help." I gasp in another breath.

His whisper caresses my cheek. "Nice and slow, Ms. Winslow." There's something sensual in the way he says it. "Nice and slow."

He breathes again, as if to demonstrate. On the next breath I match him. Soon we're breathing together. It's strangely intimate, like we're two wounded creatures under the forest canopy. It's almost like dancing.

Almost like having sex.

I crane my head around just enough to see that he still has his eyes shut tight, dark eyelashes wet with tears from the irritation of the spray. Did I hurt him? Did I burn his eyes?

"Stop moving around," he growls. "Lie still."

Like I have any choice with him pinning me. My heart pounds under his weight.

Breathe in, breathe out.

It's as if we're in some kind of time-out, a no-man's-land with the two of us fucked up and lying on the forest floor on a bed of pine needles that actually feels sort of soft and nice. The moments stretch on and on. I wonder how long it will take him to recover.

Maybe I really injured his eyes. Could I have hurt his eyes permanently?

He shifts, and I think maybe he's getting up. But he doesn't.

In a weird way I'm glad. If he got off me, that would end this strange, relaxing time out. It would bring back the harsh reality of who we are to each other.

For now, there's nothing I can do with him lying on my back, and I let my limbs go soft, let my breathing calm, giving myself permission to relax. I feel like jelly suddenly, spread underneath him, spine flattened out. Us breathing together.

My eyes drift closed. The warm patch on my neck feels lit up every time he breathes out, and I imagine his lips hovering just over my skin.

I imagine him kissing me there, and a wave of forbidden feeling swells through my core.

My eyes fly open. There is no way I'm turned on.

Except I am.

My heart races. My breath gets fitful again.

"Hey," he says. And then more softly. "You're okay."

I become aware of a hardness against my thigh. An erection. A melty sensation pulses through my pelvis. I'm trembling deep down, and it's not just fear; it's excitement.

Horrified, I try to shake him off, and he tightens his legs and arms around me. I feel his weight and warmth keenly now. "You don't want to give me any more trouble, do you?"

"No," I whisper huskily.

The energy of sex runs wild between us, and I don't know how to stop it. Does he know? I flash back on him in the prison waiting room, the way he looked at me, and all that power and beauty barely contained in shackles. How stupid I was to think he was beautiful.

"No, you don't want to give me trouble," he affirms. "So we're going to stay just like this until my eyes can recover."

"So you can kill me?"

"If I was going to kill you," he says, warm and tickly beneath my earlobe, "don't you think you'd be dead?" There's something about the way he says this that makes my belly quiver, and I can't stop focusing on his erection. His big, strong heart beats against my back, beating my heart like we're conjoined in some primitive way.

His breath feels soft on the side of my neck, and heaven help me, I want to feel more of him. I imagine his skin on my skin. Dimly I'm aware that my breath is changing, speeding, shallowing.

I stiffen as he presses his lips to the warm spot; it's a kind of kiss. Or is it? And then he whispers, "Penny for your thoughts, Ms. Winslow."

Oh God, he knows. This man who's going to kill me, this man I've been breathing with, he *knows*.

I close my eyes, panting now, pulse wild. He shifts his legs, forcing me to press my thighs together, and a wave of desire rolls through me.

He slides one hand up my arm and fumbles his other hand into my hair. I can tell by the way he moves that he doesn't have his sight back, but that's not what alarms me. The feeling between us has changed. He's different.

We're different.

It's as if we're connected, and I can feel him shift, like the terrible desire between us changed something in him. He fists my hair and pulls my head sideways, exposing my throat.

"Don't," I gasp.

"Don't what?" he whispers, lowering his lips to my neck, pressing them to my tender skin. He scrapes his teeth across my pulse point. "Don't what, Ms. Winslow?" He rubs his hands up and down my arms, soft through my sweater.

I let out a puff of air I didn't know I was holding. Maybe it's desperation. Maybe it's desire. All I know is it's fucked up. "Just don't."

He slides his hands up to cover mine, locking his fingers over mine, balling my hands into fists. It's a little bit like he's holding my hands and a little bit like he's controlling me, and it feels like a metaphor for everything between us now.

He lifts himself off me, nudging me over.

"No," I say, but in one rough, efficient movement, he makes me turn over. A lack of sight doesn't seem to hinder him whatsoever. He clamps his legs over mine, and I'm trapped, staring up at his shut eyes. Tears dot his dark lashes like diamonds.

"Grayson," I say. "Don't."

He grips my wrists in just one of his huge hands now, and he runs the other hand down the side of my chest.

I gasp.

"A class I recently took—because as you know, I'm the scholarly type—stressed the importance of using just the right word." His hand is a heavy weight on my belly. "A precise word over a vague word. *Don't.* That's not very precise."

"Don't do this." I'm scared now.

"*This,*" he whispers. "That's vague too, don't you think? *Don't do this.*" He shifts off me a little more, sliding a hand over my breast now. "You're better than that, Ms. Winslow. Dig deep and find that precise word. I know it's in you."

The electric feeling of his hand on me blazes through my sweater, my bra. It's like I have nothing on, like I'm laid bare to him. Even my glasses are off. He simply helps himself to me, roaming a gentle hand over to my other breast.

I need it to stop feeling good.

"Don't what? Don't touch you?" His gentle fingers make me feel all lit up. He shifts a leg between mine.

"Grayson," I whisper.

He moves his hand back down to my belly, and then I feel rough fingers under my sweater, trailing over my tender skin. I gasp when he hits the sensitive place below my belly button.

"Get off me," I say, twisting, which just allows his leg to press farther between my legs. The press of his thigh to my sex sends a pulse of feeling up through my core.

"Is that really what you want, Ms. Winslow?"

"Fuck off," I say. "Yes, it's what I want. You off."

He grips my wrists more tightly, anchoring them to the soft pine needles. I close my eyes as his fingers travel ever upward under my sweater, up my belly to my chest. He reaches my breast, slides his fingers lazily back and forth over my nipple. "You'll lose this fight, you know," he says matter-of-factly as he slides his calloused fingers over the thin fabric of my bra.

"Congratulations—you can dominate somebody half your size."

"That's not the fight I'm talking about. You'll lose the fight you're fighting with yourself." He kisses my neck. "The fight to not feel this. The fight against desire."

The fight against desire. It feels like a well-worn phrase. He kisses my cheek—a gentle kiss.

His gentleness contrasts wildly with his iron grip on my hands, preventing me from gouging his eyes out.

"It's always how it goes." He kisses me again. "Always. It's okay to lose. Everybody loses. The toughest fuckers I know lose this fight."

Dimly I wonder where this comes from—my memoirist's radar tells me there's something in there. But I can't care about that now. "I want you the fuck off," I say, panting as he pulls the fabric of my bra aside, as a rough finger circles my nipple.

"It's okay to lose," he whispers. "Be okay with it."

I feel like I'm sinking into his touch, like he's taking me over. Worst of all, I can feel the wetness between my legs; that's what makes this evil. I *am* losing the fight. "Fuck," I say, trying to jerk my hands. "Why don't you just kill me?"

He laughs softly and kisses me. "You don't mean that."

Oh God, his hand is heading south now. Maybe it's perverse, but I don't want him to touch me there because I don't want him to know I'm aroused. I try to kick out from under the press of his legs as he plunges his fingers under the waistband of my skirt.

He slides his finger into my panties. It comes to me

that we're breathing together again, but it's not the calm, measured breaths from before; it's something darker.

"Ms. Winslow," he whispers as he strokes my core. Tears of shame burn through my closed-off eyelids as he finds my sensitive nub and begins to strum the feeling higher.

"I don't want it," I pant.

"I know," he says in a strange tone. "I know, but sometimes it's better if you tell yourself that you do." He kisses my neck and keeps on touching me, stroking me higher. I feel like I might be losing my mind, like my brain is a plane that's just taken off from the runway, soaring up into the air, out of touch, out of communication. Something turns in me as he touches me, pushing the desire further.

He hears a voice, and then I hear it too—a call in the distance.

I suck in a breath, about to scream *Help!* when his heavy hand clamps over my mouth, preventing me from calling out.

"Oh no, you don't. We're going to stay very still right here."

I look around. The foliage is thick enough to hide us.

And all the while he hasn't stopped touching me, stroking me, making me feel this terrible pleasure. Usually it's good, but now it's hateful.

His hand is tight on my mouth. I breathe through

my nose, control fraying, and I go for his eyes with my newly freed hands.

Too slow. Before I can get at him, he has his face tucked, burrowed into my chest, making it so I can't get at his eyes or even his neck. Like he knew that's what I'd try. I tear at his ears, but he seems impervious to that.

I bite the finger of the hand over my mouth. He swears and shifts his hand, squeezing my jaw shut. I grab at his hair, pulling, but the feeling between my legs is building; my mind is melting.

He won't stop stroking me, won't take his hand off my mouth, and before I know it, I'm holding on to his hair instead of pulling it.

I don't know what's crazier—the recklessness of him staying on top of me, getting me off instead of running, or the fact that my fingers are tightening in his hair. Or the fact that he's nuzzling my breast through my soft sweater, like he knows I'm done going for his eyes and throat. I'm feeling dizzy from breathing fast through my nose, or maybe it's from what he's doing to me.

Maybe it's just that he's hit a place with the right pressure and I can't believe how good it feels, and I never want him to stop.

Can he tell? He continues his circling motion as I writhe under him, pushing into his hand. He tightens his seal over my mouth, stroking slowly. I can't stop arching into him, pulling his head into my breast by his hair, wanting, needing.

And suddenly I shatter with feeling. Sharp, bright, intense. It goes all through me in waves, this beauty, this wildness. I'm breathing hard and he is, too, and nothing matters except that feeling, pulsing on and on. His fingers stop as the intensity fades, leaving me boneless, because it was wonderful. Too wonderful. Too wild. An orgasm. I'm aware that I'm crying. I feel bewildered.

He shouldn't have done it. I shouldn't have liked it.

He pulls away from me, grabbing hold of my arm with one hand so that he can wipe his eyes with his sleeve.

And I'm coming down from an orgasm. The best of my life. And coming to my senses.

That's when I call out. "Help!"

"Hello?" A man's voice. "Someone out here?"

"Fuck!" he whispers. And then he does something crazy—he lets me go. I scramble for my glasses and leap up, running toward the voice, putting them back on as I go, getting myself back.

I can see a figure up ahead through the trees. "Help me!" I scream, pressing my skirt back down as I dodge around trees and right into a pair of strong arms. A policeman. I'm sobbing hysterically, pointing at where Grayson was. "He's...he's..."

Suddenly the man stiffens.

"On the ground. Slow." Grayson's voice.

PRISONER

The cop lets me go, and I back off. Grayson's behind him with a gun to his head.

"You're not going to get out of this," the cop says. But I can see that the cop's holster is empty. Grayson took his gun.

"I think I'll get out of this just fine," Grayson says.

The cop spins, and suddenly they're fighting.

Help the cop!

But I don't know how to help. They're a fury of fists and snarls, wolves fighting over a carcass—or deadly fighters grappling over a gun. Grayson catches him with an elbow, smashes a fist into his face, and the man's down. I gasp. *No.*

"Run and I'll kill him," Grayson says, pulling the man's arms around a tree and cuffing them, the cop is hugging a tree. "Fuck," he says, ripping his black T-shirt down the middle, baring his chest like a wild animal. He pulls the shirt off and rips out a couple of strips with a glance at me. "I mean it."

"You're not a cop killer," I hiss. I want to believe that. Partly because I believed in *him* for so long, reading his work and building him up. But also because, if he'd kill a cop, he'd kill anyone. *Me.*

He slaps the stunned man in the face. "I can tell you know who I am. Am I a cop killer?" he asks as he wads up one of the strips.

"Yeah," the cop says.

"See?" Grayson stuffs the fabric into the man's mouth. Then he ties a gag over his mouth. "This worked out, don't you think?"

I'm frozen where I stand, hope draining out of me as I watch him blindfold the cop.

He turns and stalks toward me. I back up and hit a tree. His eyes look puffy, but apparently he can see just fine now. He grabs the front of my sweater. "You're not getting away, you understand? You can't get away from me."

"Okay," I whisper.

"Say it like you mean it."

"Okay."

He's staring at me weirdly. This softness comes into his face.

"What?" I ask, afraid even to move.

He lifts a hand. I flinch, but he just touches my cheekbone. Even though he's actually being gentle now, his touch stings. "You're cut. Did I do that?"

"When you pushed my face into the ground, you mean?" I bite out. I actually don't think he hurt my face at all. I think it was from when I crashed through the bramble, but he seems concerned for my welfare in that fucked-up way of his, so I let him think it.

I'll take any morsel of sympathy I can get.

CHAPTER SIXTEEN

~GRAYSON~

M S. WINSLOW IS nothing but trouble. If Stone were here, he'd drop her without a thought. He's always been more comfortable with killing than I have. I mean that with respect. He didn't hesitate to slash throats and gouge eyes when he had the chance, and it's because of his physical brilliance and love for violence that we got out of that hellhole alive.

Here I am with a cop bound, blindfolded, and gagged. And little Ms. Winslow looking at me with her big doe eyes. She looks...wounded. Betrayed. Shocked that I might be a bad guy after all.

Well, nice to meet you too.

"Let's go."

"But what about..." She glances back at the cop.

Doesn't she know the cop would give her up in a second if it meant catching me? She's nothing to him. A pawn.

"What?" I go over and press the gun lightly to the cop's temple. "Should I do it?" The cop jerks his head, pointing his face upward the way blindfolded guys always seem to do. Like if they look upward, they might suddenly see through the blindfold. I never understood that.

Her lower lip trembles. Is she going to cry? *It's going to sting her cheek.* Why should I care? I shouldn't, I shouldn't, but my stomach clenches when the tear falls over the smooth skin and splashes into the bloody streak. Like an idiot I go to her and brush my thumb over the cut, knowing the salt and grime will hurt her too. She flinches but doesn't move away.

Pain is a funny thing. We fight so hard to avoid it, almost more than death. But it's the only thing that binds us. Going through pain together and coming out on the other side is the only form of friendship I've ever known.

And strangely, I want to have that with her. In a way I feel like we do. The class. The pepper-spray episode. A little hate, a little hell.

"Should I shoot him?" My voice has dropped to a whisper. "Should we get rid of him?"

She shakes her head, hard, dislodging more tears. "Don't. Don't."

It makes me want to do it more. Maybe we'd be more connected if we went through a little more hell together. Sometimes when you're made of ice, fire is all you feel. My finger tightens on the trigger. At least then

I'd have done what they locked me up for.

Ms. Winslow wraps her arms around herself. "They'll kill you!" The words sound torn from her. "They won't just put you back in jail. They'll put you on death row."

Her words get me. It's sympathy. Maybe even some kind of warped affection.

I know what to do with the fist and the knife. I know what to do with pain and hate. I know what to do with a woman, how to run the tender, caring act just long enough to get my rocks off.

I don't know what to do with Ms. Winslow.

"Let's go," I repeat, gruff this time. Aren't we a pair? Both of us determined to save the other, even though it might kill us in the end.

A grunt comes from the cop.

I spare him a glance. His mouth is stuffed full of fabric; his hands are cuffed. Stone would probably taunt him.

"Save your energy," I say softly. "Don't fight it. That makes it worse. Wait for your chance."

Of course he doesn't listen. He strains his muscles, fighting so hard the leaves shiver above him. A vein pulses in his forehead.

"Don't struggle," I snap, but he isn't listening. They never listen.

"Let's go!" I say again, and she obeys, turning in the direction I nod.

There's enough light coming through the tall branches to tell me there's an opening in this direction. I can't risk going back to her car with the cop car there. I doubt there's a partner sitting inside, waiting to hear back; state troopers work alone. But he would have called in his position before leaving the car. Backup is on the way. Probably not for at least thirty minutes, though.

Knowing police procedure has saved my ass more times than I can count.

We move through the forest at a swift pace despite the rocky landscape. Fallen trees and deadwood block our way. She stumbles sometimes, but I always catch her before she slips. She's warm and soft in my grip. I force myself to let her go.

Why isn't she running?

Obviously I'll just catch her, but she has to know I won't kill her now. I sure as hell know it. She's mine to do what I want with, but that also means she's mine to care for, to protect.

Lying on the ground with her, calming her, helping her breathe, that was one of the most powerful experiences of my life—powerful in a good way. The feeling is so huge inside me that it scares me. And then the way she broke apart underneath me, under my touch.

I catch a flash of red on her pale cheek at one point and I grab her wrist. Her brown eyes look up at me, dark pools in the dappled light.

"Did you get hurt?" I demand to know, even though she obviously did.

She shakes her head. "I'm fine."

The blood dripping down her cheek calls her a liar and twists me in a knot. I want to say something comforting, but all I do is tighten my hold on her wrist. "You won't get away if you run."

Her smile is small. "I know."

But I know she heard everything I told the cop. *Save your energy,* I told him, and she was listening. The same way she lectured about memoirs, I taught her how to escape. How to fight back. *Wait for your chance,* I said. And she soaked the knowledge right up.

The best thing I can do for her is leave her here, but I can't. I won't.

CHAPTER SEVENTEEN
~ABIGAIL~

H E FORCES ME into the stream. Freezing-cold water swirls around my ankles and fills the insides of my boots, numbing my feet clear to the bone. I try to pull away, but he holds my wrist tight. I'm shivering. I can't believe he's not cold without a shirt on. Not that I should feel sorry for him considering he used his shirt to gag and blindfold a cop.

"Where do you think you're going?" he asks.

"The other side."

He shakes his head. "We're walking the stream."

"I can't," I say.

He pulls me closer; he still seems obsessed with the gash on my face, which maybe should be a good sign. I force my focus onto the trees in the distance, anything but the rise and fall of his hard, mud-streaked chest. It's around dinnertime; I can tell by the slant of the sun. Up close he smells like sweat. Not pine, not cologne, not musk, just man sweat.

"Bend over."

"What?" I try to yank my wrist from his hand, but he fists my hair and pushes my face nearly into the water. He splashes water onto my cheek. I close my eyes against the cold spray of it, spitting it out of my nose and mouth, trying to twist from his grip.

"God!" I say as he lets me up. I sniff and wipe my eyes.

He inspects my cut and grunts his approval, as if infection is this huge threat right now. He pulls my hand. "Come on."

"I can't even feel my feet!"

He frowns, furrowing his dark brows. "Fine." He bends over and loops my arm around his neck and just hoists me up.

I pull my arm back and struggle against his hold. "Put me down!"

"You want to walk? Or I still have that .357. I could put a few holes in you, and you could float. Is that what you want?"

I loop my arm around his neck, feeling weird, like I'm participating in my own captivity. But it seems better than the alternatives. *Don't struggle. Wait for your chance.*

A ways down he steps onto the bank and puts me on the mossy ground. I feel unsteady on my feet. He gets up on the rocky shore next to me, water streaming from his big black boots, chest shining with sweat. "Take off your panties."

I look at him like he's crazy. Maybe he really is crazy behind those dark and beautiful eyes. Underneath all that rough skin and powerful muscle. He's a loony bin wrapped up in the sexiest package I've ever seen.

I'm praying that he's just toying with me.

He smiles like it's pretty hilarious. "Do it, or I'll do it for you." He picks up a rock, rubs it in his armpit, then tosses it deep into the woods. He does the same thing again, with another rock, and then another. "Two seconds," he says. "I'm not fucking around." He raises his brows, waiting. "Am I doing it for you? You know I will."

My stomach lurches, but I don't have a choice. My hands are shivering as they reach under my skirt and push down the fabric of my panties. I place them in his outstretched palm.

"Thank you, Ms. Winslow." Like I just handed him a pencil to complete his assignment.

He tosses them into the underbrush. Then he picks me up and carries me through the stream again, heading back where we came from. My heart sinks as I realize what he's just done—pointed the search dogs the wrong way.

"You have such dirty ideas, Ms. Winslow," he says, trudging through the water.

Soon we pass the place we started from maybe ten

minutes ago. *Making good time,* I think grudgingly.

"I try to be practical," he continues, "and where the fuck does your mind go?"

I hate that he can read me. I wish I could read him. "Stop calling me Ms. Winslow."

"What do you want me to call you?" He lowers his voice, and his dark eyes meet mine. "*Abigail?*"

My belly does a flip-flop to hear my name on his lips, and I look away. It's like an invasion of my privacy or something, him saying Abigail, but *Ms. Winslow,* the way he says it, is just too dirty.

"I don't want you to call me anything," I snap.

He snorts, carrying me down the stream the way a groom would carry a bride over the threshold. It feels almost tender. I have to remind myself that he's a cold-blooded murderer.

So why hasn't he killed me yet?

Save your energy, wait for your chance, he told the cop. I wonder if my chance is coming up—surely his feet are too numb by now to run fast. And though he doesn't show it, he has to be tired from carrying me; his biceps bulge and strain under my weight. The tendons in his warm, sweat-slickened neck pop with every step he takes. Can I wear him out this way? I wish I weighed three times as much. Anything to sap his strength.

His nostrils flare minutely as he goes. He has a simple nose, a friendly, no-nonsense nose that contrasts with the sharp beauty of his eyes. And he knows how to harden those features to make himself scary. His perfect cheeks are getting just a shadow of stubble. It occurs to me that he must have shaved for his escape. Wanting to look clean-cut, I suppose.

Sometime later, he veers out of the stream and puts me down.

"Ride's over," he says, pointing through the bramble. He wants me to go first, so I go.

We walk for what feels like hours. My feet ache from my boot heels. My shins have been whipped by a thousand tiny branches. We head up the side of a plowed field, and then another, but no farmer is in sight and no cops, either.

Well, they're searching in another direction if they're searching at all. I'm coming to realize I can't count on the authorities. They couldn't keep me safe at the prison. Why should I expect them to save me now?

I'll have to rescue myself.

Grayson seems to know where he's going. As we trudge along, I get the sense he's listening—to the wind, distant noises. This is where he excels: a type of battle. Not fought between countries, but soldiers. Between sides.

We go over a hill, and I see a road up ahead. My blood races.

"I know what you're thinking," he says, leading me

down the bumpy, weedy terrain to a roadside strewn with litter. We begin to walk, just beyond the shoulder. "You want to flag somebody down? Go ahead, it's their funeral." He picks up a whiskey bottle and swings it in his right hand as he walks, takes my hand with his left. "One way to get a car, I guess."

I hear a car approaching from behind, and I stop breathing.

"Don't even think about looking," he says just when I'm about to look.

The car continues on by—a lone driver in a silver compact. And then there's silence. He makes me pick up a glass soda bottle. It's full of ants. A ways down he finds a shred of rubber that came off a tire, probably a truck tire, and he picks that up too. He points to a fallen tree, just off the shoulder of the road. The shadows have gone long. It'll be dark out soon. "Sit."

I sit, trying to think what to do. If I flag someone down or wave my arms wildly for help, will he really just shoot them? A truck approaches. "Eyes on the ground," he growls. "Act natural."

Act "naturally." It's called an adverb, asshole, I think, but I don't say it. He seems to get perverse pleasure when I correct his grammar. I wonder how much he does it on purpose, just to get a rise out of me.

He sits next to me and starts breaking the bottles we collected as the truck approaches. I sneak a look. The driver's on his phone.

Help me, I mouth.

Grayson immediately starts smiling at the truck. Almost like he's laughing. As if I'd made a joke. The driver locks eyes with Grayson as he rolls past, chatting away on his phone. My hope slowly withers.

Then he grabs my wrist in an iron grip. My blood runs cold. He speaks through gritted teeth. "You don't do things like that." He jerks my arm. "You understand? You can't." He seems almost alarmed, as if I'd darted out into traffic instead of going for help.

I stare at him defiantly, trying to keep my cool composure in spite of my racing heart.

"I'm in charge, and you're not," he says. "The sooner you get used to that, the better things will go for you."

I keep up my stare.

He looks almost sad then. "Give me your glasses."

My stomach gets tight. "No."

"Now," he growls.

"I can't," I say with a sick feeling, though I know it's true—sometimes playing along and getting used to things is how you survive. But I need my glasses to read. To make out faces. To shield me, hide me. I *need* them.

He's waiting.

Instinctively, I put up my free hand to touch them. "Please." He grabs my wrists. I twist my arms, straining to get away from him. "No!"

"I'm sorry." Calm as granite, he reaches up to take my glasses with the other hand.

"Not my glasses," I beg as he pulls them off my face.

"You think they protect you, but they don't," he says. "You think somebody out there might rescue you, but they won't. They will never help you. People out there can't protect you." He set the glasses in the dirt and picks up a large rock.

"No!" I gasp as he brings the rock down, smashing the frame and lenses. "I can't see."

"I can," he says. "I'm the one who protects you now."

I sob as he picks out the shards of lens from the frame and sticks them into the rubber strip. It looks like a snake studded with shark fins. I watch through bleary eyes as he goes out and lays it in the road.

He comes back and pulls me into the shade under a tree. Unlikely a driver would see us unless they were really looking. "We just need a vehicle now," he says as if we're a team on some caper together. I maintain stony silence. We will never be a team.

A shiny blue pickup truck heads our way. There's one person inside, but I can't make out much without my glasses.

"Hello," Grayson mutters under his breath as the truck goes over his trap. There's a pop as the tire blows out, and the driver steers to the side of the road. Grayson takes my hand and pulls me along. "You say one fucking word, you try anything, and somebody dies. Got it?"

He doesn't seem to be expecting an answer, so I don't give him one. I feel naked with no glasses and no panties. He wants me helpless. He's doing a pretty good job of it, I suppose. But he doesn't know me. And I will never get used to this.

We reach the guy on the side of the road quickly. I can see him better now—I can see middle distance, just not far and near. And I can see that the front tire is completely flat, but the rest of them look fine. "Need any help?" Grayson asks.

The man takes one look at Grayson and straightens up, squinting. Grayson's handsome face and charming, cocksure smile don't fool him. "No thanks." He holds his ball cap in his hand; with his big, puffy build and graying flattop he looks like an aging football player, and he knows Grayson's trouble.

"You got a spare and a jack?" Grayson asks.

"Yep," the man says. "I'm good."

"Excellent." Grayson pulls out his gun—the cop's gun. It's giant and scary. The man stills. His eyes dart to me, but I don't have any answers. "Let's have the phone. Easy."

"I don't want any trouble," the guy says as he pulls his phone from his pocket.

"That's the right attitude." Grayson plucks the phone

from the guy's hand and tosses it in my direction.

My hands come up by reflex—a decades-old reflex that kept me from getting hit with dishes or books or whatever my mother decided to throw at me.

I catch it. The phone is still warm from the guy's body, and my stomach turns over. It feels like I'm complicit in this, like I'm an accomplice instead of a victim.

But Grayson still has the gun.

My eyes plead my case to the guy, but he's all apprehension. His gaze darts back and forth. He's trying to figure us out. *Bonnie and Clyde,* that's the conclusion he comes to. He thinks I'm part of this. *No, no!* I want to yell.

Grayson gestures with the gun. "Now take off the shirt and toss it to my woman."

My woman. Disbelief rolls through me.

The man unbuttons his blue plaid shirt, eyeing me fearfully, and tosses it to me.

I catch it, shaking my head, short and fierce. *I'm not his woman. Get help.*

He looks confused, scared. Maybe angry.

"Where's your jack?" Grayson barks. The man mumbles that it's in the back, and again Grayson gestures with the gun. "Go get it. We got some work to do."

The man has some work to do, as it turns out. Gray-

ANNIKA MARTIN & SKYE WARREN

son, ever the enterprising criminal, forces him to change the tire for us, which the man does with incredible efficiency, jacking up the truck and switching out the tires. He has all the right tools. He's that kind of guy.

I feel like an idiot for not doing anything, but every idea I come up with seems more likely to make things worse than better. Only one car passes by in the time he's working on the tire. It slows, maybe thinking about stopping, but Grayson just grins at them like everything is just fine, and they speed back up. It's a dream. Or a nightmare.

It's dark by the time the man finishes, bare chest dripping with sweat. Grayson makes a big show of testing the tightness of the bolts. Then he nods. "Get out of here."

The man looks at him with disbelief.

"Go," he says. "There's a gas station a few miles down. Can't say it'll be open by the time you reach it, but…"

The guy takes three rapid steps backward, covering more ground than should be possible. I don't want him to go, to leave me alone with Grayson again.

The man turns and runs. He was definitely a football player, maybe twenty years ago. That's how he runs, like he's going to tackle something. Not like the truth, which is that he's scared.

Anyone would be scared. A big tough guy is *terrified*

of Grayson.

Horror and frustration bubble up inside me.

He winks. "The FBI won't know which way is up. Were you helping me all along, Ms. Winslow? Are you secretly my lover?"

I throw the phone at him, which he catches, of course. One-handed. "I will *never* touch you," I say.

He turns to me. "Yes, you will." There's no triumph in it. He says it like a statement of fact. He takes a step forward.

I back up until the truck stops me. I'm sweating, but the hot metal is almost a relief. Warmer and more human than the flesh-and-blood beast that looms in front of me.

But I have something to say too. Something true. And I want *him* to listen. "You might hurt me. You might touch me. But I will never, *ever* touch you. Not of my own free will."

I'm shaking by the time I'm finished talking. Tears are threatening again, but I don't care about them. They don't make me weak. I know what real weakness is. I saw it inject itself with drugs and hook up with abusive men just to get its fix. I watched it die. That will never be me. Never.

He reaches up to cup my cheek—the side without the scrape. On purpose? I don't know. He trails his thumb over my eyebrow and down my temple. Places he couldn't touch when I had my glasses. Like he's learning me, mapping my face. The inside of my chest feels bright and quivery, but I keep my frown.

"So I can touch you?" he asks gently. "But you won't touch me back?"

My voice trembles. "I didn't say that."

"Didn't you?" His hand trails lower, down my neck. Goose bumps rise all across my chest and over my arms despite the heat.

He caresses my skin right where my collarbone is, softly, with the back of his knuckles. I clench my fists at my sides, dreading what comes next. He's going to keep moving lower, until he's touching my breasts. And then what will I do? Cry? Scream? There's no one to hear me. The guy from the truck has disappeared over the ridge.

I let my eyes close. "Stop."

"You don't want this." His tone is conversational.

"I hate you."

"What *do* you want, then?"

"I want you to die. I want to hurt you. I want you to let me go."

He laughs softly, a puff of breath against my forehead. "In that order?"

My teeth clench together. "Take your pick."

"You know what I think, Abby? I can call you that, right? It's cute. Like you." His hand curves to the side, feathering light touches along the cashmere of my sweater. He grips my hip as if we're dancing. And we *are* dancing. It's a sick song he plays.

"I think you want to fix me. That's what you were doing at the prison. That's what you're doing now. But the thing is, Abby, it's not going to work. You can't fix people. Not with bullshit writing assignments, not with anything."

"They're not bullshit," I spit out, angry suddenly because, yeah, he can take my freedom, but he can't take the things that I know. Or the things that Esther taught me. "Some of the guys in there, it meant something to them to tell their stories, and for their stories to be heard. Telling our stories is what heals us and makes us whole," I add, parroting Esther's words.

His beautiful lips twist in a sardonic smile. "That's really what you think?"

"Yeah," I say.

His voice flattens out. "Some people can never be fixed," he says to me. "Some wounds can never be healed. Not ever."

CHAPTER EIGHTEEN
~GRAYSON~

SHE'S SLUMPED AGAINST the opposite door. Her hair fell down from its bun. Dirt and blood are smudged on her face. She took off her fancy sweater to use as a pillow when we started moving, and her nice blouse is torn and soaked with sweat. But she looks beautiful anyway. And tragic. It's hard to keep my eyes on the road; I want to stop the truck and just stare at her, drink in the sight so I'll never forget.

That might not be a problem. Even when I close my eyes for a second, stopped at a stop sign, I can see her face. She's etched in my mind, her fragile body, her prim features. And underneath, a core of fire.

What made her so adaptable, so brave in the face of threats and violence? There's something. I don't know what it is, but something made her this way.

"You got a boyfriend?"

She gives me a dark look. "Yes."

My blood boils, although I don't know why I'd be jealous of some half-baked accountant who goes to church on Sunday. That's the only kind of man I can see her with.

Liar.

I can see her with me. Under me. Over me with those firm little breasts moving as she rides me. But that's just sex, and I figured out a long time ago not to trust my own body. Stimulation. Physical reaction. It can be anyone rubbing me, *fucking* me, and as long as they do it the right way, I'll orgasm. That doesn't mean I won't kill them.

"He must be worried. Are you usually home by now? Cooking dinner for him?"

She purses her lips during the brief pause. "We don't live together. I live in a place on campus."

"And he lives—where? Not on campus?"

"He's... Yeah, he's off campus. He lives...with his parents."

Disbelief rocks through me, along with a healthy dose of relief.

Even though, why does it matter if she's got a boyfriend? Some lame-ass boyfriend waiting at home does not matter at all. But the weight off my chest proves it does.

"There's no boyfriend," I say.

She scowls at me, proving me right. "Is too."

God, she's such a shitty liar. I love it. I want to watch her lie about everything. I want to watch her do everything. "Circumcised or not?"

Her mouth gapes open. She closes it and then opens it again. Nothing comes out. "He's...he's..."

"He's made up."

"No, he's not! He's a communications major in his junior year. And president of the history society. He has brown hair and...and freckles."

I snort. "I'm sure there's a guy you know like that. Maybe you even had a little crush on him. But you're not dating him. And you're definitely not fucking him."

Her eyes narrow. "Not everyone thinks about...you know."

"*You know.* Is that what you call sex?" Now I'm sure she doesn't have a boyfriend. In fact...is she a virgin? Because damn, that's pretty goddamn innocent. For the first time with her, a whisper of concern runs through me. What if she's *too* innocent?

What if I break her?

"Be specific, Ms. Winslow. What is it you're not thinking about?"

Her blush spreads up from her chest to bloom in her cheeks. "Stop pretending you know what I'm thinking. You don't know *shit* about me."

I'm surprised by the bite of her words. I take another look at her, all wrecked and hot and dirty, head resting on the passenger window, hair tangled around her shoulders, out of that prim bun. There's something natural about her like this.

You don't know shit *about me,* she said.

My questions just make me hungrier for her. It feels like physical hunger, like thirst, a craving so deep I wouldn't even know how to quench it. I can only make her talk and make her cry and make her *hurt* and hope it's enough.

"You're the good girl. The quiet one. The do-gooder. What's there not to know?"

Reverse psychology. It's clumsy and stupid, but when her eyes meet mine, I think maybe it's not so stupid.

"Perfect Ms. Winslow," I taunt.

"Maybe you're not the only killer in this truck. How about that?"

I snort. "Did you forget to feed your goldfish one time?"

Abby stares out at the taillights of the car up in the distance, thoughts heavy, lips zipped. Yeah, I know how to wait.

I look back at the road. Back in the foster home, I forgot to feed my two goldfish once and they died. I cried like a baby, and I felt like shit for weeks.

After I got taken, sitting down in that basement in my corner by the metal locker, I'd be scratching designs on the floor with a nail while Stone and the older guys played cards or whatever and I'd think about those fish and I'd still feel like shit. But then we'd hear the footsteps up at the door, and if it wasn't mealtime, we knew they'd be dragging one or two of us up there.

Or worse, the sound of Dorman's car outside the window, because that would mean me getting called, and the whole thing would start—making you eat the drugged candy, and then they put you in the creepy outfits—sailor suits and short pants and shit. And I'd think about those goldfish, seeing nothing and feeling nothing with their huge dead eyes, and be all jealous. Like a fucking idiot, jealous of some dead goldfish. Floating around above that stupid little castle I once saved my pennies to buy back when I was a free kid.

I glance at the dashboard clock. It's been an hour since we cut the driver loose. I'd meant to switch vehicles by now, but she's got something on her mind, and she wants to spill. Abby's eyebrows move inward a tiny bit when she has something to tell. She used to do that in class too. The guys never noticed that, and they'd talk when she had that expression, but I never did. I care about what the fuck she has to say.

Right at the point where I think maybe she changed her mind about what she needed to tell, she says, "I let a man die." Her voice gets a little gravelly as she continues. "I stood there and watched him."

I should keep my eyes on the road, but I'm riveted—to her hate. Her beauty. Her total powerlessness with me. And now she's telling me a secret.

"He was in a drug overdose," she continues. "Foaming, the whole bit. My mom told me to call 9-1-1. Paramedics could've saved him. It wasn't too late, you know?"

"Yeah," I say, but I know she doesn't hear. The look on her face tells me she's back there. It's a look I know real well, having been in prison, a place filled with guys who spend half their time *back there.* I need her to continue now more than I need my next breath. I look at the darkness beyond our headlights and glance back. "And you refused."

"No. I grabbed the phone like a good girl." Her voice is trancelike. "I tried so hard. I always did." She pauses. "I really did." She seems badly to want me to believe it.

"Of course. Kids want to be good," I say, not sure where that came from or even if I believe it, but I'm desperate for her to continue, and she does.

"I punched three numbers. Just not 9-1-1. It was 4-1-1. She made me call because she didn't want them to know she was there. She goes, 'Don't say I'm here. It's just you, Ab.'"

Ab. It's no kind of name. I resolve never to call her *Ab.*

"And I talked into the phone." She demonstrates, putting her fist to the side of snarly hair, eyes wild. "We need an ambulance—hurry!" she pleads. "My stepfather—he's not breathing. W-what?" Her voice gets small, scared. "At 247 Larkin. Hurry. Uh—he overdosed on drugs! He has spit on his lips. Kind of gurgling." She widens her eyes, gets on this mask of panic to match her voice that does something funny to my chest. "He *is* on his side! No, he is... I don't know. Make sure his mouth is open?" She eyes me, nodding urgently, just as she must have done to her piece-of-shit mother. "His mouth!"

Chills run up and down my spine.

"Okay!" she says. And then, "He sounds weird! It's not right! He's still not right!" She spins her voice even higher. "Wait. Hold on! No, just hurry!"

She pulls her fist from the side of her head and thrusts it in her lap, suggesting she'd simply hung up at that point. The pretend 9-1-1-call she never made. She straightens out, face sphinxlike. "My mom was hysterical. She had to snort a little brown just to even out enough to get out the back door for the afternoon."

"And you stayed and watched him die."

"He took a long time. Or I don't know, maybe it seemed like that. It was the day before I turned eleven. I remember because I thought..." She doesn't finish the sentence. A birthday wish that never materialized. "The sounds... His body just really wanted air. Rattling, but kind of like a baby animal crying. I sat far across the room, and it was like he knew I was there and he knew what I was doing, but he couldn't get to me. He just sat there making those sounds."

"You couldn't risk him staying alive."

After a long time she says, matter-of-factly, "He was killing her."

I nod. Thumping on the mom, feeding her drugs, maybe whoring her. "You couldn't risk it, then. That's obvious."

She knows what I'm doing. "I *killed* him."

"You had to choose."

She snorts, full of hate and derision, and I get in a flash that she never told anybody before. But she told me, now, and I can't fuck this up; it's like she's given me something fragile and I have to hold it and care for it.

I see her as that ten-year-old kid, scurrying to school, holding her little world together. I see her trying to make up for it. Repenting with her Sunday-school boyfriend who will never really touch her or make her feel anything real. Pulling stories out of guys like me because she knows how they scorch you inside.

"Hey," I say, "look at me." She finally looks at me, face lit by the dashboard lights. "You had to choose. Sometimes you have to choose between one shitty thing and another."

"Is that personal experience talking, Grayson?"

She's trying to push the spotlight back on me. It makes her nervous, me seeing her like this. And that's how I know this is real. When she's flustered and angry, that's when I'm seeing the real her. "You saved your mother. That's what matters. Some people have to die."

ANNIKA MARTIN & SKYE WARREN

"Like me?" she snaps.

"Dying's not what you'll be doing, Abby."

She looks away, but not fast enough to hide the flush on her cheeks. "I didn't even feel bad after," she murmurs, almost to herself. "I always felt bad about not feeling bad, but never for killing him. Not ever. It's psycho."

"Why would you feel bad for saving your mom?" I'm starting to get pissed because she shouldn't feel bad about any of it. In fact, I want to rip somebody's face off, but that's not helpful, either. "To a kid that age, listen— saving your mother is the same as saving yourself. It's the same fucking thing."

"Don't try to make me feel better," she says.

"I'm not. I'm being straight with you."

She glares at me, but the glare just covers the torment sunk deep in her eyes, and panic flares in my heart because I'm failing her.

I reach down, desperate for something good to give her from inside my worthless self. Something real. "Sometimes, Abigail, you have to punch a fucking hole in your soul to survive." I might be driving like a maniac, I don't know. We're off the highway, but I'm still going highway speeds. I reach over and grab her, pull her clear across the seat to me. "Most people never have to find out what kind of shit they're really capable of. Most people don't have to turn themselves into something they hate just to make sure they can get that next breath."

I might be digging my fingers into her upper arm, but I need to feel her. Her eyes are like mirrors in the greenish light. I can see myself in them.

"You're going too fast," she whispers.

I slow slightly. "You know who doesn't do that? Who doesn't do the fucked-up thing?"

She's crying now. I think it might be relief. That's what it feels like inside me as I watch the tears roll down her cheeks.

I answer my own question. "The kid who ends up dead, that's who." I slam on my brakes. I nearly ran a red light. We're two feet into the intersection. *Keep it together.* But I'm coming apart.

"Where are we going?"

There's a town just ahead, and I'm going for it. This truck is near expired. "Switching vehicles."

She sniffs out a breath. Some kind of subtle cut.

I'm way beyond subtle. "You and me, we survive, okay?"

She's watching me, but she doesn't seem to hear, sitting there, dark hair tangled around her pale face, red-rimmed eyes shining. "You are so fucking beautiful," I say.

The light turns green.

And then I kiss her.

Chapter Nineteen

~Abigail~

TEARS SWIM IN my eyes. I'm underwater but still breathing.

I don't see his eyes darken or his head lowering. I can't see the signs of a predator closing in, especially when he doesn't look anything like a predator. He looks concerned—about me, when almost no one has ever cared. Definitely not a man like this. Virile and strong. Powerful. He renders me breathless with just a low-lidded look. There's no time to be afraid before his lips touch mine. They're softer than I could have imagined. His words are jagged shards of glass, accusations and threats. *Lies.* But his lips tell a different story.

They're warm and comforting, pressed flush against my mouth. Even an hour ago I would have jerked away. I would have slapped him. But this kiss tells me he understands. Death and kisses. Blood and sex. They twine together in a dark braid I bury deep inside. He pulls it out of me, rips it from my heart and leaves my throat raw and tight.

He parts my lips and slips inside. There's a moment of hesitation. *Do I let him?* A rough sound of impatience vibrates from his lips to mine. His hand tightens on the back of my neck. He's not asking; he's taking. He takes my air and breathes it back into me. He takes control of me, and I can finally give in.

I can finally let go.

He rubs his tongue against mine, raising goose bumps along my arms. I never want him to stop, and as if he hears my deepest desires, he tightens his hold on me. One hand fisted in my hair. The other on my hip, pulling me closer.

I'm losing myself. The thought stops me cold.

What have I done? I told him about my mother. I told him about my past. I've told him everything about me, tearing off strips of my skin like it doesn't matter. Like everything will be okay. But it won't. He's going to kill me. He's going to rape me. Though just now, with my tongue curling against his, it doesn't feel like rape. Is this what death will be like? Will he make me want that too?

A car horn sounds behind us, and I jerk back. His eyes are dazed with lust and something deeper…

I push the thought aside. He doesn't feel anything. He's an animal, reacting with snarls and the snapping of teeth. At least that way I can understand what he's doing. No one likes to be put in a cage.

At least that way I understand why he's hurting me.

He accelerates, but he still has me, fingers digging into my arm. I whimper.

That seems to snap him out of his haze. *You're beautiful,* he said before he kissed me. But the way he looks at me now, I'm not pretty. I'm an alien, something he can't quite comprehend. There's wonder and wariness. Hesitation and hope.

The scariest part wasn't when he pressed a gun to my rib cage while my heart beat a staccato rhythm. The scariest part is right now, wanting to fulfill his hope. Believing that I can. It's that nightmare that follows me down.

✧　✧　✧

I JOLT AS the truck rocks me awake. My cheek bounces off the window. It's night. Did I fall asleep? Looking around, I see we've pulled into a motel parking lot. The place is dark, deserted. The neon blue and red light from the vacancy sign casts a ghostly glow on Grayson's profile. My insides turn cold with dread. A motel means a bed. Me and him—in a bed.

"Why are we stopping?" My voice comes out rusty.

"I need to sleep. You can keep watch."

A joke. If I saw anyone coming for us, I'd more likely call them over than give Grayson a warning. By his dry tone, he knows that very well. But he's taking the risk—

so he must really be exhausted.

This is my chance to escape. I just have to keep watch for an opening. It will come.

It has to.

"Don't get any ideas," he says, reading my mind.

Too late. "If you think I'm going to cooperate with you, you're insane."

He laughs, low and a little bit wild. "What ever gave you the idea I'm sane?"

Then his hand is on my wrist. He yanks me halfway onto his seat and grabs my chin. His eyes are dark pools swirling with anger, guilt—but most of all, determination.

"You're hurting me," I say through clenched teeth. His grip on my wrist is twisting my skin. Even his hand on my chin is going to leave a bruise if he clenches it much longer. Everywhere he touches me, I burn.

He doesn't ease up. "It's a warning, sweetheart. You know what I'm capable of, and I'm at the end of my rope here. Got no more patience left."

That was him being *patient?* "Let go of me."

"I don't think I will. I'm going to hold on to you. All night even." He grins, a little cocky. I can imagine him using that grin in a bar and having every woman there at his feet. I can imagine being at his feet, especially now. I already am, just not by choice.

My heart pounds with fear, thinking about that bed

in there. I have to get away.

He pushes me back into my seat. "See that guy inside the window?"

I look through the lit windows of the motel office and see that there is somebody at the desk in there, but I can't make out much else. There are no other people in the tiny office. No cars in the lot or buildings nearby. *No one to hear me scream.*

"Yeah," I say.

"I know you can't see him that well, but he's just a kid. Seventeen? Eighteen? And he's counting on you to be good for him. You can do that, right? You can sit here, nice and quiet, and he doesn't have to get hurt."

Really, the only thing more annoying than Grayson threatening me is Grayson being condescending. I glare at him.

He chuckles. "So we understand each other."

I watch his back as he goes inside the tiny motel office and up to the counter. I have no idea what he's telling the guy, but it wouldn't be his real name or the fact that he just escaped from prison.

Grayson must seem like a completely different person in there—less scary, less intimidating. The guy's head bobs up and down—is he nodding? Laughing at some casual joke?

He's got the guy fooled. Well, he doesn't have me fooled.

So we understand each other, he said, but what he doesn't know is that I've built my life around reading people. As a child, it was how I stayed alive. One step ahead of the junkies my mom hung out with. I learned when to fight and when to lay low. And I'm going to use the same skills to get away.

I can't run now, even though it's what I want to do more than anything. But I already found out what happens when I run, and it's not pretty. He'd catch me. He'd *punish* me. Or maybe he'd just make me come again.

Plus, he really might kill that kid.

I have to be smart and not let fear take me over. Wait for my chance. I won't get many of them. Later, when he's sleeping, that's when he'll be vulnerable.

He comes back and gets in. His smirk makes me itch to hurt him.

"Good girl," he says.

Oh, I definitely want to hurt him.

Chapter Twenty

~Grayson~

I LOVE IT when she's angry at me. Back at the prison she always seemed kind of sad. Beaten down, like some of the lifers. But when I make her angry, her eyes light up like firecrackers. I watch her *boom boom boom* like she's my own private show.

The room is as small and shitty as I expected. It's a good thing because it means no one will be eager to fill up the rooms around us. I can't trust her not to scream. It would be a stupid move, but captive animals do stupid things sometimes. The brain shuts off, and then they're pure panic. Right now, she's thoughtful. Watching me carefully for a sign I'm slipping up. Ordinary people can't cope with this kind of stress. She's not only coping, she's impressing the hell out of me.

I can't afford to be impressed with her.

"I want to take a shower," she says, just as regal as can be. Like the Queen of England, and I'm one of her subjects.

"Your wish is my command," I reply just to watch

her eyes spark all over again.

I let her have the shower. I even let her close the door—which is a gift on my part. Plus it gives me time to scout the motel room without her watching me. There's only one bed, and thankfully it's got a post I can tie her to.

The door is bolted shut with the chain lock in place. The only chair slides right under the knob—keeping intruders out as well as keeping her in.

The shower has been going for a long time. An old motel like this—the water will be cold by now.

I don't bother to knock; I shove inside and find her huddled in the tub, knees pulled to her chest. She's making little stifled noises, as if she's drowning underneath the spray. She's not drowning; she's crying. Something strange weighs down my chest, sudden and heavy. I'm not one of those guys who's allergic to women crying. I don't care if they like it, even though they usually do. But something about her curled up in a ball like a wet kitten makes me want to dry her off with a fluffy towel and tuck her into bed.

"What are you doing?" I ask her even though I don't expect an answer. She doesn't give me one.

The water is freezing, so I shut it off. There's no fluffy towel, just a thin one. I use it to dry her. She's shivering, not looking at me. Her hair forms a heavy damp curtain around her face. It's a shield, but I'm done letting her hide. I tuck the wet hair behind her ear. On impulse, I kiss her cheek.

She flinches like I slapped her.

I touch her gently at her temple—the same place I'd put a gun as a threat. We're in for the night. She knows what's coming.

I trail my finger down, down, down her cheek and across her lips. I follow the line of her profile. She becomes two dimensions to me, a cutout silhouette of a real person. The line of her neck is an edge, something I can cut myself on. When I get to the tops of her breasts, she grabs the towel around her and pushes away.

"That's right," I say approvingly. "Fight me."

The back of the neck is a sensitive place. It's where one animal grabs another to bend them into submission. It's where I place my hand. I use it like a leash to guide her to the bed. Each step feels forced, and that's the way I like it.

"Lay down," I say.

She glares at me.

"Lay down, and I'll let you keep the towel."

She hesitates, then complies, fastening the flimsy towel just over her breasts.

"Let's be clear," I say as I tie her wrists to the headboard. "If I want to fuck you, I'll fuck you. If I want you to suck my dick, you'll suck my dick. And if I want you to lie there quietly and go to sleep, you'll do that too."

But that's not in the cards, and we both know it.

Her wrists are tied tight enough to press her hands together as if she's in prayer, with a cloth connecting them to the bedpost. I move to her feet, fastening one ankle to the metal frame under the mattress. Best if the other one's free.

I stand and survey my work as she glares up at me. And that mouth. That pretty pink mouth with the tongue that darts out and wets her lips. Yeah, I could do a lot with that mouth. She's mine to do what I want with, and it's hard to know where to start.

With a huff she turns and curls on her side, away from me—as much as she can be with her hands and one ankle tied, anyway. I run a finger along her arm. Goose bumps rise.

"You gonna pretend you like it?" I ask.

Her fists clench, as much as they can, anyway. I don't really want her to pretend. I like her how she is. Real. I think about the library, when I took off her glasses. How real she felt. Like we were standing on the edge of something.

I want her to talk, so I goad her. "You gonna pay your way? Maybe if you fuck me good, I'll let you go."

She makes a hissing sound. "Never."

"Yeah." My smile dawns slow. "Maybe you'd rather stay with me."

She jerks her head around, and there go her eyes

again. *Boom boom boom.* Suddenly they seem important, those fireworks. Like I have to keep them in her eyes. Can't let them fade out.

But then she turns away from me again and goes very, very still. I sit on the bed next to her and run a finger down over the rough, cheap towel that covers her torso until I hit the end of it, skimming the top of her silky thigh. I continue down toward her knee, two fingers now, enjoying her warm, soft skin, enjoying that she's mine. I'd always known I would fuck her when I got the chance, but being with her in this shitty little room, it already seems better than what I imagined and I'm not even inside her, yet. She gasps when I change directions, back up.

When I hit the edge of the towel, I slide my hand up under it, finding the curve of her hip, fitting my hand around it, fingers finding her hip bone.

She sucks in another breath. Like she's so surprised this is actually happening. As if she'd thought I was somebody different. Somebody better. Did she hope her class broke me of my darkness? People like her want to see the best in people like me, and she'll probably want to think the best as time goes on, but it's important that she doesn't think the best of me or hope for me to be something different. Misery is wanting what you don't have. Misery is wanting what a rat has, or really, anything different. It's important to me that she sees what this is and what it's going to be. Deep down, she already knows exactly how we fit, which was why she was nervous around me in class. Even with my wrists chained up, she knew I'd fuck her someday.

"Turn over," I say, pulling at her hip, encouraging her to turn onto her back.

"Don't," she says.

"Come on."

She doesn't move.

"Do it," I say.

"Why?"

"You know why," I whisper. I tighten my fingers over her hip and pull firmly, guiding her. She kicks backward at me with her free leg, but I'm ready—I catch her leg with my other hand and make her turn over, pressing her leg and her hip down, putting her how and where I want her.

She stares up at the ceiling. The towel only half covers her. Her pulse pounds in her neck. Frightened. Her eyes are vacant—she's gone somewhere. I slap her thigh. "Hey."

She ignores me, like she's not there. And she isn't. With a jolt, I recognize what she's doing—she's keeping some little piece of herself away from me. I know all about that.

"Look at me."

She won't.

"I know what you're doing, and it doesn't work. It never works. In fact, it works against you."

"What the fuck do you care?"

My heart's pounding like crazy. I care because I care. I need her to listen.

I touch her hair. "You just can't do that, okay? We're together now, and there are a few things you need to learn, like if you keep something away, it just makes it harder on everyone. On you. On me. That's not something you want."

No answer. She looks exhausted, empty. Just how I feel. I keep my hand on the thigh of her kicking leg. I imagine pushing it aside, spreading her apart and pushing into her. And yeah, she's gone somewhere, but I would fuck her until I find her again, in that place where she's gone, or maybe until I find some missing part of me, some part that isn't empty and hollow and wrong.

And suddenly I'm imagining something else—I don't know if it's the exhaustion in her eyes or what, but I realize I could give her the kind of help I never got. It's crazy, but I'm talking now. "You want to sleep? Is that what you want?"

She rewards me with a pointed look. The anger. She's back.

"Answer."

She makes her look go darker. I take it as an answer.

"You need to give me something real. Like what you

wanted from us in class. But I'm not talking about a vignette here. I want something, Abby. I want something from you."

She takes a bit to figure out where I'm going with this. "I'll never touch you, ever. Not ever."

"Yes, you will," I say softly. "You'll touch me if I want you to." That's the real thing, for her to learn this.

"You can't make me."

"I won't have to. You'll make yourself do it." She looks at me in hate as I stand up, making myself bigger than her, no longer on her level. She's back, and I'm the devil, breathing in her fire, consuming little bits of her soul. It feels wild and good.

"Never."

But she needs to understand that I'm in charge, and that there's nothing wrong with that, and I need…what? Something to patch up my wrecked soul. I even make it easy for her, moving up to the bedpost, a position that puts me between her and the bedside lamp. I cast a shadow over her. That seems just about right. I prop a hand on the wall, leaning, just casual, like I'm talking to a friend.

"Hands only. And I won't fuck you tonight."

"Do your worst, because I said I wasn't going to touch you."

"But you will, because that's the fastest way we get to sleep. You're going to take me out, and do me nice—and

I mean nice. And then you're going to thank me." I can't believe I'm giving her this option after all that time imagining this opportunity in prison. I'm disgusted with myself, but it's what I've said now.

She's breathing hard.

"No? So I do my worst? That's what you want?"

Silence.

"That's your choice? This is a limited-time offer, I can tell you that much, Abby." I don't know what's going on in her mind but…

She closes her eyes. She looks miserable.

It's better this way.

I make my voice low, as if she's a wild animal I have to coax to eat from my hand. Like the rat in the basement. He was real, even if his name wasn't. "It's okay to lose. You've got to understand, you lost a long time ago."

"I'm not touching you," she says, and it pulls at something in me, because I know that she *will* touch me, and it'll be better than fucking her.

"You lost before it started," I say. "Hands only."

She's the one tied up. She's the one captive, and I'm hard as a rock. I can have any hole of hers I want, and she can't do a damn thing. Instead I take the hole of my own creation, the space between her palms. I reach down and show her what I'm looking for, just to show her. First I slide my two fingers inside, as if her clasped hands are a cunt I have to prepare.

She gasps when I touch her like that. Imagining my cock there. Maybe she's even thought about it, but probably not quite like this.

I look down at her, running my fingertips gently between her palms. It's a sensitive place, her hands and mine. Warm with our shared heat. But nothing compared to how my dick will feel.

"You're not just going to touch me, got it? You're going to take me out and jerk me off," I tell her. "And then you'll thank me."

For not fucking her. She *should* be grateful. It was what I'd planned to do. It won't kill me to fuck her, but it's this I really want.

"Take me out. Do it nice."

She squeezes her eyes shut. And it's like that electric line from class is still connecting us because I can feel her caving in to me, now—I recognize it with a rush of emotions I can't define. She moves her hands down to my pants. I watch as her nimble fingers undo my button, and then my zipper.

"Nicely," she says.

"What?" I ask, heart pounding.

"Do it nicely. The word is *nicely*, motherfucker."

Oh, Jesus. She's pulling me out and I almost come right there. Her wrists are flush against each other, but she can still squeeze me in both hands and push down to my root and that's what she does. A grunt escapes me.

She closes both fists around me and begins to jerk me off for real. It's a little too fast, even considering how turned on I am. That's how much she wants this over with. I understand that—God, I understand that too well. The way she's moving fast reminds me of other hands. Greedy, grasping hands.

I grab her wrists. "Take your time."

Her gaze meets mine. "I hate you," she says between clenched teeth, but she's slowing now, stroking while she watches me. It feels good when I focus on her face, when I stay in the present instead of the past. It helps to hear her voice too.

"Yeah, give me more of that sweet talk."

"Fuck you," she says, her hands moving in nice, solid strokes. I watch her lips, and I think about leaning down and kissing her, but it would be too much. Too sweet.

"More," I grunt. Shadows from my past are constant-ly stalking me, and never more than when someone else's hands are on me. I need something to ground me here, in this shitty motel room, with the pretty teacher we all imagined fucking. "Talk more."

"Why don't you go find someone who actually wants you?"

It's so fucked up, but her words are doing it for me. I kind of love her being this hard ass, this bitch, while she's making me feel so fucking good. So I push her. "I think you love how I feel. You love this—admit it."

Her hands tighten, and I shudder with pain and pleasure and a sudden reluctance. I want to jackhammer inside her and I want to draw a line in the sand that will keep me from her.

I want to hurt her and I want to protect her. Break her and shield her.

Determination fills her eyes, and my dick gets that much harder. "Why do you want me to slow down?" she taunts. "A little desperate from all that time in prison? A little dry?"

"Fuck," I say, teeth clenched tight because her hands are moving even faster. "Yeah." She's racing me to the finish line, and she's winning.

"Or did you get some action after all?" she says, her voice full of venom. "In your cell? In the showers?"

God, the kitten has claws. She's using them, and I'm on the edge. She's cutting me open. I can't even say the right answer. *No, I've never fucked a guy. I've never been fucked.* Because it's not true, and she'd be able to see that. Though I was never fucked in prison.

She sees all of me, everything. She sees my weakest points, and she attacks them.

"Get yours back." My voice comes out so thick she probably can't even understand me. "Make me hurt, baby. Get me back."

For all the times I hurt her, insulted her. For all the

times I'll do those things in the future.

And she does, tugging on my cock like there's no tomorrow. It hurts but it feels too damn good to stop. I watch her little hands work furiously, full of anger and desperation. My balls pull tight into my body. It feels like an explosion at the bottom of my spine, and all the lava comes pouring out of my dick.

At the last second, I grab the wet towel off her and use it to catch my come. It would have gone in her face, in her hair. It would have gone in her eyes and made a statement about who was in charge here. But by catching it in a towel instead, I've made a different statement. The opposite one.

She doesn't seem to see the move as weakness though, which is a good thing. I sigh with relief—four fucking years of relief—as I tuck myself away. She looks just as pissed off as when I started, maybe more, but that's better. At least she's not wide-eyed and huddled in a shower, staring vacantly into space. I know what that means in a person. As long as she keeps fighting me, she'll survive.

I come around the other side and roll into bed. I'm so exhausted, I'm nearly immune to her naked body, stretched out beside me. And we made a deal. My word has to mean something to her. I cover us both up with a blanket.

Just in case she has any ideas about trying to get out

of her binds, I slide one arm underneath her head. The other one I fling over her waist. And last, I slide my foot over her tied-up leg, tangling us together. If she so much as coughs, I'll feel it. There's no way she can escape.

Her skin is soft. I listen to the sound of her breath, hoping she'll sleep now, and wanting her like crazy.

"Thank you," she whispers into the dark.

CHAPTER TWENTY-ONE

~ABIGAIL~

I LIE IN his arms, thinking about all the ways I'll hurt him once he's asleep, once I get my hands free. Scratch out his eyes, maybe punch my knuckles into his windpipe. I don't need to beat him up, just disable him enough to get away.

So I wait, lightly pinned under his arm, his leg. He thinks he can keep me. He doesn't know how small I can be, how quiet. The way I'd huddle in my room with my mangy cat, listening to the sound of fists on the other side of the door. That's a form of weaponry, being small and quiet. He'll never know what hit him.

The AC here has two settings—freezing and nothing, and it's on freezing. But the parts of me he's touching are warm, and his breath is warm on the nape of my neck.

My toes feel like little blocks of ice, and I shift my foot so that it's under his huge calf, and then I tuck my other foot under that one. He stirs, pulling me closer, warming me, and it feels good, like somebody on this wasteland of a planet is saying, *Let me keep you warm.*

I never had anyone rock me to sleep before—my mother was too beaten up or strung out on coke to even recognize me most nights, but maybe this is how it would've felt. Calming. Soothing. Like somebody saying, *I'm here.*

For a split second, I imagine giving in to the comforting weight and warmth of his limbs on my body like I did in the woods, but I don't—I'm not stupid. I keep myself as stiff and distant as possible. Except for my toes. He's just so warm.

I wonder if that's how it was for my mother. Hating and wanting the drugs at the same time.

Until it killed her.

It's maybe a second later or hours later that I jerk awake—all I know is that I'm losing my battle with sleep. And my eyes are wet with tears. But he's still holding me, and his heartbeat is steady as sunshine, and he has sandwiched my toes between his heavy legs and they're finally warm. It's like I'm tumbling. Falling.

How could I have softened toward Grayson for even a second?

Carefully, slowly, I extract myself from his hold. It's like a real-life version of the game Pick Up Sticks, where I have to remove my limbs, one by one, without disturbing him at all. I untie my ankle with my toes.

It feels like a ten-foot drop out of the bed. My feet land too hard on the thin carpet. Pain shoots up my shins, a burst of white in the red streak of my thoughts. *Escape. Get away.*

Only my hands are attached to the bed, tied up with cloth. The bonds are tight but not cutting off circulation. I made my wrists clench, pumping extra blood through them, tensing the muscles without looking like I was doing it, when he tied me up. That way I'd have a better chance of getting out. Now I relax myself, willing my wrists to grow slimmer. I pull at them hard, trying not to yank and wake him, but I'm frantic to get free. He left enough room in the knots that I wouldn't wake up with bruises, but I'll have them now.

I twist against the fabric, trying not to think about the way he washed my cut. The way he carried me in the stream. How he could have demanded a lot worse than a hand job. There's some kind of code he's following, a twisted form of honor that I find almost endearing.

Except I can't find him endearing. I can't think he looks almost vulnerable, sleeping in the dark like a dangerous prince waiting to be woken with a kiss.

I lean in and try to loosen the tie with my teeth, then I pull and twist some more, wincing as the cloth cuts into my flesh. Little by little, I'm getting free.

I almost can't believe my careful movements aren't waking him, but I bet he didn't sleep last night in the prison, all pumped for his escape today. And he fought in that riot. He carried me through the stream, and I may be small, but I'm not light. Then he drove for hours without stopping. He's been on an adrenaline high for twenty hours, capped off by a hit of endorphins from the orgasm. He sleeps on.

And suddenly I'm loose.

I kneel on the floor, staring at my raw, swollen hands, no longer attached to the bed. I wait for Grayson to snap his eyes open and laugh his dark, gravelly laugh and tell me it has all been a test. But no. He sleeps on, and my heart twists as I watch his chest rise and fall. He's a horrible human being, but he's still a human being. That means something to me. It *has* to mean something, or I'm a horrible human being too.

I find my clothes in the bathroom and dress quickly. My body moves like a train leaving the station—slow at first and then building speed. Then racing. I hold my breath as the lock snicks. The hinges squeak, barely audible over the eager AC. I step into the darkness outside, breathing in that inimitable smell of nighttime and pine, and quietly shut the door.

Safe. Safe. Safe.

My heart beats heavily in my chest, triumphant and terrified. The light is off in the motel office, but I rush down and I try the door. Locked. I wonder if the teenage kid who worked there is staying in one of these rooms or whether he's left the property. Either way, I'm not planning on banging on any doors to find out. That will give Grayson too much time to wake up and find me.

The road is long and empty both ways. I pick a direction and walk fast. With any luck, I can find help. With any luck, I can be free.

I pass an abandoned farmhouse, but no people are in sight. A truck passes by, but I'm too afraid to flag it down. What if the truck driver is as evil as Grayson? I can't trust anyone. I stay in the shadow of the trees until the red taillights fade to black. I am alone here, disconnected.

It's like with every passing mile, I am farther and farther away from safety—and farther from myself. From being human. I'm turning into this other type of being, one who jerks off criminals in crappy motel rooms. One who wants to be kissed in a getaway car.

I need to get away from him, away from this. It doesn't matter if he kills me. I understand now why he had to escape prison. Even the threat of death won't keep me locked down.

I follow the line of trees in case I need to use them for shelter, but I don't go deep inside. The woods couldn't protect me last time. They'll only cut my skin. They'll only make it easier for him to track me down. No, I'm going to walk until I reach people. Civilization. Safety.

Buildings appear like a mirage, and I almost can't trust them. A small town. It's like heaven. I walk faster.

By the time I reach the town, blue and purple hues streak above the horizon. Dawn. I'm running out of time. Cars are parked diagonally in front of old-time shops. A pharmacist. A lawyer's office. Who can I trust? I hear the rumble of a truck. It could be anyone. It could be *him.* An uneven sidewalk trips me, and I fall, gasping at the jolt to my knee. I scramble up; I have to keep going.

My breath is loud in my ears, every puff an explosion. And then I see it down the street. A police station. A little police station with only a single cop car parked in front of the building, but it's enough. If I can get there, I'll be safe. Grayson won't be able to touch me inside that building. Or will he? Will a small-town cop be able to stand on his own against Grayson? But he's my only hope. And he'll have a gun and probably a partner. He'll have training. He'll have backup. Grayson has nothing but his fierce will and ingenuity—though I have to admit, those things have gotten him further than anyone expected.

I imagine the crunch of gravel behind me, and I take off running, afraid even to look. There's only now. No later. No future. No being open and honest and vulnerable with anyone else—not ever again.

My lungs burn. My legs are screaming in pain. It feels like my own body is holding me back. He's gaining on me. I can hear him. *Feel him.*

I dart between cars in a parking lot, heading toward the little police station, and it's like running through a fun house. Pale clouds are reflected in windshields. Endorphins twist my vision until everything looks wavy and strange.

The door to the station opens before I can reach it. Blue uniform shirt. An older man, graying hair. And a gun. God, *yes*. Finally. It's wrapped up in black leather and tucked beneath his belly, but that's fine. This man—this gun—is going to make things right.

"Help me," I say in a burst of breath. "Please help me."

The cop's hand goes to his gun. He doesn't pull it out; he just holds his hand there as he moves away to inspect me, gaze snapping down my body and then up again. "Miss? What's happened? Are you okay?"

There's a hint of suspicion in his voice; he doesn't like that I ran up to him like this. It makes me laugh, half with freedom and half with hysteria. "He's after me."

With dark brown eyes set deep inside folded lids, he scans the street, the cars.

No one is there.

"Ma'am, are you in trouble?" the cop asks. "What happened?"

"It's him. He escaped from a prison—the Kingman Correctional Facility. There was a riot and… His name is Grayson—Grayson Kane," I say, recalling how proudly and painstakingly I typeset his name above his vignette in that stupid journal, making the margins just so.

The cop's gaze turns sharp. "Kingman Correctional?"

"He was back at the motel, but I escaped. I thought he was chasing me."

The cop scans the empty horizon, and finally his eyes fall to my red, swollen wrists. "Come inside."

Relief fills me as I step into the cool office. The smell of stale coffee mingles with lemon-scented floor cleaner, making my stomach lurch. The cop introduces himself as Sheriff Dunham. He points to a swivel chair with pilling fabric.

"Sit down while I call this in."

I follow his instructions, my hands shaking in my lap. I'm not sure why. This is a good thing. Now I can go home to…a room with bare walls? A string of endless classes? The only meaningful thing I've ever done is *The Kingman Journal,* and even that is tainted with what Grayson did.

My gaze goes back to the door, and I recognize what's twisting my stomach: fear. Part of me thinks I'm safe now, but the other part of me remembers that Grayson did the unthinkable. He escaped from prison. He can do anything.

Sheriff Dunham grunts in response to whatever the person on the phone is saying. The conversation takes a long time, and my nerves begin to rise. The sheriff isn't watching the door while he's on the phone. He's watching me instead.

He murmurs something that sounds like assent, and a chill runs through me, like the cold sound of chains. Like the heavy double-barred doors clanging shut in the prison.

Apology glints in his eyes, faint enough to tell me he won't be swayed from what he's about to say. "Ma'am, I'm afraid I'm putting you under arrest."

My mouth gapes open. "*What?*"

His expression firms. His eyes harden, as if no regret had ever lurked deep inside. "There's a warrant out for your arrest. Aiding and abetting a felon."

I NEVER IMAGINED I'd be looking at the bars from the inside of a cell. The funny thing is they look the same from the outside, round black cylinders, impenetrable and forbidding. In the prison, they'd been a reminder that I wasn't as safe as I thought I was. The sight of them that first day had slammed into the sense of security I'd worked so many years to build.

And now that I've been locked in a small-town jail, they shatter that security completely.

I refuse to sit on the mold-blackened cot or go near the toilet without a lid. It smells foul, even if you flush it.

So I stand in the only corner left, huddled, miserable. And angry.

My mother was arrested countless times. She'd told me things designed to help. *Don't fight; you'll only wear yourself out. Be nice to the guards, and they'll be nice to you. Make your wrists tight when someone's slapping cuffs on you, so you have a chance of getting out of them.* She assumed I'd end up as lawless and beaten down as she was.

I never thought she'd be right.

The sound of shuffling comes from outside. The phone rings, and I hear the low tones of the sheriff. He must be talking to the cops near Kingman—or maybe even the FBI. They're probably giving him credit for catching a dangerous criminal like myself. A hysterical laugh threatens to escape me. I force it back down, because once I start, I might not stop.

I told them the name of the motel where he was. They thought I was lying.

Footsteps *click-clack*, slow and steady from the front offices back to the single cell where I wait.

I glare at the sheriff as he stands outside the bars, holding a bottle of water.

"You thirsty?"

I glare some more. I'm horribly thirsty, but the thought of accepting help from this man makes my stomach churn, even though I know he's only doing his job. He's not allowed to decide who's guilty or innocent; he just puts them in jail.

"They won't be here for another six hours, so you may as well have a drink. Go ahead. You hungry? You look a little pale. You're entitled to a lunch. We usually send out to the bagel place—"

It's lunchtime already? "I'm not hungry," I snap. Though I should be. I feel a little feverish, actually. "I didn't help him," I say, my jaw clenched so tight I can barely get the words out. I know it's useless to argue with him, but I can't help it. Something about being innocent, about being unjustly accused, makes my blood turn to lava. I was the one held at gunpoint and dragged across the state. I'm the one with bruises on my wrists. Now I'm the one locked up behind bars.

He sighs. "If that's true, then they'll sort it out."

I think he believes me, but I still have to stand in this cold, dank cell. I still have to accept a bottle of water like it's a scrap of bread and I'm a stray dog.

And I *want* to believe that they'll sort it out, but how did they even tangle it up in the first place? "What's the evidence against me?" When he doesn't answer, I push. "They must have evidence to get an arrest warrant, right? They can't just take one out without any kind of proof."

Something flickers in his eyes, almost like worry. He knows something isn't right here. "It's not for me to know the details, miss. I'm not involved in the investigation."

"You seem pretty involved to me," I shoot back.

He doesn't meet my eyes again. He sets the water bottle on the floor and moves away. "I'll check in later," he says before returning to the front.

How can they hold me here? I've done the right thing for so many years. Even when it hurt. Especially when it hurt. I tried to be the good student, the good girl. The unfairness of it rises like bile, sharp and acidic. I think about Esther. Does she think I helped him escape?

How can anybody think that? I barely know him.

But that's not quite true. I do know him.

A dark stain spreads at the base of the water bottle, turning the dusty concrete black. Condensation drips down and adds to the pool of water. I let my mind drift as I watch the drops fall and slowly dry.

Now that I've stopped running, now that I'm safe—at least I'm safe from him—I feel sleepy. All the tension that was holding me up leaves me, and now I'm boneless. Shaky.

Shadows lengthen across the dingy cot and the gray mottled floor. I don't want to contemplate using the toilet, so I don't want to drink too much. Half the bottle and I'm done.

But God, I'm so tired. And hot.

I curl up on my side. The concrete feels cool on my cheek, and it's probably more sanitary to touch than the cot. I tell myself I'll take a little nap.

The next thing I know, I'm startled awake by a crash. I shoot up from where I lay.

Above me, there's a dark shape. Sunlight streams around it, giving it an unearthly halo. The clink of keys.

"I told you not to run."

Grayson. He sounds pissed.

I scramble back and hit the wall.

He opens the cell door and stands above me, looking down, his expression black.

"How did you get in here?" I look around. Try to listen for signs of life. "Where is…"

"Don't worry, nobody's dead. Yet."

I don't know who he's threatening—me or the cop, or maybe the whole damn world. He's capable of anything.

"Up." Something flashes in the gloom, and I realize he has a gun in his hand. I stiffen. "That's right," he says with a sparkle in his eyes, still seeming to track my every thought. "You ready to be good?"

"What are you doing here?"

"What does it look like?"

"I've had hours to tell everything I know—what your friend looks like. The license plate."

"Did you?"

"They didn't question me yet, but—"

"Didn't think so."

"But you didn't know that!"

He gives me this look, calm and sure. It's as if I've been out there buffeted by wild ocean waves, and he's a strong, solid rock outcrop. He's sharp in places too—maybe touching him will rip me open. I don't know how to feel.

"Why?" I whisper.

He kneels, putting himself at my level, and something like concern flickers in his eyes. "Because I had to get you out of here." He closes his hand around my upper arm and pulls me up. "I'll always come for you. You're mine."

CHAPTER TWENTY-TWO

~GRAYSON~

ABBY SLEEPS, CURLED up where I set her in the passenger seat. It would make my life easier if she never woke up, but I can't stop looking at her, worrying over her like a damned mother hen. God, she needs water. And food. She seems feverish, but that could be exhaustion. Her wrists are raw from where she pulled against the ties. I should've heard her. I should've stopped her.

I've been doing a shit job of taking care of her.

That's unlikely to change much, but there is one place I can take her. I take the back roads past closed-down shops and empty trailer parks, keeping a careful eye on her. Sometimes I touch her, just to make sure she's breathing, that her pulse is there.

Her face looks peaceful now, but it makes my gut clench to remember her in there, caged up like an animal.

Why the fuck did they arrest her?

I tried to get an answer out of the sheriff, but I suppose I didn't give him enough time. Doesn't matter. I already know it's the governor. He just keeps fucking me over—framing me for killing that cop. And now he's framed Abby.

It's like he knew she was important to me.

I make a quick call on a pay phone when we stop for gas, then hop back in and keep right on going, even though my eyes feel full of gravel.

A small-town sheriff doesn't mean anything to me, but they'll bring in the FBI on this. I'm supposed to be much farther away by now, but Abby's escape attempt set me back. I've been awake for forty-eight hours except for those two or three hours in the motel. This isn't the kind of exhaustion a Mountain Dew will fix; it's the kind that will get me killed.

And get Abby killed.

I don't know when she started to matter. She does, though. She matters. I couldn't shoot her in the back as she ran away from the truck. I couldn't let her suffocate in that damned jail.

Something has changed inside me. A weakness? I'm not sure yet.

I'm driving and keeping an eye on the rearview mirror, but I decide I don't like how she's sleeping, with her neck all crooked. In a way, it would serve her right to wake up with an ache in her neck, but I shift her anyway, her cheek to my thigh, which is as close to a pillow as she'll get. I press two fingers to her throat, and only then do I realize my hand is shaking even though there's nothing to worry about: her pulse is strong and even.

She's going to be okay.

Everything is going to be okay. I survived three guys in the shower room trying to pin me down. Yeah, I broke a couple of ribs and cracked my skull, but I made it out alive. That's my mantra. I can survive anything. Even her.

I stroke her hair. My voice starts out thready. "Why did you run? Could've gotten yourself killed. But then, you knew that, didn't you?"

She doesn't answer, of course. That's okay. If she can hear me, if she recognizes my voice, maybe she'll feel safe. But what am I thinking? She'll always fear me. Always associate me with darkness.

The way I do the governor.

"How'd you get out of those knots, huh?" Either I was sloppy or my little bird knew a trick.

She shifts and her hand rests on my thigh just above my knee. Maybe she thinks it's a pillow, I don't know. I just know how bad I want her to keep it there. I trace the curve of her ear, the hollow of her neck. I should be watching the road, but I can't take my eyes off her.

I imagine her waiting for me to sleep, her breathing so even that my senses would be fooled. I imagine her ripping her wrists from the ties, clenching through the pain. I can't help but like her.

"Where'd you learn that, baby?" I murmur.

Her calm expression is my only answer.

Even a shitty motel would feel like a luxury at this point, but that's too risky now. I force myself to drive the extra hundred miles.

It's night by the time we reach Nate's place. The gate leading into the long driveway is unlocked, which tells me Stone got my message and let Nate know we were coming. I turn in. Dr. Nate is set up in an old farmhouse with different barns, pens, and outbuildings scattered around. He's a large-animal veterinarian. Cows, horses, pigs. And guys like me.

As soon as we hit the gravel, Abby pushes herself off my thigh, looking around, dazed. And agitated. Her hands go to her face, her arms, her movements still jerky and uncoordinated.

"You're okay," I say, doing everything I can to keep from touching her. It wouldn't calm her, me touching her right now.

She's looking out the window. You can't see shit except the porch light up ahead. I know what she's doing—assessing the place, maybe thinking about making a run for it. I take her by the arm so I don't have to hurt her wrists any worse. She yanks back, nearly ramming herself into the door of the car.

"Don't," I say wearily. "Just don't."

"Where are we?" Her voice is slurred, but at least she's awake.

"Visiting a friend."

"Where?"

"Michigan."

A shocked breath goes out of her, like I took her to Mars or something. "How long have we been driving?"

"A long time."

Her eyes dart to the dashboard clock. The beater I stole from the motel has an old-fashioned clock with actual hands, and it says 10:52. "Yeah, it's right," I add. We're near enough to the porch now to see bugs buzzing around the light. A light inside flips on too.

Nate won't like me bringing her here, but he won't do anything about it. Because we go way back. There are some bonds you can't break.

"I need you to do something for me." I hand her the strip of cloth I dug out of the backseat some hours ago. "I can't let you see this guy."

"I already saw your other friend."

"Do you *want* me to kill you? I'm clearly still caring what you see and what you don't see. Right? Maybe that should tell you something."

"Or maybe you just like messing with my head. I'm not stupid. I know you can't keep me with you forever, and I know you can't let me go."

Frustration surges through me. Because she's right.

Because that's what my crew is going to say. Because I need some water and some food and some goddamn sleep.

"Here's your choice right now—you spend the next few hours in the trunk of this car, or you put on the blindfold and come in with me."

She throws the cloth at my face. "I'll take the trunk."

"Really? So you're not hungry? Not thirsty? Not in the mood for a nice, cold glass of lemonade?"

She swallows. Salivating. Deliberating, when we both know what she'll do. She sticks out her hand.

I give her the blindfold. "And you definitely don't want to make me chase you again."

"Fine." She puts it on. I go around and open the passenger door and guide her out and up the three steps to the big wraparound porch and up to Nate's front door, which swings open.

"The fuck?" Nate mutters under his breath, glaring as we walk in.

"Don't mind me," Abby says.

"No talking," I growl.

Nate widens his eyes.

"It's fine," I tell him. Then I shake Abby a little, partly to get her attention and partly in punishment. She's got a mouth on her. "You need to use the bathroom?"

She shakes her head, but I do have to go. I need to

shower while someone else watches her, since I can't trust her by herself.

My body demanded rest several hours ago. I ignored it. Now it's forcibly shutting down on me. I've lost whatever thin hold I had on politeness or patience. I guide Abby into Nate's kitchen and push her into a chair. *Stay,* I tell her with a squeeze of her shoulders.

Her soft sigh promises that she will. Never can believe her.

I set my hand on her forehead. "Does she seem feverish to you?"

"I'm fine," she says, jerking her head away.

Nate scrubs his hand over his short, kinky hair, eyeing me unhappily.

"See what you think," I urge him. "Go on."

He sighs and presses his hand to her forehead. "Are you hungry? Thirsty?" She doesn't answer. "Aches or pains?"

"Besides the obvious?"

He turns an accusing glance at me. "I'd imagine she's just overwrought."

"I need a few minutes. She hasn't eaten for... She needs to at least drink." Then I turn to her. She sits primly. Even blindfolded and with that cut on her cheek, she takes my breath away. "If you run, he'll shoot you. He's not nice like me."

Her lips firm.

I exchange glances with Nate, who isn't amused. He's a good guy—or he tries to be. That's what makes him different. But the past...that's the part we have in common. And you can't escape your past. Not Nate. Not me. Not even Abby.

CHAPTER TWENTY-THREE

~ABIGAIL~

I FOLLOW GRAYSON'S footsteps as he goes into some other part of the house. He's leaving me alone with this other man. I should be thinking about escape, but it turned out so badly last time…

There's a small knock, and then the light rumble of heavy glass over wood.

"Orange juice in front of you," the stranger says.

I ignore him. I want Grayson back, perverse as that sounds.

"You should drink. You can't think straight when you're dehydrated."

"Why should I trust you?" I demand. "I don't know you."

I can almost hear his shrug. "You don't want to keep up your energy? To fight at a moment's notice?" He has a deep voice. A nice voice.

"Is that what you think I should do? Fight you? Fight Grayson?"

He doesn't answer, and I get the feeling he isn't so

comfortable with this.

"But you're not going to help me." The words come out bitterly. Grayson wouldn't have brought me here if he didn't trust this man.

"I'm not going to help you, no," he says.

I wonder how he and Grayson met. I wonder what happened to make this man loyal to Grayson, and make Grayson trust him completely.

"How long have you known him?" I feel like a supplicant at his secret stash of answers. But I can't help going to him, empty bowl in hand. Whatever truths he might give me about Grayson are food for survival, and I'm starving here—dying.

There's silence, and I think he might not answer. But then he does, with the weight of reluctance in his voice. "A long time." I feel each word drawn out of him, heavy with meaning. "Since we were children."

"Did you go to the same school?"

"No," he says simply.

"You were neighbors or something?"

"No," he says softly, thoughtfully. "We...wound up together, that's all."

The darkness in his tone grips my belly with an icy hand, because I'm suddenly thinking about the rat. The basement. *We wound up together.* I assumed the rat story was a lie, created to get a message out. Grayson laughed and let me think it was a lie. Wasn't it?

The sound of pipes stretching in the walls tells me Grayson is finishing his shower. I need more, in whatever minutes I have before Grayson returns.

"I get it." I set my hands flat on the table so he can't see them tremble. "The basement."

The sound of a quick inhale fills the quiet. "He told you?"

I stiffen. *It's true, then? He didn't make it all up?* "Of course," I say in as natural a tone as I can manage through the shock. "He told me." Which is true. In a way.

He pushes the glass toward me. I can feel it cold against my knuckle. My heart pounds as I think through his vignette in this new light. *Kept in a basement. They broke my arm.*

"Just tell me one thing," I say softly. "How long? You won't help me. Fine. Just tell me that."

"If Grayson didn't feel like telling you that…"

"Oh, come on," I say, trying to think what might sway this strange honor-bound friend of Grayson's. "He told me the whole thing. Even the rat."

I wait, straining to know so much more, to know everything. But I can't ask too much. How long; that's an easy question.

"Please," I say. "I don't want to hate him."

I regret the words as soon as they're out of my mouth—they feel too true, and I shouldn't feel bad for him. Being trapped in a basement as a kid doesn't give him the right to kill people and take people captive.

After a long silence where I think he won't even answer me, he says, "Six years."

My heart stops and then begins thudding wildly. Six days, I wouldn't have been shocked. Six weeks would have made sense. There would have been time for him to go missing, time to have those cartons printed and distributed to schools, for other children, safer children to wonder over at lunchtime.

Six months...well, that hurt to think about.

I can't even fathom six years. In a basement for six years. Captive for six years. No TV. No games.

The stranger's laugh is rusty. "I've shocked you. And now I think...I think you let me believe you knew more than you did. Smart. Know your captor."

"Is that what Grayson is?" I ask, and I know I've gone too far.

The air shifts. I feel the man moving away from me. "You'll have to ask him," he says.

Then he's gone. But there isn't time to contemplate an escape, because just as quickly, the kitchen is filled with familiar footsteps. I guess I already took the stranger's advice, because I do know my captor. And even though I'm blindfolded, I know it's him in front of me.

Chapter Twenty-Four

~Grayson~

NATE DOESN'T QUITE meet my eyes when I pass him. He's just outside the kitchen, checking his phone, well in my line of sight but removed. Separate. As if an extra four feet can keep him apart from what I'm doing to Abby in here. The way he's acting, he must have said something about me, something I won't like. But I'm not worried about it. We'd never move against each other. We'd kill for each other. We already have.

Abby is sitting where I left her, in the kitchen chair, blindfolded. The glass of orange juice in front of her is full. She hasn't touched it.

I need sleep. Which means she needs sleep. I crush the pills I pulled from Nate's stash. A sedative meant for dogs and cats. I stir it into the juice.

She'll be able to taste it, but that won't matter. I'm not trying to hide the fact that I'm drugging her.

"Here," I murmur, taking her hands and showing her where the glass is, making sure she has a grip on it.

She takes a sip and makes a face. I catch the glass

before she can knock it away.

"What is that?" she asks, sputtering.

"Something to help you sleep."

"You drugged me?"

"Not yet," I say evenly. "One sip isn't going to do anything. You're going to drink this whole glass."

"Like hell."

Her swearing gets me hot. And that's a problem, because in an hour she's going to be asleep. "You are going to drink it, because the alternative involves cages and metal handcuffs. And then I'd probably stick a needle of horse tranquilizer in you for good measure."

Because judging from her bruised wrists, she might be willing to break her arm to get out. Most people think they'll do anything to escape, but they won't.

Something about her is different. She's fierce and a little bit crazy. It means I can't trust her. It also means I really, really want her. To have all that wildness beneath me.

"But why?" Her voice is thready, afraid. She's afraid. It twists something in my chest.

"It's just a light dose, Abby. But the truth is, I can't trust you after what happened at the motel."

She flinches as if I hurt her. Maybe I did. But I can't risk her getting loose from me while I sleep here. I can't make Nate watch her.

And, above all, I don't want to have to tie up her

wrists when they're already fucked up. I won't hurt her any more than I have to.

"Drink it," I say, more gently. "It's just enough for a dog. Twenty pounds. It's going to make you groggy. Not unconscious."

And just like that, she obeys me. Her hands are shaking as she lifts the glass to her lips. I help her hold it in place while she drinks it down, almost greedy now that she's decided to give in.

I think she wants oblivion as much as I want to give it to her.

I watch her drink, watch the way each sip leaves shiny little specks of pulp scattered across her top lip like stars. And then she licks them off.

"That's good," I tell her. "You won't cause me any trouble tonight."

"Yeah," she says softly.

I look up and find Nate staring at us with an expression I can't quite read. I don't care. Let him think whatever fucked-up thing he wants. I peek into his fridge. "You like blueberries?"

She nods.

I pull out the bowl and pick the biggest blueberry, fat and almost purple. "Here," I say, pressing it against her lips.

She opens for me, and I imagine the sweet-tart juice bursting against her tongue. I wish I could see her eyes, watch them flicker and spark.

But there's only my heartbeat and the faintest sound as she swallows. I imagine her tongue turning a deep purple, stained by blueberry juice. My body reacts almost violently. Exhaustion has drained every part of me except my cock. That part of me is ready to go, ready to press into her, ready to rub against that dark tongue, hungry for the soft, wet friction. Years of being locked up are finally taking their toll. I've been so long without a woman that even a woman eating fruit is a pornographic production.

The phone rings. Nate answers tersely.

Someone on the other end of the line is worked up. Nate has mastered the balance of soothing and authoritative. When he hangs up the phone, his expression is grim. "I've got a surgery out in Blainsville. I need to be on the road five minutes ago. Not sure when I'll get back."

"Got it."

Unable to help myself, I smooth the back of Abby's hair. She doesn't even react. She's exhausted and drugged, no fight left in her. She'll be mine for the night. Helpless. The only question that remains is what I'm going to do with her. I'm still not sure about the answer.

I walk Nate to the front door. We stop on the porch, where I can keep Abby in sight through the window.

Nate lets out a long breath. "You got a plan? Because

I don't know what that is in there."

"Get to the Bradford. Do the governor. That's the plan." But he knows all that.

"The *girl*," he clarifies.

"I know."

"She's innocent."

That's why I like Nate. Stone doesn't give a shit about innocence, but it matters. It has to; otherwise justice doesn't mean anything. Vengeance doesn't mean anything.

"I'm just tired," I say finally. It's the best I can do. Bone-deep tired. Razor's edge tired.

He studies me with world-weary brown eyes. I'd trust Nate with my life, and he trusts me the same. We figured out a long time ago that no one else was going to protect us.

"I've never seen you like this," he says.

I laugh, low and rough. "You don't remember? Fucking sleep deprivation. Fucking starvation. The whole nightmare."

He looks surprised that I'd mention it. "*Her*. We're not them. We don't have to be like them."

"This is different. I'm not going to hurt her." I lower my voice. "I'm taking care of her—I'd do anything for her," I add, surprising even myself. Not so surprising considering I raided a police station to get her back a few hours ago. Probably broke twenty laws.

He gives me a strange look.

"She's mine," I say like that explains it. "You don't have to understand."

"Oh no, I understand perfectly," he bites out. "It's not what we *do,* Grayson."

"Not what *you* do," I say.

He gives me a dark look. He's always been the upstanding one. Blending back into society has always mattered to him.

Fuck society. "She's mine," I say again.

There's a look of warning in his eyes.

"She's mine, and that's just how it is now."

"Vehicle's in the shed," he says.

Then he's gone, and it's just me and Abby. I go back in and fix us some toast. She doesn't ask for her blindfold to be removed even though she knows the good doctor is gone. Maybe she gets that I can't let her see where she is—a kitchen full of clues. Or maybe the drugs are already making her a little docile.

That was the genius of whatever they gave us back in that hellhole of a basement, just enough drugs to knock the fight out of you.

Nate doesn't want to remember, but I'll never forget the lesson—that you're either strong or weak. You dish it out, or you take it. Doesn't take a rocket scientist to figure out what side of that equation I'm planning to stay on.

I smooth her soft hair again. "You're okay," I say. "We're both tired. Let's get some sleep."

She nods.

Is she being too pliant? It might be a trick. She could be plotting to escape as soon as I'm out. I hope to hell one pill was enough, but I didn't want to risk more. Nate might have been able to give me a more specific number, but I didn't want to involve him any more than I already had. A small amount. Enough for a few cats. She seems almost catlike now. Slender and restrained.

And clever too.

I go to Nate's utility drawer and cut a length of string and shove it in my pocket. Just in case.

"Come on." I pull her up. She's steady enough on her feet, but I can tell she's a little off-kilter. *Good*.

I guide her up the staircase, the blindfold a handy excuse to help her. I just want her to feel good and drift off like she doesn't have to care about anything. At least one of us should get that.

I take her to the guest room where I slept after Stone got shot. I fling the covers aside and lay her down on the smooth sheet.

"Ahh," she says. It's practically a moan, and the sound ripples over my skin, hot and carnal.

"Yeah," I whisper, lowering the blinds. "It'll feel good to sleep." I turn on the bedside lamp and switch off the glaring overhead light.

I pull off my shirt and pants, stripping right down to my boxers, and I sit on the foot of the bed and start untying her prim little lace-up boots, caked in mud. I'll leave the rest of her clothes on. She wouldn't like me undressing her.

She still doesn't have panties, a fact I've been intensely aware of ever since I made her take them off at the river. It was an asshole move, but that's what I am now. An asshole who drugs sweet young women. Who drags them across the state and binds them with metal and chemicals. Hey, it could be worse.

She turns on her side, tucking both her hands beneath her cheek. "Feels so good," she mumbles.

My hand is cupping her delicate foot. I roll off her sock, knuckles grazing the little indent between her heel and her ankle bone. I've never been a foot guy, never seen the appeal, but if I started down that route, her feet would definitely be my gateway, because they're smooth as silk and perfectly formed. I have a newfound fetish for her feet, her hands...even her eyes, with their gorgeous, wise, soft sort of allure.

Too bad Nate didn't get to see her without the blindfold, but maybe that's for the best. I like her being all mine.

No one can take her away from me.

Gently I pull off the other sock and rub my hand over her skin, telling myself I just have to check to make sure she's warm enough, but really I need to fucking touch her a little bit, and what the hell, it's only her feet. How wrong can that be? I've been violated in every place, hurt in the softest place, and all I'm doing is giving her a foot rub.

"Grayson," she whispers.

She likes this. *She wants this.* It's an illusion, but that might be enough for me. My cock swells at her lazy, husky tone.

I press my hands on either side of her cool little toes, pancaking them between my palms. I want to devour her. "You warm enough, baby?" Like the Good fucking Samaritan I am, just needing to make sure the girl is warm.

I watch myself warm her with a detached fascination. I need to stop touching her, but I don't. I need to leave her alone, but I won't. I have my hands on her feet, her ankles, and it's just the beginning. My body wants more. She wants more.

An illusion.

Instead of pulling her foot away, she pushes it toward me, pressing it into my hands like she really wants my touch. I know it's the sedative, making her seek out warmth and softness. I know that's what it is from firsthand experience.

Still I rub her toes, knowing she'll like that. "Mmm," she says. I move to her other foot, full-on massaging it.

"Mmm," she says again. I can tell she's in a place where even things you don't want feel good, as long as they come along with warmth and softness.

I spent a lot of time in that place.

It wouldn't hurt her if I fucked her now. I was always going to fuck her—what better time than now? There were days I would've given anything for a dose of painkillers, but I had to go without. It's a gift, that sedative.

Remembering it sparks a white-hot fury inside me. Fury at myself, at the governor and his minions. The men who ran that house. Perversely I'm even mad at *her* for making me want her this much.

Instead of climbing onto her and pressing her legs open, I push her feet away and pull the wad of string out of my pocket.

One soft loop around her ankle and one around mine. We're connected now. She won't know it's there unless she tries to take off. After what happened in the motel, I probably don't need the extra layer of alert, but I'm not taking any chances. I have to take care of her. That's important. She's mine, and I have to watch over her.

I climb into bed next to her and ease off the blindfold. Then I pull the sheets over us both, tucking her in next to me, pressing the blankets around her, getting her into a protective cocoon. I think about how she looked in that cell. The governor probably got her named an accessory. Maybe he figures it's how he'll get to me. Anger flashes through me. Fucking putting her in that dirty cell.

She's on her stomach, head resting on one arm, hair a dark halo around her pillow. I tuck her in tighter, but it's too much, too tight, and she stirs. "Grayson," she whispers. Then she fights her way out of her cocoon and finds me, nestling her head into my chest. My arm goes around her, and she snuggles into me.

"Don't let go," she whispers, and my heart surges.

"I won't," I whisper, pulling her in and kissing her forehead. She presses her body alongside mine, and I drink her in, cock like steel.

"Grayson," she says, and she kisses my neck.

She doesn't really want this. It's the drugs making her soft and desperate. But when I look at it in a certain way, it's as if she *does* want me.

It's like that hundred-dollar bill they put out with that inkwell hologram. If you tip the bill one way, it's just an ugly-ass inkwell, but when you tip it another way, the Liberty Bell appears inside the inkwell, like there's something shiny and special in there when you know there isn't.

That's how I feel now. Because I'm just the piece of shit who kidnapped and drugged her.

And I know the only reason she's enjoying being in

my arms is that she's drugged and uninhibited, giving in to animal needs for comfort and warmth.

But it's like the fucking Liberty Bell appearing inside me when she slides against me. And suddenly I want the illusion. I love the illusion. So I just fucking take it. I take her mouth and get a taste of her. And I push my hand up inside her sweater, finding the lacy edge of her bra, feeling the swell of her tits underneath.

She makes a soft sound of pleasure and there's the fucking Liberty Bell, clanging like crazy.

CHAPTER TWENTY-FIVE

~ABIGAIL~

ONE MINUTE HE'S feeding me blueberries. The next he's dragging me up some stairs. Or maybe it only feels like dragging me because my feet aren't working, maybe because I can't see anything.

A bed. Soft, wonderful, with sheets smoother and cooler than sheets have any right to feel. Everything is a little dizzy and off center. *So tired.*

My shoes are off. My feet feel warm and loose, like taffy. *So good. So tired.*

I blink, but he's just a fuzzy shadow in the dim light of the room. I can't make out Grayson's dark eyes or his cocky smile. I want to. He's beautiful to look at, but all I can do is close my eyes and sink into his touch.

I sigh as the musky scent of him surrounds me and hands tuck me in safe and sound, but the covers are too tight, so I fight them off, which isn't easy; my limbs feel heavy and disjointed, but I get free and find him. He's soft grass and damp earth, and I want to lie flat on the ground of him and breathe in deep, but I can't move.

His arm is a heavy band over my waist. *Trapped.* For some reason that seems okay.

The tart flavor of berries lingers on my tongue.

I'm heavy and warm and a little bit floaty. I think I should always feel like this.

He drugged me.

"Don't let go," I whisper.

"I won't," he says, and I sink into him. I just want to crawl inside him... And suddenly I can't breathe.

At first I'm not sure what's wrong, and something hot and smooth is inside my mouth, but then I realize he's kissing me, frenching me. I'm not sure if I like it, but then I do, because it shocks me with feeling. And his warm hands are weights on my skin, under my shirt, pulling at my bra.

I move against him. Our bodies are two animals, sliding against each other with perfect rhythm. Something rubs my shin, just a little rough. It takes me a century to realize it's his leg on mine, and there's something a little magic about his skin, his warmth. I say his name.

"I got you," he whispers. I feel this strange coolness on my breasts, exposed, like my arms are tangled up and my face is warm. I try to get free, but my arms still aren't working, and then it doesn't matter because they're free, and this new sensation is even more delicious, all the cold, all the heat, all at once.

I know my breasts are bare, but it's wonderful in the darkness. I'm dimly aware that he's kissing them, touching me. Rough hands on my thigh make me move and squeeze my legs together, and I think how wonderful it is to have things feel amazing. I'm trying to stay aware—I don't want him to think I'm not paying attention, but I go somewhere off in the floaty distance, and when I come back to him, I realize I'm totally naked, and I can move and feel and be with him.

I sigh at the sudden sensation between my legs, the sparks of his fingers. I kiss some nearby skin, and the feeling in my belly builds with stars, and I move like a snake against his warmth.

His breath sounds sharp, in little starts and stops, which seems funny when everything else is so slow and easy.

He says my name, and kisses me all over my face. I feel good, and I laugh.

"What is it, baby?" he whispers.

"I don't know," I say, because how am I supposed to know? And maybe I only imagined laughing, because my attention has moved on, and I realize his fingers are actually inside me now, and the second I realize that, the entire universe explodes in a dazzle of color. I ride that, on and on, and then all I feel is him pushing my legs apart, and I don't like it, because he's away from me, but like magic he's back, inside me, pushing into me.

"Yes," I whisper.

He's in me; he's *through* me. As if he's light and I'm air. My brain is split apart with walls where pathways should go. I'm wandering through a maze in my own mind. There's an answer, somewhere here. *What's happening?* But all I can see is the brick wall right in front of me, over me, between my legs, pushing me down into oblivion, holding me like walls, making me want to stay.

Chapter Twenty-Six

~Grayson~

S HE'S SOFT UNDERNEATH me. It's like fucking a cloud, if a cloud could clench tight and wet around my cock. In the dim light I can see the curves of her breasts, the hollow of her throat. Her expression is dazed.

Because she's drugged.

"This is so fucked up," I mutter, the mantra in my head. She is fucked and I am fucked, but I don't stop. I've never been so turned on in my life, and she's barely conscious.

Abby, Abby. She's not even Ms. Winslow anymore. Ms. Winslow is buttoned-up and careful. Ms. Winslow is safe—but I'm not even sure that girl was real. This girl in my arms rocks her hips against mine and moans until I'm so worked up I growl against her neck.

I could have driven away with Stone. I could have put a goddamned bullet in her brain. Instead I thrust into her swollen cunt and hope it never ends.

"Please."

My cock flexes inside, hearing her beg. But I stop

and pull out. I dig around in the drawer by the side table until I find what I'm looking for.

"Please," she mumbles, her hands grasping. Does she even know what she wants?

I tear the condom package and sheath myself quickly. This is part of taking care of her. Part of owning her. Then I press back inside, all the way to heaven.

Her lips part. Her lids lower. She's going to drop right out of awareness, asleep and pulsing around my dick. I tighten my grip on her hips, and I slam into her hard enough to wake her up again. Her eyes open wide as she whimpers. Her eyes roll back, but it's not the drug this time.

It's pleasure.

I've found the place inside her that makes her body jerk and her thighs quake. She can't even help it. I plunge my dick inside her, again and again, finding that spot, battering it. *There, there, there.* Her mouth opens around a choked cry. I don't think she could form words if she wanted to. She can't ask me to stop, and that's just as well, because I'm not going to.

Her eyes fill with anxiety. Even in her confused state, she knows the orgasm is coming. I almost feel bad for her.

Almost.

I know what it feels like for your body to betray you. I know what it feels like to climax when you're being ripped apart. I know what it is to hate yourself. I hang there, with the tip of my cock parting her flesh, holding my breath.

Her eyes focus on mine. "Don't stop," she says, slurred and urgent.

I tear into two pieces. The one who wants this girl and the one who's taking her. Then I slam into her and find home, find my release in a blur of shadows and light.

I stay inside her when I'm done, resting on her—not so heavy as to crush her, but she didn't seem to like it when I pulled away before.

That's how this thing works. She's mine to care for. Mine to have. Nate understood it all too well.

Her breath evens out—not fake even but real even. Sleeping. I brush a strand out of her eyes. There's a kind of furrow in her brow I don't like; maybe she's having a bad dream or something.

"Shhh," I whisper. "I won't let anyone hurt you."

Anyone else, that is.

Still that furrow. Is she having a bad dream? I stroke my fingers along her forehead, smoothing out the skin, showing how I want it, and she seems to like that, because she shifts and then the furrow disappears.

I wonder if I've chased some shit dream away. It gets me hard that I could do that. Literally. I'm still inside her, and I realize with a sort of weary surprise that I could fuck her again. What is it about this girl? I move in and out, working up a little steam, testing it.

But then I pull out. The whole point here was to get some rest. I need rest. She needs rest.

I WAKE UP with a pounding headache...and a light tugging on my ankle. With effort, I keep my body relaxed but not unnaturally still; that's the trick to pretending to sleep. I learned it early on as a kid, not that it did me much good.

The bed shifts slightly as Abby sits up. She pushes the covers aside. The slightest tug and a whisper of air tell me she's trying to untie the string. I stay very still and let her do it. The string tickles my skin as her end of it falls to the bed.

She makes it to the door before I spring up and push her from behind, pressing her into the wall with my body—not hard enough to hurt her. Just hard enough to send a message. I clench my fist in her hair and pull back.

I wrap my free hand around her neck and squeeze gently, to get her attention.

"Good morning," I whisper in her ear.

CHAPTER TWENTY-SEVEN

~ABIGAIL~

M Y MIND IS like one of those old film reels, black-
and-white stills flashing in front of me, out of
sync with the music. And there's static. So much static in
my own brain that it scares me. Did I bump my head?
Am I hallucinating? But one fact registers in the
onslaught of imagery: I'm naked.

"Let go of me."

His fist tightens in my hair. His other hand presses
against my neck. I feel a puff of warmth against my skin.
"I think I like where I'm at."

I struggle, kicking away from the wall and jerking my
head in his hold. He doesn't ease up. No, he leans
against me, using his weight to press me against the wall.
My cheek flattens against the smooth, cool surface. I'm
panting, and so is he—but for different reasons, I think.
His breathing is labored...and aroused.

Then I realize something else: he's naked too.

His cock is hard against my butt. The image fills me
with raw heat, flames licking my body from the inside.

And anger.

He's touched me with more than his cock. And I don't remember undressing. In fact, I'm pretty sure I wouldn't have agreed to that.

I would have lost.

"What happened last night?" I'm near tears, but I fight them. I can't look weak now. Power is the language he speaks, and the waver in my voice is already a disadvantage. A single tear would be surrender.

He sighs like I'm overreacting. I want to kick him in the balls.

"What did you do to me?" I demand again, louder. Almost hysterical, really, and I hate how much I sound like my mother in her crazy moments.

"I didn't hurt you," he says.

A chill runs down my spine. Did he *touch* me when he undressed me? Then a steel door slams down on my thoughts. Of course he touched me. I don't want to know what happened after that.

Except I can guess, especially when my thighs brush together, a little sticky. A little wet. More wet than I've ever been when having sex. It doesn't make sense that I'd have been turned on. It also doesn't make sense that I would *still* be turned on, after sleeping for hours.

But I know that's what happened.

Humiliation runs through me like a river, filling every empty space inside me, reflecting light on places better left dark. How could I have been turned on by him? Embarrassment swells to fury, and I twist my head violently. My hair would pull right out of my scalp if he didn't let go—but he does. He releases me, and I snap at him with my teeth. I wish I had fangs to sink into his neck, right where the scruff fades to nothing.

He laughs. "You're a little wild. I'm not letting you near my dick with that mouth."

I go crazy, hitting and punching like a maniac. I think I'm hurting myself more than him. Everything hurts, but I can't stop. Stopping means I'm okay with what happened, that I enjoyed it. "You're a fucking caveman. You're barely even human!"

He picks me up and suddenly I'm spinning, then sailing through the air. I land on the bed with a bounce. I roll away and push up but the sheets tangle around my ankle, and I fall back onto the bed, limbs uncoordinated. I could hear the horses on the way into the house yesterday, and this is how it must feel, being born and expected to stand right away.

Grayson's on top of me, yanking my wrists up over my head and pinning them beneath his hand.

He straddles my chest. I'm helpless, and he's looming over me. A kind of pleasure roils deep in my belly—my body betraying me. "I hate you," I say, and a hot tear slides down my cheek. *Surrender.* Now he knows how scared I am, and I hate myself a little for giving it away.

The bed creaks as he leans down. Is he going to do it again? Have sex with me? Of course he's going to do it again. But he just places a kiss on my forehead, chaste and almost sweet.

"Calm down," he murmurs.

I'm the opposite of calm. I'm naked and crying, and with Grayson that's almost the same thing—both vulnerable and broken.

He caresses my arms, my sides. "Shh, no one's going to hurt you. Not as long as I'm with you."

"Don't lie to me," I snap. I'd rather he threaten to kill me again. I want him to be a monster.

"Am I lying?" He sounds amused. "Are you hurt right now?"

"Yes!" I say because now that I'm still, I can feel the twinge deep inside me, the slight ache that means he had sex with me.

He trails two fingers from the base of my neck, between my breasts, down toward my belly. "All right, I touched you. I fucked you. Did you think I wouldn't?"

No, I knew he would, even before he escaped from prison. Everything in me pointed toward him.

"It's how this works, baby," he adds wearily. "It's just how this works."

I stiffen. *This? It's just how this works?*

I go silent for a second because of how much he admitted in one simple sentence. That what's happening is a thing he understands all too well. A thing he learned when other kids were learning baseball.

The final piece of the puzzle falls in. The basement. The other boys. All those years.

It wasn't some custody dispute that got him on that milk carton. I know what happened to him sure as I feel his hand pressing my wrists together. I'm filled with a sense of grim triumph.

"What would you have done," I whisper, "if I hadn't picked your story for *The Kingman Journal*?"

He smirks. "I knew you would."

"Why?" I demand.

His eyebrows shoot up. He's surprised I'm not freaking out still. But I have a long history of coping with insanely violent situations. "Because you're easy," he says.

My indignant huff only makes him smile, a little smug.

"I knew that if I gave you a sob story, you'd fall for it. And you did."

"It was pretty genius," I say. "By focusing on the most peripheral details, you could leave the horror at the center to the reader's imagination."

"Thank you for your kind assessment, Ms. Winslow," he says mockingly.

"You only had to get those details just right, and the reader fills it in for you. It's the best kind of lie to tell. One that's true. Nothing's quite as effective as truth, is it?"

Grayson freezes. Wondering what I know.

"It's what Hemingway did. Stayed on the edge of it. One raw line of truth and then another."

His hands tighten on my wrists. "And now I'm free."

But I'm not through with him. "How does it feel?" I ask. "To be on the other side?"

"Don't."

A shiver runs through me at the fury in his voice. But when you're stuck in a ring with a crazed animal, you'll use the weapons you have. I need him emotional. Not seeing straight.

"Six years. That's a long time. Are you strong enough and bad enough yet that they can't touch you ever again?"

His expression tells me I made a direct hit. And I know I can hit him as much as I want and he won't hurt me—not physically. In a perverse way I know that I can trust him because of his thing about protecting me. His code. It's a fucked-up code, but it's a code all the same.

I frown. "No? Not quite?"

He sneers. "You think you know me?"

"I know how it feels when your stomach hurts like it's trying to eat itself. I know what it's like to fight with a grown-up and lose."

His draws his lips close to my ear, so close it tickles. "Like you're doing now? Fighting with a grown-up and losing?"

"Yeah," I whisper, knowing that this is a dark and powerful line that connects us. "I know what it's like to hate what's happening. And to hate that you like it."

I feel him soften. He keeps hold of my wrists but he's loosening. My words are potent. Powerful. I can use the truth as a weapon, just like he did.

I say, "I know what it's like when you want something so wrong. When you crave it."

"It's okay," he says softly, as if to comfort me, gaze tender. "It's okay to feel like that. It's not your fault." Everything's shifting, and I know he's going to kiss me.

I watch his eyes close, see the dusky curve of his lashes against his skin. He doesn't have any right to look both sexy and sweet. Doesn't have any right to sink on top of me—but God, he does.

His lips are soft and warm, so incongruous it makes me sigh against him. And even though he's broad and heavy, especially because of that, it feels like a caress. His whole body embraces me, his mouth on mine, his hands on mine, his legs straddling my thighs. I'm wrapped in a cocoon made only of Grayson, where it smells like musk and tastes like man and wipes away every thought I should have.

Like getting away. Like fighting him. I had a plan here—to lull him with a sense of comfort and connection. That connection he so badly needs.

But the truth is a double-edged sword. Because I do crave him when he's heavy on me, kissing me. I don't want him to stop.

And his words made me feel better somehow. Or at least less alone.

His tongue nudges my mouth open, and I let him in. This is what he did to me in my memoir class, paying close attention, turning in every assignment. He thinks I want this kiss, because I do. It's the best kind of lie to tell—one that's true.

"What happened last night?" I whisper. It's the same question I asked before, only different now. Different because I already know.

His voice is rough when he answers. "It didn't hurt. I didn't hurt you."

He drugged me…and he fucked me…and he knew it wouldn't hurt. There's a sick kind of tenderness in that. A twisted sort of care. My heart breaks a little, because I think this is the only way he knows how to be kind. And that's what makes me reach for him.

He doesn't ask why I changed my mind. Maybe he doesn't care. He just pulls a condom from the drawer and slips it on. He flips me over, drags my hips up, and pushes a pillow underneath.

That's the only warning I have before the hot, blunt head of his cock breaches me from behind.

My body opens to him, wet and soft and willing. My

mind understands him, why he is the way he is. But it's my heart that aches for him, wanting whatever shards of love he can give me, jagged, even knowing I'll get cut in the process.

"You want this," he says, breathless.

It's not a question, but I answer him anyway. "More."

His fist twists in my hair—like earlier, only hotter now, because he's pressing my face into the cool sheets. The wet sheets, made damp with my tears.

"It doesn't hurt," I manage to say. I can't stop crying, but I need him to know he's not hurting me. It's important to him, not to hurt me. I don't even know why I'm crying, but it's not because of his cock or his fist or his warm weight covering my back.

"Why?" His voice grates, a rough burst of air against my cheek. He's holding me down completely, every part of him covering every part of me.

Why am I crying? Why do I want this? I don't know what the question is exactly, but I reach up and hold his wrist. I use it like an anchor as the storm of him batters me about. His cock drives into me, relentless, bordering on pain but never there.

He's careful even in his fury, almost tender as he shudders over me and groans his release.

Then my body clenches around his, sudden and wild, and I can't breathe at all. It doesn't matter; I could die this way, warm and wet, protected like never before, the salt of my tears on his lips as he leans down and kisses my cheek.

And now I know why I'm crying: because I'm losing, just like he said I would, because I want to be in this prison of his, enclosed by him, the object of his intense focus, and I know it's wrong—it's a wrong thing to like. Maybe it's myself I'm losing. Maybe it's my sanity.

I just know I have to get away.

Chapter Twenty-Eight

~Grayson~

A PHONE RINGS, startling me. I realize we fell asleep after I fucked her this morning.

That was careless. I can't believe I made that kind of mistake. I detach myself from her warm body, hating every inch I put between us. I reach over to the bedside table, fumbling around, trusting she'll lie there, waiting. Wanting. Docile. Everything between us feels new. And right.

So I'm sure it will end wrong.

Nate is all business on the other end. "Guys in nice SUVs crawling around town," he says. "A few guys at the diner asking questions."

"How long ago?"

His tone is urgent. "Now."

"We're gone."

"Take the Suburban that's in the back garage. It's not mine. Red key chain on the hook. Money in the safe."

He gives me the combination, and the line goes dead. I scrub my face with my hand. I needed to move out way earlier. I should have already secured supplies and fake identification. And I spent what cash I had at the motel. There's no time for that anymore.

I turn to face her. Maybe a normal guy would be moved by the sight of her red-rimmed eyes. I'm not normal, though. The sight of her broken doesn't make me want to help her. It makes me want to fuck her all over again.

"Get dressed," I say, and for some reason, maybe because she's soft and well fucked, she obeys. She asks to go the bathroom, and I drag her to the one in Nate's room. I hear her open a drawer. Taking a razor. Scissors, maybe. Sad little weapons. I'll allow it. I shove the clothes in his closet to the side to reveal his safe. I twist the knob to the combo he gave me, but it doesn't open. Did I get the numbers right? I try again. Nothing. Fuck. A third time isn't the charm. Fuck it. I grab a shirt from a hanger and nick the change off his dresser just as she's coming out.

I should blindfold her, but there's no time if guys are already asking around in town. Someone might have seen us drive through; eventually they'll expand their radius to search here.

The last thing I want is a fucking standoff, dragging Nate into the mix. And her.

I take her hand and drag her down to the kitchen where I grab the red key chain from the hook; then I stuff a box of cereal and the half empty OJ carton into a bag.

"Let's go," I tell her.

"What's happening?" she asks.

"Trouble."

I lead her to the back. The sun is high, telling me it's near lunchtime. I pull up the old wooden shed door—one of those old-fashioned jobbies where it tips out and up.

The beater I stole from the motel is in there next to a Suburban. I'm not surprised. Nate probably came back between vet gigs to move it. He's thorough like that. Part of what makes him an awesome healer.

I wait until she climbs into the truck and buckles herself in before I press the gun into her neck, letting her feel the cold, hard tip of it.

She stiffens and leans away.

I follow her with it, keeping metal on skin. She needs to know that fucking hasn't changed anything. The thing isn't even cocked, but we're about to head onto the road. I need to know she's with me. This isn't a fucking fairy tale. I'm not going to turn into a good guy because her cunt is made of velvet and rainbows.

"We good?" I ask.

Her lips move without sound. She's getting the message, and even if it feels like knives inside me, that's the important thing.

She gets out a whisper. "Yeah."

"Okay." Sometimes you have to make a gun real to a person, and it's for her own good, because I don't want her to run. She'd finger Stone and maybe even Nate, and the governor would be their problem too. They'd be lucky to get twenty-five to life.

So I just have to make sure she doesn't run, simple as that.

I go around to the driver's side and fire up the engine. I pull out, put it in park, jump out to close the garage door, and we're off. I breathe easier once we've cleared Nate's driveway, and even more when we're on a two-lane highway without anything to link us up. I'm guessing the vehicle is stolen, maybe by another patient of Nate's, but I'll take my chances on the interstate all the same.

"You should've just killed me," she says when we're ten minutes out from Nate's. Her voice sounds hollow. "It would've been better."

My insides twist up because of how well I recognize that tone. *Fuck.* "Don't be stupid. You never want to be dead instead of living."

She's sitting as far away from me as she can. Beyond crying. "It would be better."

"Stop it," I say through gritted teeth. I want clever Ms. Winslow back. The fighter, the woman who tricked me into telling more than I ever meant to. The woman who understands things other people can't.

I want her not to feel like this. And not to be the one who made her cry. All because she got fucked? "You need to reach the hell down inside yourself and find that little corner in there where you know things are okay. That part of you nobody can take away."

"Not even you?" Her voice is quiet.

Not even me, I want to say. But my attention is snagged by the four-way stop in the distance. There's a car sitting up there, right at the stop sign, and no other cars are in sight. It could be somebody texting or looking at a map. Somebody harmless.

Or somebody watching. Waiting.

"I don't even know what you're talking about," she mumbles.

"Don't bullshit me. You're okay." If nothing else, she's talking with me. Communicating. It's the quiet ones you had to worry about. They were liable to swallow a razor blade when you weren't looking.

God, the bleeding. The bleeding never stopped. I push the memories back where they belong.

She glares at me. "Is this you giving me advice on how to survive a guy like you? Because that's a little fucked up, even for you."

I'm glad to see the bite. Even directed at me, I'm glad to see it.

The car's still there. I'm too far away to see how

many people are inside, or even if the windows are shaded. I could do a U-turn and get going the other way, see if they follow. But that's like waving a red flag if it's the governor's guys. I grab the ball cap and stuff it over my head. "Get down."

She looks around, sees only the sunny blue skies and fields and the blue sedan in the distance.

I grab her neck and push her down. They don't know this vehicle. A lot of guys ride around in ball caps. I slow at the stop. Shaded windows. *Shit.* I wait, then go.

The shiny blue car follows. It still could be nothing. Or it could be that they suspect, and they're calling their friends.

I knew the FBI could track me, and I trusted my evasion skills enough to get away. Hell, they had always worked before. Only once had I ever been caught, and that was because of the governor.

The governor, whose guys are following me now. It's got to be them. This is bad.

My hands tighten on the wheel. "If the shit hits the fan, baby, you run like hell, okay?"

"What?" She sounds incredulous.

It makes me smile, just a little. She thinks I'm the biggest and the baddest guy here, which is kind of sweet. But she's wrong. "If something goes down, you run. And don't trust anybody in a big shiny car or SUV. Don't trust these small-town badges either. Get back to the city. Call the FBI. Tell them you were taken hostage, that you got free. They'll come get you."

"What's going on?"

"I told you, baby. Trouble."

Her eyes flicker with disbelief, and I know there's some irony there. I'm trouble. But I don't want her going down with me. It's important. She's important.

The car is still back there, a little close for comfort. I jerk the wheel and pull over, slam onto the gravel and stop. The car passes me, then skids to a stop in the middle of the street up ahead.

So they were following me. Game on.

I do a U-turn and scream down the road the other way. The Suburban has shit for pickup, and the blue car is on me.

Abby pops her head up, peeking over the seat, right as a shot blasts out.

"Jesus!" I swerve the car to throw them off.

She's back down, huddling in the seat. I run my hand over her hair to reassure myself. They didn't hit us, didn't hit *her,* but now I'm pissed. Nobody shoots at Abby.

There's another shot, and my tire blows out. And then another and something breaks; the steering's out. I slam on the brakes and go into a spin. I'm reaching out and grabbing her to keep her safe, keep her from smashing her head, trying to control this piece-of-shit ride. There's a bone-shattering jolt, and everything comes to a stop. The world comes to a stop.

The nose of the car is smashed sideways into a tree.

"You okay?"

She looks at me, dazed. Her eyes are wide. Scared. How did she get mixed up in all this? But that's life—it'll drag you down no matter how sweet and innocent you start out. I grab my piece. I see the blue sedan in a ditch on the other side of the road.

I jump out. Everything's quiet.

A shot explodes the silence. I duck behind our vehicle. He's behind his, behind the engine block. Only one of us will be getting reinforcements soon, and it's not me. Things are only going to go downhill for me from here, so I charge his car, right across the road, shooting. *Shoot your way out.* It's desperate and ballsy. It's something he won't expect.

I run right up, one boot crashing onto the middle of the hood, and I'm landing right on him, feet first. He gets a shot off, but he's moving—he expected me from a side. So the shot goes wild. I've got him under me now like a stomped sack of potatoes. I grab his head and ram the hard plate of my forehead into the delicate structure of his nose, a vicious head butt that breaks his face and knocks him right out.

He slumps onto the dirt. I wipe his blood from my eyes.

ANNIKA MARTIN & SKYE WARREN

Our truck is fucked up now, so I get into his car, making a U-turn and screaming up right next to the Suburban. I get out and clamber in the still-open driver's side door. She's there, cringing against the passenger-side door. She didn't run like I told her to. In shock, maybe.

"Let's go," I say.

The way she looks at me, I'm guessing my face is pretty bloody. She fumbles her door open. I reach for her wrist, but she's too nimble. She takes off down the road.

Now she runs.

I've got a functioning car. I could get us out. But the governor's guys are on their way. If they catch her up and she tells them her story, it's not just Stone and Nate in trouble. They'll figure out she means something to me, considering I didn't kill her, considering I fucked her. And before long her fingers will be showing up places where I'm most likely to hear about them.

I look at the barren landscape that will soon be crawling with the governor's vehicles and the cars of dirty cops. I go back to strategy, because it doesn't fail me. What's the best thing to do? The smartest thing? *Shoot her.*

I tear out after her instead, down this road barely wider than a single lane, a straightaway for as far as the eye can see. Catching up to her is not a problem. Hours upon hours of physical exercise in the yard and in my cell means I'm on top of my game. But dragging a fighting girl back to the car, all before the governor's guys show up? I'm sweating that.

A shiny town car comes tearing up the road from far ahead. She's running, waving her arms for help.

"No, Abby!"

She keeps on going, and I keep after her even though it's crazy. I could still make it back to the blue sedan.

"No!" I shout. "Don't trust them. Abby!"

She speeds up, thinking she has safety in sight.

Fuck. It's just the opposite.

The car pulls over some ten yards ahead.

The guy's in a suit. I recognize his red buzz cut and pinkish complexion from the last time the governor's guys cornered me. I don't know his name, but it doesn't fucking matter. History is repeating itself, and the scariest part is that Abby's here for it. He takes cover behind his car door, piece flashing in the sun.

"Get away from here!" I yell. She could still get away. It's me he wants to kill.

Shots ping around my feet. I dive for the ditch and roll, shoot back. He ducks behind his door.

She's like a deer, frozen at the side of the road, not quite between us but too close for comfort. "Abby! Get to the blue car and take off—I'll cover you. Come on, you want to be free, right? Drive out of here. I'll deal with him." I'm revealing her value to Red Crew Cut, but he'll figure it out anyway. "Go!"

She just stands there, probably more shocked by the sound of me begging than the gunfire.

Hell, I should turn around and head back to the sedan myself. I could still do that while Abby's out there creating confusion. It's a good plan. "Get out of here!" I yell.

It's then, I suppose, that he catches on. "It's a trick, Abby," he says. When he says her name, it feels like spikes in my spine. "I'll keep you safe."

"Abby," I yell. She looks back at me, eyes full of regret.

There's fear too, because some part of her knows it's not normal for a guy in a suit to stop his car and start shooting. He didn't announce himself as a police officer because he's not one. Her survival instinct is telling her she isn't safe, but her mind is overriding that. Because of me. What I did to her.

"We'll put Grayson back where he belongs," the governor's man says, voice smooth with authority. "Come on back here where you'll be safe."

"He's lying, Abby!" I picture her relief when they take her into custody. She'll think it's over. And then her horror when they start hurting her.

"You shouldn't have done it," she says, backing toward the town car, voice cracking. She takes another step toward him. Then another. She's five feet away from the car.

This is my punishment. That's all I can think about. Her soft flesh sucking me in. Her moans filling the air like goddamn music. I took what wasn't mine, and this is my punishment: watching her get destroyed.

"Abby," I plead, voice hoarse.

"You would have to kill me eventually," she says, so damn sadly that my chest aches. The tears on her cheek flash white in the sun. "In the end, that's how it would be."

Helplessly I watch her turn and run to the town car, to the open door that's shielding the man in the buzz cut. He pops up and grabs her by the neck, shoving the nose of the gun into her cheek so hard it distorts her pretty features. Rage stabs through me, and it's all I can do not to barrel out of the ditch.

She coughs and struggles as the coward marches her out, using her to cover him.

Strategy. Shoot her.

Her cry is hoarse. "Grayson!" Her terror blinds me. It's all I can see—he's hurting her, choking her.

Shoot them both. Mow them down.

If this had been a trick to draw him out, it would've been brilliant. Because there he is, out in the open with only her for cover.

She's clawing at his hands. He's choking her, and the fucked-up thing is that I can barely breathe now, and my pulse pounds so loud I can't think.

Red speaks. "Throw the weapons and come out, hands knit on your head. Then I'll let the girl go."

He won't let her go. He'll kill her for the same reason I should've. But the pain of him choking her out slowly is too much to bear.

"Help me!" she gasps, and I'm powerless to resist.

CHAPTER TWENTY-NINE

~ABIGAIL~

I'M PULLING AT his fingers, trying to get air, scratching his arms and hands, but he doesn't care, he just squeezes tighter until it feels like my tendons are separating from bone. Even dragging me around the woods, even *fucking* me, Grayson didn't hurt me like this.

The tip of his gun is grinding so hard into my cheek that my mouth tastes of blood.

"Grayson!" My cry is a whisper in the wind.

Come on back here where you'll be safe, the man said. A lie. For once Grayson was telling the truth. But then, he was telling the truth all along.

Through my tears I see something flash in the sun out in the weedy ditch where Grayson took cover. I watch the gun slide onto the road with a loud clatter and come to rest a few feet over the painted white line.

"The other." The guy in the suit shakes me like it's nothing. He's a big guy, almost as big as Grayson, so I guess it is nothing.

My brain feels scrambled when he tightens his hand again. I can't get enough air. I gasp and claw at his fingers. Another gun sails out of the weedy ditch onto the road.

"That's it." Grayson's voice. "She can't breathe! Ease up."

The man loosens his hold on my neck, and I gulp in the air. The haircutting shears I got from the bathroom lie on the ground near my feet. He didn't see them fall. I try to twist out of his arms, but they're like rock. If I could get to the scissors...

My heart twists as Grayson rises from the weeds, hands over his head. His stance is wide and proud. And then he starts toward us.

He's coming for me. Just like he did before.

My heart skips a beat, and everything slows. I forget the hands around my throat, the burn in my lungs. All I see is him. The borrowed gray T-shirt shows off his lean, muscled body. His expression is fierce.

The man tightens his grip on my neck again, and I can hear the smirk in his voice when he says, "Fancy meeting you here."

Even from far away I see the change in Grayson's eyes—they're like steel, peering out of his bloody face.

He shrugs. "The way I remember it," he calls out, "I said the next time I saw you, I was going to kill you."

The man jabs the gun deeper into my cheek. "Yeah,

you said that right before they stuffed you into the back of a squad car."

Grayson smiles, and it sends chills down my spine.

"Close enough," the man says.

Grayson doesn't stop.

"I'll kill her," the man says.

"Oh, I was going to kill her myself," Grayson says, moving steadily toward us like a thundercloud or a battleship.

I feel the man's fingers stiffen over my throat, press in. I sputter. "If you were going to kill her, she'd be dead," the man growls.

I cough, but Grayson doesn't flinch. I'm right in the middle of them, two men who want to kill each other.

"Any kid who grew up on a farm knows," Grayson says, moving ever nearer, just a bus length away now, "you should never name the animals. It makes them too hard to slaughter. But you go ahead."

Name the animals? I twist and kick, landing one on the man's shins.

In a flash Grayson's hands are off his head, and he has a gun pointed at us, having taken advantage of the distraction I'd provided, I suppose. "You've got one shot, the way I see it, before I take your head off. So how about you do her, I'll do you, and we'll all be on our merry way."

The man starts pulling me back toward the open car

door, but then Grayson starts counting. "One. Two." And I know we won't make it. "Three."

The gun is off my cheek, and the blast shatters my ears. At that exact moment he lets me go, and I stumble back, clutching my neck, gasping for air. I lose my footing and fall to the ground. There's another shot, and another. I wait for the pain, but it doesn't come. Who's hit?

I scramble to my feet and see Grayson lying there, curled on his side, grabbing at stones around him, trying to get to his gun, which is too far away.

The man who was choking me is on all fours, like a cow. He rises to his feet, unsteady, clutching his belly, gun in hand, taking jerky steps toward Grayson.

He's going to kill Grayson. And then he'll kill me. The shears that dropped glint in the sun. I roll over and snap them up, and without thinking twice, I run for the guy, jump on his back, and jab them into the side of his neck.

They go in with sickening ease.

Horrified, I pull them out. My fist feels wet. Warm. He raises an arm and his gun goes off, and then we crash to the ground together, but I don't let go. He's crawling, dragging himself. I have this idea in my head that I have to hang on, I have to stay behind him and ride him, because he might shoot me if he can see me.

I can barely hold on, my one hand is so bloody. A car

passes, slowing, then speeding, a blur of metal and glass out of the corner of my eye, but I don't let go. This is how I'm going to beat this asshole. Not with physical strength. Not with fighting skills. By never giving up. It's how I always win.

He's on his hands and knees, and then he just collapses. I jump off him, arm soaked with blood. The man seems dead. Then I look over at Grayson. He isn't moving.

Something lurches in my chest. I know what I should do—take one of the cars. Take the car and get out, like Grayson said. Get the FBI.

It has to be the FBI, because that's what Grayson told me. And then he groans.

Before I can think better of it, I'm at his side. He blinks rapidly. "Fuck," he whispers.

"Grayson." His whole shirt is full of blood, there's blood on his face, but he was bloody even before he got shot. Sirens in the distance. "Can you walk?"

He tries to get up. "No. Go. Take the car. No time." The blue car is a ways off, but not the black fancy car. If nothing else, being with Grayson has taught me about taking what you want. He's injured now. I'm in charge.

I run to the fancy car and get in. The keys are still in the ignition. I start it up and drive it the few yards to where Grayson is, navigating so my tires don't go over the man's body...the man I *killed.* I should probably leave Grayson here. I know I should.

I get out and open the passenger door and go to Grayson. "Come on." I pull on his arm, and he grunts in pain.

"No! Other—" He uses his left hand to push himself up.

I grab his left shoulder and help him, though it's him doing the work. It's only a couple of feet to the door. He flops onto the seat and I shut the door. Then I race around and get behind the wheel and drive.

The seat is so low I have to sit up to see out the window. I lay on the gas, increasing the speed, using the steering wheel not only to steer but also to keep me forward. I'm not the best driving without my glasses, but I can make out the road, the red blur of a stop sign, other cars.

He's curled up on his left side in the passenger seat, the top of his head grazing my thigh. The curled-up position seems to ease his pain.

"Fuck, baby," he whispers. "You are so beautiful."

He's delirious. "I'm taking you to a hospital."

"No."

"You don't have a choice." Because I have the power, though I don't feel powerful. I just feel scared. More than when Grayson put a gun to my side and forced me to help him escape. More than anything.

"No…just…" He fades off. My heart pounds.

"Just what?" I press. Does he have a game plan for when he gets injured? "I'm taking you to the hospital."

"Bradford Hotel," he grates out. "Get on the interstate."

"Are you crazy? What about your friend?"

"No. Can't go back there."

I look down at him. He seems to be pressing on his shoulder; the white scar design on his thick forearm gleams with sweat and blood. The words *chest cavity* float into my mind. How bad is he hurt?

"Grayson?"

The only sound is sirens in the distance.

I drive for a bit and say his name again. "Grayson." Again he doesn't answer.

Don't leave me alone.

"Don't name your farm animals?" I ask. "What the fuck is that? So I'm a farm animal you shouldn't have named?"

He makes a breathy noise. Maybe it's supposed to be a laugh. It doesn't comfort me.

"Here's a farm animal name. How about 'You're lucky I pulled your sorry ass out of there after what you did.' What do you think about that for a name?"

I look down. He's smiling. Maybe grimacing. Either way, it's better than him sliding out of consciousness. I want him with me. I have to know he's okay.

The road winds. Trees obscure everything beyond

ten feet. "Where's the interstate? I'll get on the interstate if you tell me where it is."

He hisses out a breath, like this is a monumental task. "Which way're we going?"

"Which *way?*" I look around for the sun. It's up there, but I don't know what time of day it is. Afternoon? Yes, afternoon. The sun sets in the west. "Uh, east."

"Okay," he says, voice light and shallow, a pond instead of the ocean. "That's what we want," he says. "Interstate's east of here."

"Should I speed up and risk, you know—"

"Getting a ticket? Fuck, yeah!"

"You hang in there," I say. "I'm doing ninety."

He doesn't answer.

"If at any point I think you're unconscious, you *will* be dropped at a hospital."

No answer.

Don't leave me alone.

"Or I'll just drive you back to the prison myself. Straight to the clinic and check you in." I reach down and touch his dark hair, damp against his clammy forehead, inches from my thigh. "Got it? So stay with me."

"Yes, Ms. Winslow." The words are faint, but they've never sounded sweeter. My chest expands with relief. At his core he's a fighter. *A warrior.*

And he fought for me.

Nobody ever came for me or fought for me, and it means everything that he did.

Everything.

I come to a four-way stop and let my foot off the gas. He grunts in protest, like he can tell I'm slowing.

"Okay, okay." I check all directions—there's nobody around. I check again; then I blow through it, pulse pounding.

Sirens don't sound. No cop car tails me. Nothing at all happens as I drive down the empty lane. "I just ran a stop sign." Exhilaration pulses through me. I feel so *alive*.

I rest my hand back on his forehead. I have to save him because we're connected.

The corner of his mouth lifts in a smile. He's aware...barely. My lips press together.

His skin is ashen. And God, the way he's curled up on the seat. Even sitting is too much. There's a lump in my throat the size of a baseball.

My mind goes to the day my mother OD'd. I called 9-1-1 for real, and I did CPR on her lifeless body until they arrived. I couldn't save her.

"Grayson?" It comes out as a whisper. When he doesn't answer right away, his name forms a chant in my head. *Grayson, Grayson, Grayson.* When did he start mattering so much? Why do I care about him?

"North on the interstate. Don't stop," he finally says,

his eyes still closed—and I know he means the car. *Keep driving. Get away; get safe. Don't stop.*

I grip the steering wheel with both hands and speed up. But my mind goes back to last night.

Did I tell him to stop last night? I remember flashes of fear and relief. I'm not sure what it means, except that he was over me. Inside me. The worst part is, I can't remember if I told him no.

My eyes prick with unshed tears, because I could have cared about him. I already do.

"Did I say no?" I whisper. It's eating at me, not knowing.

He's injured now and only half-conscious. It's the worst time to question him about something so important. Or maybe the best time. He knows exactly what I'm talking about. He knows what's important here. "Doesn't matter," he grates out.

Heat flashes through my body, white-hot and incandescent. I think it's anger. It might be arousal. "Of course it does."

A sound comes from his throat, like a growl. "It wasn't your fault, understand? It doesn't matter if you say no. Doesn't matter about right or wrong. You do what you need to do to survive. That's all that matters." He cuts off with a hitch of breath. His hand presses against his shoulder.

His other hand rises like he might reach for me.

Before last night he might have held my neck in that possessive, controlling grip he uses to steer me. And I think that much hasn't changed. Sex is no guarantee of tenderness. Maybe I don't want it to be. At least when he's cold and cruel and strong, he's alive.

I tighten my hands on the wheel. "Where do we go? Where can I take you?"

"The Bradford Hotel…safe house…two hours from here. Get to the interstate and head north."

I'll have to really squint to make out the signs. He presses his fist to the glove compartment door, knuckles white with the force. I feel an answering tug in my gut.

"South Franklin City," he continues, "176 Gedney."

Will you live that long? I can't ask the question.

He seems to hear it anyway. "Whatever happens, don't stop. Just drop me there and leave."

"A hotel is your safe house? Grayson?"

He goes limp. I think if he dies, I might just keep driving forever. North past their hotel. Past the Canadian border. I'll drive right off into the Arctic Ocean because I can't deal with another dead body beside me.

But as the afternoon light limns his body through the window, I can see his broad chest rise and fall, even from the corner of my eye. He's alive…for now.

God, what a pair we make, both running for our lives. Both tripping over ourselves to escape the past. But you can't—that's what I figure out as I speed along in a luxury car with this delirious man beside me. I can't escape my past. I'm stuck in that movie, *Groundhog Day*, doomed to repeat my mistakes until I finally get it right. That means keeping him alive.

And after that? I don't know. I've never made it that far.

✧ ✧ ✧

WE DRIVE FOR an hour. When I'm well rested and well fed, a two-hour drive is nothing. Maybe my legs get a little stiff or something. But right now there's a knot in my back. My hands are actually shaking on the steering wheel. My eyes are tired because of not wearing glasses. Things are getting blurry. And we need gas. That's what finally forces me to stop. I pull into a gas station. That's enough to rouse Grayson.

"Are we there?" he mumbles, and he sounds so much like a grumpy kid I have to smile.

"Not really. What kind of safe house is the Bradford Hotel?"

"Drop me there and get away. Don't stay." He's been in and out of consciousness for some time. It's been a straight shot. I managed to find Gedney Street on a map, though I'm not sure if I can trust his mumblings on the address.

From here I can see the soda displays and an ATM inside the store. It doesn't look welcoming. In fact, it's exactly the kind of place I would have avoided in favor of cleaner, brighter stores. But it's either this or run out of gas. "Do you need anything?" I ask.

He grunts. "Probably need gas."

"Thanks, Einstein," I say. "Do you have any money?"

"Not enough," he whispers.

We're not going to make it much farther with half a gallon. I squint at the window, trying to get a read on the guy inside. Not much to tell. It's a semirural gas station. I have some experience in hocking stuff when the money's run low.

I put my hand to my neck. "I have this. It's worth something."

His gaze slants to the rearview mirror. He moves like he wants to sit up, then he winces.

"Stay down," I scold, though he couldn't get up even if he wanted. "I've got it under control."

"Where're we?"

"Keppelsville."

"No," he whispers.

"This is a diamond. It's a universal language." I smooth my hair back, try to get myself looking civilized.

"Bring the gun."

"And right there, that's the difference between you and me. I don't behave like a caveman."

Not anymore, anyway.

He's protesting, but I don't have to listen. I get out and shut the door. "I treat people as I would want to be treated." I give him a look. He knows exactly what I'm talking about.

He fumbles the gun out onto the seat next to his head. He can barely move, damn it. A pang of fear slides through me.

I spin around and head into the dingy little station, angry with myself. How did I get back here? I pay my dues. I go to college. I'm not that girl who pretended to call 9-1-1 and watched a man die. I'm not the girl who stole food from the corner store or slid bills out of my mom's junkie friends' wallets.

That's not my world anymore. Damn it.

Inside the store, the guy is looking through a porn magazine. He's big and whiskery like he can't shave right, and he wears thick wire-rimmed glasses, and he makes no attempt to hide the racy cover from me. In fact, he gives me a long once-over that leaves no doubt as to his thoughts.

Nice.

I put on a businesslike attitude. "I seem to be running low on gas. And cash." I hold up the small diamond on my necklace. "Would you be willing to trade?"

He smirks. "I'd be willing to trade. But not for the diamond."

"This is worth a couple hundred dollars." I take it

off. "You'd make a serious profit."

He eyes me like a spider eyeing a fly. I get what he sees. A woman alone on a lonely stretch of highway. Dirty. Desperate.

"That's what I'm offering. You don't like it..." I shrug. "Somebody else'll see what a good deal it is."

"I don't see anybody else around, though, that's the thing." He stands. He's a lot bigger than me. "You won't find another station for miles. So how's about you get on your knees back here. Fifteen minutes," he adds as if that wasn't enough. "Fifteen minutes for all the gas we can fit in that little tank of yours."

This guy is foul, and I'm talking about more than the smell coming off him.

"The diamond or nothing."

His eyes shift to the side. I follow his gaze to what might be unrecognizable to most people; a thumbnail of polished wood. I know exactly what it is: one edge of the butt end of a double shooter, favorite weapon of convenience store clerks everywhere, big on stopping power and beating power. Maybe he's thinking he can get the diamond and his fifteen minutes too.

But not as a trade.

And this weird feeling rises in me—heat, flashing up my neck and into my eyes. It's not anger, it's something else. Like I'm fed up with people thinking I'm some weak little girl. With people pushing me around.

I'm not afraid of him. I'm pissed.

I turn and beat it to the car, running all the way around it. I reach through the open window and grab the gun off the seat just as the guy clears the station door. Grayson is slouched sideways, eyes closed. Unconscious? At least he's out of sight.

I crouch behind the engine and wait. I haven't shot this kind of gun before, but I know how. The gas station guy comes barreling out with his shotgun. I let him get good and close—then I pull the trigger.

The shot goes wild, like I meant it to. He skids to a halt. Out in the open. My heart races. It felt kind of good.

"Don't move," I say, surprised my voice sounds steady.

He turns and runs back toward his shop.

I shoot again, shattering the window. "Don't move!"

He freezes.

"Throw it down." Of course he doesn't listen. That would be too easy. "I swear I'll shoot you. You think I won't?"

"Fine, bitch." He throws down his gun and puts his hands up.

I'm shaking with fear and rage and something else. Something that feels wild and out of control. Power. Is this how Grayson felt when he escaped that prison? "Now you're going to fill up the gas."

"I'd have to go back in and enter the release code," he calls out. "The release code."

Crap. It feels like a trick. I decide I can't let him go back in there. But what to do? What would Grayson do?

I walk several paces from the pump area and make an X in the open gravel with my foot. "Lie down right here, spread eagle, or else I'll kill you."

I move a bit away from the X and widen my stance, aiming at his head, shaking like crazy. I don't know if I'm being convincing, but he saunters over—slowly—wasting time. He feels my fear.

"You want me to kill you, Mr. Fifteen Minutes? You go ahead and give me an excuse."

That speeds him up.

It's all coming back to me, like it was in my bones the whole time—the *fuck you* attitude. The confident command, just an edge of bravado to keep them off balance. It's the way my mom faced down a big dealer one time. The way muggers talk when they've got you far from help.

He gets on the ground, right on my X like I told him, staring at me, eyes full of hate through those thick lenses. Is he just waiting for his chance too?

"Give me your glasses," I say.

He frowns. I feel like I'm channeling Grayson. I haven't forgotten how vulnerable it made me feel, getting my glasses taken away. I also need to see his cash register.

He takes them off and throws them to me.

There's a brick propping open the door. I go over and grab it and hurl it through the other plate-glass window. "That's so the bullet doesn't slow down when I hit your sorry ass if you move."

I rush in and get behind the register. There's video going. Shit! But then I see the record light isn't even on. Okay. *Breathe.*

His glasses are way too strong—they make me feel dizzy almost, but they magnify the words when I tip them a certain way, and that's all I need. I hit the *no sale* button on the cash register, but it doesn't open. I stab at it.

Nothing.

I glance out. He's still there, on my X. I almost can't believe he's staying there like I told him to. I must be more convincing than I thought.

"Not one move," I yell, just to be sure.

I finally see it—the code, taped to the window—356. I enter the numbers, hit the *no-sale* and the thing opens. I take out the money and examine a bank of buttons coming from a console. I find pump two and set it to 30 gallons. A light goes on. I push the glasses over my head, and I run out and start the thing pumping, heart pounding out of my chest.

I run back in and pack a bag with waters and first-aid supplies. I eye a package of rope, covered in plastic, on

PRISONER

one of the displays, thinking to tie the guy up, but I can't
do that alone. I'd have to put down the gun, and he'd
overpower me for sure. But he'll call the cops the second
we're out of here. Unless he decides to chase us himself.

Knees shaking, my gaze rests on a key chain. There's
an old Ford parked off to the side. His? It has to be! I
grab them and head out.

The keys work. I open the trunk. It's full of tools,
which I throw onto the ground. "Come over here and
get in that trunk or you die." I watch the options roll
through his mind. It's a cool spring day. He'll be fine
inside this trunk until someone comes for him. Or he
can take his chances with a madwoman.

He chooses the trunk. "Bitch," he mutters as he hauls
his ass inside.

He glares up at me, and I watch myself through his
eyes. It's like an out-of-body experience. Is this really me,
locking someone in a trunk? I pull his glasses from where
I'd perched them on the top of my head. I watch him
focus on them. They're probably special and took a long
time to get made. He needs them. Maybe Grayson
would smash them, just to keep the guy weak. Grayson
thinks there are only two choices in life: weak or strong.

Fuck that. I toss them in. He catches them, and I
close the trunk.

It's here I know that I'll never be as far gone as Grayson.

Two minutes later I'm back on the road. Grayson is still out.

We near the on-ramp.

Decision time. No more operating on fear and adrenaline. No more running simply because someone is chasing me. No more reacting. I need to decide what I want. I need to decide whether I'm really driving him to his safe house.

Because, why *shouldn't* I leave him at a hospital? Why shouldn't I drive him straight to the nearest FBI office? He told me himself that he killed a cop. He fucked me when I couldn't control the situation. He deserves to be behind bars even more than I do.

But when I imagine dropping him off, it feels like a kind of loss. I think of the raw need in his voice this morning as he pressed me to the bedroom wall. All that raw need when he told me I didn't know anything about him, but really meant the opposite. I think of the way he came to me in the jail. *Because I had to,* he said.

I feel it too—the link we have is as unforgiving as barbed wire.

I touch his soft, dark hair. His color isn't good, but he's breathing still, and I think maybe the bleeding's stopped, because the wad of cloth he's been holding to his chest isn't fully soaked, and he's held it there a while.

"Grayson?" There's a long quiet, and I can barely breathe. I lay my hand on his arm.

He grunts.

My heart soars because he's still fighting. "I'm taking you home."

IT'S DARK WHEN we get into Franklin City. It was once a booming industrial metropolis, but now whenever it's on the news, it's just about how ruined it is, how everybody is leaving or how it's out of money. We pass through a downtown part that seems shiny and modern and inhabited enough, but as I head south toward Gedney Street, the landscape turns post-apocalyptic.

Most of the lights are burned out or broken; where they're still working, they illuminate abandoned buildings, some surrounded by chain-link fences, most with their lower windows all boarded up. Some have their entire first stories blocked off with cement blocks. Others are half crumbled down with bushes and trees growing around and through them. A lot of it is a blur of dark colors.

I start to wonder if Grayson gave me the right address; this is not an area where anybody would ever have a hotel. Am I seeing the signs clearly? Sometimes sevens look like ones.

I pass shadowy figures huddled around a garbage-can fire. I lock the doors.

I'm tired. Tired enough that I don't know if I'm even

driving in a straight line, but I can't stop. I need Grayson to wake up and be okay.

And then I come to Gedney Street. Clearly it was a grand street at one time; now the buildings that line it are boarded up and half consumed by vines. This street is actually scarier than the others, somehow, because there are more vacant spaces between buildings, full of trees and junk—maybe old cars; I can't tell. Even the moon seems to shine less brightly here.

I catch an address: 345. Getting close. Or is it 845?

I set the gun in my lap. I can't believe I'm acting this way—just a couple of days ago, I wouldn't have touched a gun. Until a couple of days ago, I rejected everything about this sort of life. Rejected everything about him.

Finally I get to 176 Gedney. It's a five-story stone building on the corner, surrounded by a chain-link fence. The windows and doors along the bottom are boarded up and grafittied, like most of the buildings here, but it's ornate at the top. There's even a turret way up high, like a castle. Old-style architecture. This place was beautiful once.

There's a vintage-looking sign above the once-grand arched entrance; most of the letters have fallen off, but the few that remain suggest it said Bradford something. Hotel, maybe? Bradford Hotel.

I slow the car. No way does anybody live here. The place looks abandoned, just like everything else in a ten-mile radius. I know the address is right—it's in huge numbers on the front.

"Grayson." When he doesn't answer, panic rises up. "Grayson!"

Still nothing. I squeeze the steering wheel. There's still a half tank, but there's nowhere else to go.

I pull around the corner and park at the side of the building and pat his cheek. "Grayson!"

He mumbles.

"I'm at 176 Gedney, and it's not right. Nothing's here!"

"It's right. No passing," he says. "Find no passing. Rattle it, and leave me there."

He's not making sense. I drive around to the back, through an alleyway. Shivers crawl up my spine; I feel like I'm being watched, but nobody's around. There are certainly no cars around to pass. "There's nothing here," I say. "It's nothing."

"No passing," he says.

I look nervously around, imagining hordes of half-wild people descending on our nice shiny car like in *Mad Max*; that's how this place feels. I have to get us out of here! I pull out, and I'm just about to turn back to the inhabited part of town when my headlights flash on a metal sign. In another lifetime it said NO TRESPASS-ING, but some of the letters are gone, and it says NO PASSING.

I stop. Could it be what he meant? *No passing.* Maybe they're squatting, and that's their safe house. People do that, right? Criminals do that. Though I can't imagine how anybody would get in. The car is only a few feet from the gate, though. He said to rattle it.

I look nervously around, and then I scramble out on shaking legs and rattle the thing and then run back into the car and lock the door.

Nothing.

I have to head back. But to where?

I lean my head on the wheel, so exhausted and scared for Grayson. I need to make a good decision for him, but my options all have dark price tags.

Thump. I jerk my head up and see somebody trying to break the car window on Grayson's side. I pull out my gun with one hand and slam the car into gear with my other.

Thump thump. He pounds on the window. "Abby!"

I look harder. The man draws his face closer. It's the man we met after the escape—Stone. Short, jet-black hair and bright green eyes, neck thick as a tree trunk and a scowl deep as hell. The one who wanted me dead.

He pounds on the window, and I unlock the door, swallowing hard. He won't still want to kill me, will he? But I don't have a choice. Grayson needs help.

The guy yanks open the side door and kneels next to Grayson, shoving his gun in his waistband. "What the fuck happened here?"

"He's shot."

"Fuck." He touches Grayson's throat. "Buddy? Hey!" He whistles over his shoulder. Another guy appears next to him, checking over Grayson—a blond, muscular guy like Stone and Grayson, but with longish hair. He makes a quick phone call, and they pull Grayson out of the car and prop him up between them, drunk style, with Stone holding the cloth to his chest.

A dark figure pulls aside part of the chain-link fence.

"Gotta get that car the fuck out of there," the figure whisper-yells. "Call Nate! Get Nate in the air."

Another guy comes and yanks open the driver's side door. "Out."

There are too many of them. Some of my fear for Grayson gets pushed aside to make room for fear for myself. "I need this car," I say.

"Follow them in. Go!" The guy points with a gun. Going in seems only slightly better than staying out on the dark street or fighting for the car, so I follow Stone and the blond man. The car pulls out behind me and heads farther back, where they must be parking it.

"How long ago?" Stone barks as I follow them through the gap in the gate.

"A little over two hours?"

"Jesus!"

"He didn't want to go to a hospital."

"Fucking goddamn," he growls.

I follow them around the side, trying not to trip over the chunks of rubble, architectural detailing that fell off the place. We head through some thick ivy, and somebody pulls aside a wood board and pushes open a door made of wrought iron.

Everything's dark. Somebody replaces the board behind me, and flashlights flick on. I catch glimpses of torn wallpaper, muscled forearms, guns, thick necks, scuffed boots as we move through. Chains clank nearby.

"You couldn't've called us?" Stone seethes with danger and darkness.

"No," I snap. "What with the fleeing and not knowing your number and him delirious. No."

Three of them work together to carry him across the dark space. Somebody opens a door. I follow them into a brighter, more lived-in-looking space.

These guys are maybe around Grayson's age, if not older. They're a breed apart from guys I know in regular life. Like battle-worn barbarians or something. There's a soldierly quality to them. Medieval. Cavemen, even, like Grayson, but they handle Grayson with absolute strength and care. I find myself feeling grateful to them for that.

The blond slides a set of bars aside and leads us up some stairs. We go up two flights. I cringe at the way they must be jostling Grayson's wound. Not like I can object.

We get into a large room lit dimly by a lamp in the corner. This space is nicer, with marble and intact woodwork. It's almost cozy, with furniture and rugs. Then I see something flash on the far side, and I catch sight of a row of automatic weaponry. Okay, *almost* cozy. There's a sink to one side—the metal looks shiny and polished. Is it possible they have functioning plumbing in here? Though apparently they have functioning electricity, because in the far corner I see an array of computers and other electronics, glowing with the neon blues and greens of technology, incongruous in the vintage space. They've invaded this place, but they share it with the past.

Guys are pulling down shades and blocking off windows. Three guys set Grayson onto a table. The blond brings over a pair of utility lights, the kind in little cages, and clamps them to something on the ceiling, trailing cords like tails. Like workmen use. I catch a flash of white on his forearm. The scarification mark that Grayson had. And none of them have tattoos, just like Grayson.

He adjusts the lights to hit Grayson's still form like a spotlight, making his face half-blinding, half-shadowed.

"Buddy." Stone pats his cheek. "Grayson. Hey." He grabs Grayson's non-shot shoulder, shaking him.

Grayson mumbles.

"Once?" the blond one asks. "Shot once?" he barks.

ANNIKA MARTIN & SKYE WARREN

"I think," I say. "It happened fast. It was one of the governor's guys—that's what Grayson was saying. When he was still making sense."

The blond's expression goes dark and his nostrils flare, like he's sucking in a breath of hate, like he wants to kill somebody with his bare hands, which he could easily do, judging from the size of them. Then he kneels next to Stone and touches Grayson's forehead, and it's the tenderest thing I've ever seen. "Nate's coming, Gray. Okay?" he says. "Hey!" He gently slaps Grayson's cheek, rousing him.

I'm relieved to see Grayson react. Still conscious, barely. I look around, hugging myself. Things are worn and simple but clean. It's surreal, this nice place in the midst of an urban war zone.

Like a home for a lost tribe of guys.

Stone and the blond are attending to Grayson, cleaning his wound. He calls the blond Calder, and they seem to know what they're doing. I don't want to leave him, but I'm starting to get scared. After all, Stone wants me dead—I can hardly forget what he said at the parking lot, and Grayson's not exactly in a position to help me now. And he knows where to find me. If I can get back.

"He feels cold," Stone barks, and somebody goes off, presumably to find another blanket.

It's been a while since they called Nate, to get him in the air. Does he have a helicopter? Do veterinarians do that?

"Where's the car?" I ask.

"Hidden," Calder says.

I move quietly back the way we came. I don't like the idea of going out into that scary, dark neighborhood, but I figure coming across people who *might* kill me is better than being with somebody who clearly wants me dead. I have the gun, but something tells me it takes more than a scared girl and a gun to outrun this group.

Calder rubs his hands over his blond hair and looks at me. I stop moving and try to look innocent and not like I'm sneaking out. A tall guy comes in and tucks a blanket around Grayson.

I edge toward the stairs, planning to break for it. Then Stone spins around and asks me what the guy looked like. What the gun looked like. I tell him.

Calder pulls him aside and talks to him in low tones. He's distracted. I eye the exit. Is now my chance?

Stone gives me a dark look. My heart pounds in visceral alarm. "Going somewhere?"

"I need to use the bathroom," I say, aiming for casual. "Where is it? If you just tell me…"

Stone and Calder exchange glances.

"I'll show you." Stone stalks over and pushes me deeper into the interior, down a hall, and into a little windowless bathroom lined with old-fashioned tile that gleams in the low light. And he stays out there—I can tell by the shadow his boots make under the door. He thinks I'm going to run for it. I've seen him. And now I've seen the blond—Calder. And the two other guys. I know the Bradford Hotel, their safe house. They won't let me live.

Well, my question about plumbing is answered. I splash water on my face and drink a little from the faucet.

Stone doesn't even bother stepping aside when I emerge from the bathroom. He blocks my way, hand out. "Gun."

"Excuse me?"

"Give it or I'll take it."

"It's mine."

He grabs my wrists and spins me around, pushing me face-first against the wall like a cop would.

"Hey!" I shout. Is he going to kill me now? My pulse pounds. I'm shaking inside, but I'm mad too. "If it's me talking you're worried about, look, I brought Grayson here. I've aided and abetted a fugitive every bit as much as you did. I probably broke even more laws than you did. You don't have to worry about me, okay? Your secret is safe with me—I swear it."

My voice sounds high. Frightened.

He practically rips the gun out of my waistband. "Sorry, but you are a threat. You can't help it."

"What?"

"You can't help it," he repeats. He has both wrists in one hand behind my back, and I feel something hard press against the back of my head. "We're going on a little walk."

I try to pull away, but he's ready. He has me. "No! I saved his life! Grayson wants to keep me alive!"

"That's why I have to kill you," he mutters.

I pull and pull, but he's strong as a rock. Tears fill my eyes. "I saved his life!"

He leans closer to my ear. "How did he get shot?"

"The governor's guy was going to shoot me, and Grayson tried to stop him. He didn't want me shot. He wants me alive!"

"Exactly. If it wasn't for you, he wouldn't be on that table half-dead."

My heart sinks. I have no defense for that. If it weren't for me, if I hadn't been there, Grayson wouldn't have been shot.

"You're a threat. You make him weak, and therefore you make all of us weak. I don't want to kill you. I don't kill for fun. But you've got him fucked in the head." He jerks me away from the wall and pulls me toward a dark stairwell.

"No!" I kick him and try to pull away from him. "No!" Nothing I do gets me away from him. He's done this before. "Grayson wants me alive."

"Yeah, yeah, yeah. But he'll thank me later."

Will he?

When I think about dying, I think about not seeing Grayson anymore. Like I've just crossed a border into a country that's somehow magical and dark and amazing, and I don't want to miss it now. I don't want to lose my connection to Grayson.

"We're together. I'm his." I don't realize the truth of it until I actually say it aloud. I'm his. And that makes him mine too, and it's messed up and beautiful. "I'm his and he's mine."

"No, honey," Stone growls into my ear. "He belongs to us. We're his crew. Not you. Just because he fucked you, that doesn't make you his." He drags me down some stairs and into this side building. A parking area, I realize. It's dim, and I can make out maybe a dozen cars, most covered in shrouds of some sort. I wonder if the car I brought is down here. Even if it is, I don't have the key anymore.

Plus Stone is holding me in an unbreakable grip.

The only weapon I have left is my voice. I look around, desperate to stall him. I recognize one of the emblems on the beige cloth-like cover on a car. It's a little shield. I don't even remember what the car is called, but I know it's expensive. The kind of car these guys shouldn't be able to afford.

"Is that yours?" I gasp out.

Stone stills. "Don't drag this out."

"What is this place?" They all look expensive. Different shapes, some like tiny coupes, low to the ground. Others massive and boxy. And all I can think is: keep him talking. Anything to keep him from putting a bullet in my brain. "Do you sell them?"

He snorts. "They're ours. Like this place is ours. Everything you see."

"But you don't drive them." The tires that peek from underneath the covers are gleaming black with deep treads. Unused.

"We can't drive them. They'd attract too much attention."

"So why do you buy them?"

"To have them," he snaps. Then his voice softens. "It's not going to work, honey. Stalling."

A tear drips down my cheek. "I can be like that, for Grayson. Something to keep."

Maybe it's pathetic to compare myself to a car. When you're faced with death, dignity doesn't mean much.

He shakes his head. Sighs. He raises his weapon, and I try to twist away. I should've sped off. Should have driven off when I had the chance. "He saved my life! He doesn't want me dead."

"Wait," says a cold voice. Calder appears. He looks like he's going into battle—a vicious Viking. "You can't."

"She's a *hostage*," Stone says. I kick at Stone, but he

keeps me off somehow. "We don't keep hostages."

Calder's expression is impassive. "Nate wants her to assist."

"He's here?"

"Yeah. And he was asking about…" Calder tips his head toward me.

"I'll fucking assist," Stone says.

"Your fingers are too big. So are mine. He says the bullet was a dummy; it's all over in there. He needs little fingers. Fine work."

Stone swears.

"Will he be okay?" I ask.

"Shut up," Stone barks.

"Let's go," Calder says. "He wants her scrubbed up. We'll kill her after."

Stone simply reverses course, dragging me back up the stairs.

I try to pull away. "Fuck you. I'll help, okay? Let go of me."

He lets me go and points a gun at my head. "If he dies, you die. Slow."

"Fuck you," I say. I'll die anyway. His little demonstration in the parking garage proves that much.

I reach the brightly lit main room, heart pounding. They've ripped Grayson's shirt off; his whole chest is dark with blood, some of it shiny and sticky. A lanky black man is rigging another utility light to a chandelier, and when he flips it on, you can see how pale Grayson is.

"Is he going to be okay?" I ask.

"We'll see," the man says, and I recognize the voice—it's Nate. "You drunk or anything? Squeamish? Too upset?" he asks.

I look down at Grayson. His eyes are half-open like he's fighting to stay conscious. "I'm okay. I can do this."

"If he dies, you're fucked," Stone says from behind me.

"Shut up," Nate barks at Stone. He turns back to me. "Are you good to help? I'm serious. If you're too emotional, you're no use to me."

"I'm good," I say, wiping my tears. "Just worried."

Stone snorts like he doesn't believe me.

"Hey, back off. I need her focused here. You can handle blood, right?"

Stone only crowds me closer. "Don't fuck this up."

I turn to him, pissed and torn up and scared for Grayson, like all the worry of the last hours is folding over on top of me. "You don't know me. You have no fucking idea about any of this."

"No, *you* have no fucking idea."

Asshole.

I leave him standing there. Out at the table under the circle of light, Nate has me snap on gloves and hold a clamp over a vein. I assist him, amazed my hands aren't shaking; I feel shaky inside, or maybe just inside my head. I breathe and focus, following his orders, grateful for a childhood spent patching up my mother after she got beat by her latest dealer. I'm not spooked by violence or blood or even needles. Calder is stationed across from us with a stack of super-absorbent pads; his job is to soak up blood as needed, which seems too often.

"He gonna live?" Stone asks.

Nate doesn't answer. His long, slim fingers move with speed and confidence, and he skirts around the issue with facts: "He's lost a lot of blood. Nothing vital was hit. The next five hours will tell." I get the feeling that his manner with Stone is the result of experience, as if there might have been a time in the past when he'd given a rosy prognosis only to have things go bad. Stone's a guard dog on steroids, loyal and vicious, white teeth snapping, ready to lash out.

The operation is terrifying and bloody. Nate has me depress bits of tissue inside Grayson's wound while he removes fragments of bullet, one after another, using some sort of a magnet, pausing to make tiny stitches—battlefield sutures, he calls them. I can see why he needs my small fingers—not only can I do more pinpointed tasks, but I don't block his view.

He makes Stone hold a pad to the wound while he takes a stretch break. I rip off a glove and lay my hand over Grayson's rough, stubbly cheek. He's completely out. I need him to wake up, to be okay. I want to hear his voice. God, I don't know how I got to this place, needing Grayson like this. Not just to keep me alive and safe from the guys—though yeah, there is that—but needing to be enclosed by him, needing him with me in the world.

Needing him in my world.

One of the guys appears with a bag of blood. Nate tells him to hang it from the ceiling, and everything starts up again.

The operation goes on for an hour, then two. Grayson is out cold from whatever Nate gave him. Eyes closed, mouth slightly open. At least he can't feel pain.

Good job, Nate says now and then. *Perfect. Right there…over…yeah, good.* Suddenly Nate's closing him up. Grayson's signs are good, Nate tells me. His shoulder's messy, that's all. That's how he says it—messy.

The operation is over. And with it, their incentive for keeping me alive.

"When will he wake up?"

"Not for a while, hopefully," Nate says. "We want him to sleep."

Relief is short-lived. I have to save myself. Desperate plans run through my mind. Like taking somebody hostage with a scalpel.

I sneak a peek at the watch Nate put on a nearby stool, and see that it's three in the morning.

"Come on." Nate has me help him with a final suture. Stone, who has been keeping watch from a nearby chair, stands by the table. Calder comes to join them. Nate is explaining next steps. They need to get him resting. Keep him on his back. Check his temperature at intervals.

They don't notice when I back away. I turn and run for it, making for the stairs. Footsteps behind me. Huge hands grab me.

"Oh no you don't." Stone.

An arm comes around my neck, choking me, pulling me back around.

Nate walks up. "Lay the fuck off," he says, peeling off bloody latex gloves. "I may still need her. He's not out of the woods."

"Stupid to keep her around," Stone growls. "She's seen us."

"My priority is Grayson lasting the night," Nate says. "I need her around if I need to go back in."

The arm loosens and lets me go. I wobble for a second before I can stand. I can't read Nate or even catch his gaze—I don't know if he doesn't want me killed, or if it really is just all about Grayson. Either way, I'll take it.

The three of them slide Grayson onto some sort of wheeled table and bring him down a hallway and into a room that's lit only by the moon coming in the high windows. One of the guys pulls down a thick blind, totally covering the window, and Calder switches on a lamp. It's an old hotel room, by the looks of it, with a little bed and a desk. A small pile of books sits on the floor next to the bed. The sweet computer setup is a total anomaly. I've never seen anything like this place.

For these guys, it's clearly home.

They ease Grayson onto the bed.

From the outside, the window coverings block out the light completely. You would never guess somebody lives here from the way it looks outside, the way it looked when I arrived. Stone, Calder, Nate, and a few other guys go in and out. There seem to be seven of them, all heavily armed, all with that same feral vibe, like a lost tribe. They all have that white scar tattoo and no regular tattoos, except for one guy, who is covered in them.

Now that Nate's gone out of healing mode, it's pretty clear he's one of them. They seem so connected, and for the first time I wonder if every single one of these guys go back to that basement. The moment I think it, I know it's true, deep in my gut. They're not like other men. This is a different breed of guy, raised in a different way. A horrifying way.

Then I'm alone with Grayson, no guys with guns wandering in and out. I take his hand, willing him to wake up, but he looks so weak, lying there like a wounded animal, sheets wrapped around his legs and hips, muscular chest half rough skin and half bright white and red with bandages, short dark hair pasted to his skull with sweat.

"Baby," I whisper, squeezing his hand. "I need you to

wake up. I need you to help me." My voice cracks on the last word.

His lips move. I can't tell if he's trying to say something. His lips form the words *Ms. Winslow,* but it could be my imagination. Wishful thinking.

Nate comes up next to me. "Let him sleep."

"His color's better," I say hopefully. "And his breathing…"

"He'll be back to his surly self in no time," Nate says, laying two fingers to the side of Grayson's throat. "He'll have a little trouble with his shoulder for a while, but he'll live."

Which means they won't need me anymore. My gaze slides to the door. Is Stone on the other side, just waiting for me to run? Nate protected me against Stone, but I don't know how far that protection will extend. Would he call them if I ran? Or would he chase me down himself?

He slides his brown eyes to meet my gaze, and I get the sense that he knows what I'm thinking. "You stay," he says simply. I don't know if it's a threat or a promise.

These guys can't stay awake forever. I still have money from the robbery. I can get away. I've survived too much already; I can survive this too.

But God, I'm so tired. I curl up next to Grayson and start to drift off. I feel a light blanket over me before I fall asleep.

CHAPTER THIRTY

~GRAYSON~

I WAKE UP with a head full of putty. I can barely move. It's like a train ran over me and left part of a wheel sticking into my shoulder, which is heavily bandaged; even my left arm is immobilized in some sort of sling. But worse, I had this nightmare about the crew killing Abby, and I couldn't get to her. I told Calder I'd kill them if they touched her, but I wasn't sure if he heard me. Wasn't sure if that was just a dream too.

Stone is in the chair next to me, sleeping. Nobody else is around, and I panic, wondering where Abby is, but then I spot her, curled up in the corner where somebody chained her to the radiator. She's sleeping, but she looks uncomfortable. Heat rises to my face, and I suddenly want to fucking kill somebody.

Nobody touches Abby except me. Nobody else knows how to keep her from being scared, or what she likes, what she needs. I'm the one who was supposed to keep her safe, and one of these guys locked her up? She should have a mattress. Is she hungry? Thirsty?

But it's the middle of the night. Telling time without seeing through a window is one of those handy skills you learn in prison.

I jab my fingers into Stone's neck. He grumbles and opens his eyes. "Hey," he whispers.

"Who the fuck locked her up?" I demand.

"Me." Stone puts a hand to my head like he can tell my temperature. "How d'ya feel?"

I grunt. Of course he did.

He's suited up in black, like he's been outside—getting supplies, maybe. His nine is shoved into his shoulder holster.

"Nate says you're out of the woods if you make it through the night and lay the fuck off the shoulder."

Even my good arm feels like lead. I gesture toward where she sleeps. "You don't fucking touch her, got it?"

His look is grim.

"Don't touch her."

He looks at me a long time; then he says, "You can't have her."

My whole body flares hot, like angry lightning. Every part of me answering *no*. "What's that supposed to mean?"

"It means she's seen us. She knows where we are. There's nothing you can do about it. Nate needed her slim fingers, or I would've done her last night—"

I surge up at him without even thinking. He grabs

my wrists before I can choke him.

"The fuck I can't have her," I growl. "She's mine. Got it?"

"You're supposed to kill the hostage, not drag her around by the hair," Stone says, pinning me to the bed. Damn drugs have me weak as a kitten.

"No," I say.

"It's not up to you," he says in a low voice. "I'm doing this for you, little brother."

I try again to surge up, but he has me. I'm too weak. "Fucking kill you," I say, but I can't fight him with whatever Nate has me pumped full of.

I struggle some more but he's heavy as a tank, and I'm injured, drugged.

He says, "You want to tear that shoulder and go back under the knife?"

"She won't talk," I growl. "And she's mine."

He looks me straight in the eyes. "I'll wake her up so you can say goodbye."

I give him a level look. I need him to see my face for what I'm going to say, what I'm going to promise.

Silence swells between us. He seems to know it's coming.

I deliver: "Hurt her and you're dead."

He doesn't say anything back; his expression doesn't even change, but I know there's an earthquake inside him. It was big, what I said. Stone's always been in charge, and I've always been fine with that, but I need him to get how serious I am.

He lets off me and pulls out his piece, rubs a thumb along the grip.

"You understand me?" I ask after a too-long silence.

"You saying that is exactly why I should kill her."

A feeling rises up in me, so old I almost don't recognize it. Fear. I'm scared like I haven't been for a long time. If I was in fighting shape, no one could touch her. No one ever would.

But I'm weak right now, and Stone knows me too well. A fight between us would be ugly, and I can't be sure she'd end up safe. There was a time I'd never dream of raising a hand to Stone, to my friend and blood brother, but here I am.

I look over at her, so vulnerable, chained up, curled up. And it's then I know that her vulnerability is the most powerful thing in my life—an absolute power, but not a danger. Then I realize something else. "It's about you."

"What?"

"She's a fucking danger to you, not me."

He draws his face close to mine, nostrils flaring. "No, this is about the good of you and of the gang."

"You just don't like that I took her," I whisper. "That's what you don't like. You don't like that I've taken her for mine." I check over his shoulder to make sure she's still sleeping, and I lower my voice. "Somebody I'd lay down my life for and who is mine. Not yours."

He grabs my neck and leans in, close enough to kiss me. I can feel the gun at my jaw.

"You gonna kill *me* now?" I grate.

"We said no to this a long time ago," he says. "We said we wouldn't do it. No women, except to fuck. And definitely no taking them. And you bring a fucking captive in front of our noses? I'm going to kill her for you, and there's nothing you can do about it."

He keeps me close, hand gripping my neck. I watch his eyes. Chained up there, helpless, I see the threat of her now. She's the slippery slope we've all been trying to stay off of.

"I'm keeping her. Long term."

Shock plays in his eyes. It takes a lot to get Stone to look shocked, but that did it. He jerks my head hard. "What the fuck is wrong with you?"

"You know what's wrong with me. You know exactly what's wrong with me. The only difference is I'm not pretending anymore."

"We're not them," he says.

"This is different."

He twists the gun at my jaw, warm and hard. It's killing him, her being here. But I can't let her go, not even for him. Not even for my brother in spirit.

I whisper, "You don't know what it's like when she's

yours, and you would do goddamn motherfucking anything for her."

I know he's imagined it. What it would be like. "That's why I have to kill her," he says, breath hot on my lips.

"All the girls I ever had, fucking one-night stands in some shit bathroom and wherever. It's nothing compared to—" I gesture in her direction. "That's black-and-white, and this shit is color. When you find somebody and you *know*."

"Don't."

"When you know she's yours, Stone…all yours."

He's gone still, cradling my neck, gun in hand. He doesn't want to hear this, yet he really, really does. I know what I'm doing is unfair, like describing a shot of nice scotch to an alcoholic who's denied himself for years, but he needs to know.

"Every time I thought of killing her or letting her go, I couldn't because it feels so fucking right. And when the governor's guy tried to take her down? I would've died to stop that. And when she's hungry or cold—"

"Stop it," Stone says. He's the strong one. He always has been. Like his name.

Unbreakable.

"When she's cold, I'm the one who warms her. And when she's hungry? We were at Nate's, and I had her blindfolded, and I was feeding her blueberries, picking out the best ones and…you don't know what it's like—"

"Yes, I do."

"It's not like with *them*. What we did—"

He gives me a dark look. That's another thing we're not supposed to do, talk about the bloody day we rose up against our captors. The savagery of that. "It's *just* like them," he says. "You think it's different because you don't keep her chained in a basement?"

"It's different."

"I'm killing her for you. It's the most humane thing."

"Remember when you did that carjack?" I ask. He's done a million carjacks, but only one matters and he knows it. The one where the hot blonde didn't get out fast enough for him, and he kept her captive long enough to drive her an hour out of town to meet Calder.

I knew what it was from the way he talked about it afterward. He didn't touch her, but he wouldn't let her go. He fed her, cared for her. "How did it feel?"

"Fuck you."

I press. "How did it feel?"

He waits so long I think he won't answer. And then he lowers the gun. "You know how it feels," he whispers finally. *Good,* that's how it feels.

"And that was just you taking her for a drive," I say.

"Fuck. Grayson—"

"We're not like them. She saved my life, right? It shows I'm not like them. I never would've saved any one of them."

"Jesus. Fuck!" He lets go of my neck and scrubs a hand over his face. "She has to die. Wake her up and say goodbye." He fingers his nine. I didn't think this through, how much he'd need to kill her, like the alcoholic needing to pour the bottle down the sink. Needing to set it on fire and watch it burn. Still so fucked up over what those assholes did to us.

Whatever drugs Nate gave me are dragging me under and I don't know if I can stay awake much longer. "Don't do this, Stone. Don't let them win."

"Don't let them win? Is that what you just said? Fuck you." He presses the side of the gun to his forehead and closes his eyes. "I just need to kill her. Everything will go back to the way it was when she's dead."

I reach out and grab his arm. "Come here."

He sucks in a breath, but he needs to see I'm not so far gone. He needs to see I'm still me even if I have her too.

"They're not winning," I say. "They're motherfucking dead." I move over and make room for him even though it hurts like hell. "Come here."

He collapses next to me. He's always been there when I've needed him. We're always there for each other; it's our code.

I snake a hand under his shirt and flatten my palm onto his chest, the way we used to do, feeling each other's heartbeat, like this stupid shred of humanity we gave each other, there in the basement. We didn't know how to act regular down there. Everything cramped and close and weirdly sexual even when it shouldn't have been.

Holding on to him hurts like hell, but this is for Abby. "Tell me about the plans. I want to know what they are now. If you changed them."

"I know what you're doing," Stone says. "Distracting me won't work."

But actually it will. Some kids got comfort food or a special toy when they were upset, or the loving arms of a parent. All we ever got was each other, and talking about what we'd do to the guy in charge if we ever got our hands on him. We knew early on that our captors were working for somebody. Lying together and talking about the ways we'd torture and kill him was like a teddy bear to normal kids. "Does Calder still get to scoop out his eyes?"

"No, he changed his mind while you were inside. He gets to gut him."

"Who does the governor's eyes?"

"Nobody. We decided we want him to see all the way through, because we're making him watch the films they made of us while we fuck him up. Also, Nate said that could kill him too fast if we scooped his eyes too enthusiastically."

ANNIKA MARTIN & SKYE WARREN

I nod, knowing that's the word he would've used—enthusiastically. That's a Nate word.

I ask, "You still get to cut out his balls?"

He softens finally. "And stuff them in his mouth."

"That's new," I say. I can just see them discussing it for hours, maybe over pizza and Macallan twenty-one-year-old scotch. We found a case of it hidden in a compartment in a wall when we first broke into this place, and the seven of us got drunk on it. It tasted like freedom. It's still all we'll drink.

"But you still get to kill him," Stone says. "That never changes. You earned that right."

I feel his heart slow. He's calming. Good. Stone's always been one of those guys who needs to work himself up to kill—he can't kill cold. Not like Calder.

"He'll die a hero, of course," Stone bites out.

"He'll know, though."

Our captors were portrayed in the media as innocent victims of random violence, and it always got us, that they got love and nice funerals and nobody ever knew what they'd done to us. *Carnage in a peaceful community,* one headline said. Like our captors were victims or something.

We were stupid—we assumed that when their bodies were found, it would be obvious what they were up to. But somebody got there first and cleaned out the place, taking all the footage, all the evidence we'd ever been there. Maybe the governor or his lackeys. He wasn't governor then, though. Just some pervert businessman we knew only by sight. We'd never been able to find him after we escaped from that hellhole; then he appeared on TV, running for office. I nearly shit when I saw him on TV for the first time.

Stone scratches his nose with the tip of his gun. "The problem is the governor's mansion. We knew you'd get free sooner or later, and in the meantime, we've been trying to strategize an entry. The place is a motherfuck-ing fortress."

"It's just an old mansion," I say.

"No, seriously. Thing's a fortress. Guards, metal detectors. We've tried to get in through his people. We put out feelers for bribes but nobody's soft. We've tried to get in twice already, just to scout the place out. Fucking Fort Knox laser trip-wire shit."

"Do you have the floorplan?

"We found out there was a remodel in the 1970s, but we couldn't get any intel on it. The paper trail's shit."

"We'll find a way in," I say, feeling woozy. My eye-lids are heavy. How long I can stay awake?

A voice from across the room. "Did you try the li-brary?"

Stone jerks.

Abby.

My heart swells, hearing her voice from across the

room. How long has she been up? "You okay?"

"If it's historic, there are architectural records," she says. "It's a governor's mansion?"

After a beat, Stone says, "Sure." He still doesn't look at her.

"The blueprints are probably public. They'd be in the archival section of your main library, or if you have a history center. You can learn a lot about old buildings when you know where to look."

She's so beautiful and smart and scared over there. "Baby."

"A lot of them have been remodeled a dozen times over. But if you look at the originals, you wouldn't believe how many doors and windows have likely been covered over. There could be hidden points of entry."

She pulls on her handcuffs. I wonder how much of our conversation she heard. She's working an angle—I can see it. I don't even know what it is, but I'm proud. She's so fucking strong, a survivor.

Stone snorts. "You think I can go to the library and check out—what?—blueprints to a government building that show secret ways to enter?"

"Shut up and listen," I say. "She worked at a library. She knows."

She meets my eyes. She gets me crazy when she talks like that. "It wouldn't be filed like that. It's a totally different section. You'd need to go into historical records. It would be filed by parcel numbers, and you can't check it out or even copy it. If you could sneak in a tiny camera…"

"You think they have records on this building?" Stone asks.

"Definitely. They might be stored in a section of the library that's closed to the public, but they're there."

I grin. "Oh, we'll get in. Don't worry about that. I'll get us in."

Alarm widens her eyes. "You mean breaking in?"

"That depends. Are you gonna help us?" I ask.

Stone gives me a dark look. Maybe we're being worked. But maybe not. She has us. She's fucking amazing.

"Maybe," she says.

"No maybe. You're helping us," I say.

Stone glares at me. "She just wants to get away and rat us out. She thinks she can get away."

I turn to Abby, and something like understanding passes between us. Maybe she'll try to get away. Maybe she won't. I don't fucking know anymore. All I know is that she's mine. "She's helping."

"She's not a part of this."

But I'm the one who did the time. I'm the one who was the favorite down in that hole, and not the kind of favorite you ever want to be. "I want her there."

The guys have been with me, of course, but it's different with her, and suddenly—yeah, I want her there, *need* her there. I look into her brown eyes, but I'm talking to Stone. "She comes. You said he's mine. That the job is mine. That means I say how it goes."

CHAPTER THIRTY-ONE

~GRAYSON~

W E'RE IN MAIN room, putting the final touches on our plan.

It's funny; we've been wanting vengeance for so long, but now that it's near, I don't feel happy. I look around at these guys I've gone through so much with, guys I'd lay down my life for, and I know none of them are happy either. Abby's sitting in the corner, reading. I smooth a strand of hair that escaped her bun, and I feel happy about that.

I've been spending the last few days recovering, sleeping a lot. I made the guys go out and buy Abby some nice clothes and underwear she picked out of a catalog and a crapload of books, and she's been by my side nearly the whole time, except while my guys and I were scheming.

Stone's polishing bullets at the table. He's already tasting the governor's death. Hearing him cry out in pain. Stone will hurt him, and then I get to do the honors. It means a lot that he gave it to me, because I know he wants it bad.

"Come on." I pull her hand.

"Just a sec," she says. Always wanting to finish a chapter. Always another chapter.

I pick her up and haul her over my back.

"Hey!" She struggles, and the book thuds to the floor. I'm always doing that—losing her place. I have her on my good shoulder, but it's killing my bad shoulder all the same.

"We're outta here," I growl the way that she recognizes. Primal. A little mean. The way a male lion would subdue his female.

I can feel the eyes of my guys on me as I spin around with her and walk off.

She squirms, but it's just for show now. "Grayson."

I hear the breathlessness in her voice, the arousal. She gets off on this treatment, like I do. I head down the hall, letting her struggle. I walk into my room and lay her down onto my bed. She looks up, waiting. Mine. So much mine it scares me.

"How together you guys are," she says, her eyes intense, "It's amazing. The way you survived and pulled each other through."

I don't know what to do with that, so I just shove her over and nestle in beside her. She watches my face; then she settles on her side right next to me, tracing the ridges of the scarification symbol on my arm. We lie there like two plants, soaking up the darkness like sunshine.

There's this way where I can sometimes sense the direction of her thoughts, and I know she's going to ask about it before she does.

"You all have these," she says, tracing it up and down.

"Yeah," I whisper.

"Two-sided axes in an X. You did them yourselves?"

I push a bit of hair out of her eyes with my other hand. "How can you tell?"

A faint smile brushes her lips. Because they're pretty crude.

"Battle-axes," I say. "We found the picture in one of the moldy encyclopedias we used to read out of in the basement."

She nods.

"Through the years, when we'd get in fights down there, they'd put makeup on our bruises and withhold food. We would get in a lot of trouble for getting scraped up or bruised, you know, messing up the merchandise. They had a lot of ways to control us, but we gave each other these a few days before the end. Scraped the hell out of each other's arms with sharpened nails. We were older—Stone was fifteen and strong as fuck. We'd work out down there. We were going to get out or die at that point."

"So that's what this is? A kind of war paint?"

I pause, because this isn't something we tell people outside the group, but then I realize she's not outside. To me, she's as inside as you can get. "It's part of a vow we made up: *One blade to protect my brothers, one blade for vengeance.*"

"That's your vow?"

"That's our vow."

She traces the lines of the axes with her finger. "If I look back at the newspaper reports for fifteen years ago, will I find a bloody unsolved crime?"

"Yes," I say.

She just traces it. I hold my breath, wondering what she's going to say. The moonlight streams in from the high window, adding a glow to her dark hair, splaying around her head, and her cheekbones, so strong and somehow fragile at the same time. "I think it's beautiful," she says finally.

The breath shudders out of me, and I'm filled with relief. Maybe a kind of peace, even.

She narrows her gaze. "You lived in this hotel for fifteen years?"

"Give or take. We took it right after we got out. Except Nate. He bought a guy's identity and tried to make a straight life. I guess he did."

She points up at the dingy, pockmarked ceiling where the lightbulb hangs from a cord. "You put in that light?"

"Yup. This place wasn't exactly functioning then, but... It was right after we escaped. I needed to fight with something. We all did. So we made this place into a home."

She nods as if that makes sense.

We couldn't do everything ourselves though. We took a lot of money with us from the basement, and we paid a lot of money on the black market to wire this place off the city grid. The guy probably retired on what we paid him, but the place is still humming.

"The fixture still has the price tag on it."

"So what?" I say. "It's a light. It lights things." I watch her, seeing the Bradford through her eyes suddenly, and my gut tenses. This place isn't dark and cold like a basement, but it's not that far off. My room has old furniture that would be nice except for the gouges in the wood. The walls have bright rectangles where pictures used to hang, before we got here. A thick layer of dust covers the lines in the woodwork. We've got lots of nice shit, sure. The tech, the cars, old scotch. Maybe that doesn't mean much to her.

"This place is ours. It's a good place." I turn, lying on my good shoulder. "Safe from everyone," I whisper, sliding a wisp of hair off her forehead even though I'm not supposed to be moving my arm.

"A bare bulb with the price tag on it, from fifteen *years* ago."

I lean my head to her ear. "You know I can't let you leave."

She slides a sly gaze to me. It's different when I say it now, but it's still true. I can't let her leave. My heart pounds as she looks back at the ceiling. "You deserve a nice place, that's all," she says. "I mean, it has beautiful features, but it feels kind of abandoned still. Temporary."

"Nobody's going anywhere," I grate.

She turns to me. "Right, but you can't decorate it with nice things?"

"Decorate it?"

She snorts. "Guys."

She wants to make it nice. A strange feeling comes over me, like when somebody gives you the last burger even though you've been an asshole all night.

"It wouldn't be hard," she says. "A decent fixture. Some paint for the ceiling or something. Pictures on the wall. Wouldn't you like that?"

My breathing starts to feel funny, a kind of soft heaving, because somewhere back in the cobwebby part of my mind where I never go, I remember somebody, a foster mom, maybe, caring about what was on the ceiling. Hanging toy things from the ceiling, like it mattered what the fuck I saw.

She's studying my face. "You could have anything nice you want. You could have a thousand-dollar chandelier up there."

I look away, feeling too exposed. "A thousand-dollar chandelier in a room in a boarded-up hotel?"

She turns on her side now, pursuing. "You deserve to have things nice."

And suddenly I'm wondering if Stone is a little bit right—if maybe she is too dangerous to me. Because I feel all broken apart, her saying that. And this fucking place can never be nice. She doesn't belong here. And that one fact destroys me.

I pull on her collar. "Take off your shirt."

"Grayson," she says.

I pat my belt buckle. "Sit up here and take off your shirt."

She gives me a look. I give her one back. She knows what it means.

She gets up onto my rock-hard cock, straddling me.

"Take it off," I say. "Slow."

I read the hesitation in her eyes, and I push. I don't know why; I just do, like the pain of her kindness is too much. "I said, take it off."

She pulls her shirt up by the hem—slow and shy, unaware how hot her reluctance is. She's so fucking prim, it gets me hard. She pulls it over her head. I reach up and grab her shirt before she can untangle it from her wrists, and I twist them up extra hard, yanking her arms to the front of her. Then I undo her fly and I press my thumb to her clit, holding her, stroking her.

She watches me with those brown eyes as I move my thumb up and down, getting her off, keeping her wrists tied in her shirt, twisting a little more to let her know who's in charge.

She hisses out a breath and starts rocking against my cock.

"That's good, baby." I press my thumb deeper. "You're wet for me," I say, holding her gaze, showing her there are no secrets between us.

"Yeah," she whispers.

She leans down on her shirt-tangled arms and kisses my chest. It's like heaven, and I close my eyes. It's all I can do not to flip her over and fuck her right there, but I just take her in, her kisses, all the tenderness that I don't deserve.

"Pants," I grate. She rolls off me and stands, pushing down her pants and wriggling out of them.

I watch with a funny feeling in my gut; she's so bright and good, and for a second I think maybe I could just stay with her. Maybe I don't need revenge. But the thought slips away, because killing the governor has always been mine.

Then she gets back on me and rides me sweet until I can't see or think or hear.

CHAPTER THIRTY-TWO

~ABIGAIL~

THE LIBRARY IS on the other side of Franklin City, on a dark, gloomy street, thanks to half the streetlights being out. The buildings are run-down and the sidewalks are strewn with trash, but it's not a complete and utter wasteland like the neighborhood around the Bradford Hotel. There are actually people and cars going by.

It's late. The library is closed, but Grayson walks me right up to the door like he owns the place, grip hard on my arm. Does he think I'll try to escape? I know Stone still thinks I want to.

It's the first time I've been out of the Bradford for days. Time has gone by in a blur; it seems like I spent half my time lying in bed with Grayson, reading while he slept and recuperated—and staying near him, not entirely trusting Stone and the guys not to take me out and shoot me or something, as much as Grayson insists that danger is past. Once he was well enough, he was holed up with his guys, cleaning weapons and running scenarios, preparing to hit the governor.

And while he was with his guys, I spent the time in a no-man's-land, not really a captive but not exactly free to go. And I don't know what I'd do out there, anyway. My picture is on the national news, and I'm wanted by the police. I could be in a lot of trouble. Even though I was a hostage. That should count for something.

I've been doing what I always do—hiding in books. One whole afternoon and evening was taken up in a Victorian mystery. After that, it was pirates. After that, Italian travel essays. There's this turret at the front of the hotel with amazing light, and the guys don't even use it. I swept it out and cleaned it up, and that's where I've been reading while Grayson had his head down with his guys, which is often. They're obsessed with getting to the governor—they've been waiting for it their whole lives.

They're going to kill him. Slowly. Grayson hasn't said it outright to me. Some things you just know.

"Closer," he says, shoving me to the fake pillar at the side of the big double doors, pressing against me, being a little rough, the way I enjoy.

I close my eyes, soaking up his heat, his force; the intensity of his focus on me feels like a caress. He won't ever let me go—not ever.

He's moving his arm beside me.

"What are you doing?" My voice comes out breathy, but then I open my eyes and realize he's picking the lock. I'm his cover.

The crew is around, watching from shadows. Even knowing they're out there, I can't see them.

"What about the alarm?" I ask, nodding my head at the alarm warning sign.

"City stopped paying that contract years ago." The latch clicks. He loops an arm around my neck. "Wait," he whispers, holding me close. You would hardly know he was shot a few days ago—he's strong as a bull. There's no pain in his expression when he looks down at me with something like...tenderness? Affection?

Something more?

He pulls me in, and his chest feels solid and strong, a wall against my wildly beating heart. It feels good. Maybe I can't leave. Maybe I don't want to. I grin up at him through my nervousness. We're about to break into a *library*. It's nothing to Grayson. Over the past days it has really hit me how much crime Grayson and his tribe of guys are responsible for. The expensive cars and the rest of the guy toys and all that nice scotch they drink.

As soon as the street empties of traffic and pedestrians, he leads me in.

Stepping into the library feels like going home, even with all the craziness of breaking in and Stone wanting me dead and Grayson being...well, Grayson. It's as if we're on some kind of nerdy outlaw date, picking out books together.

Grayson flicks on a flashlight, keeping it pointed low.

The cool metal racks are filled to the brim with old, dusty books. I relax a little, infused with a sense of safety. Books were not quite an escape for me.

And they were never my friends.

They were so much more than that—utilitarian and unbreakable. They were my armor, my wall against the world. Until I had Grayson.

"Where are the floor plans?" Grayson sounds grim. Impatient. Does the library make him nervous?

I like that. It makes me feel powerful. "I'm not sure," I answer. "Every library's laid out differently."

"Well figure it out," he snaps. "I'm not about to get thrown back in jail because you couldn't figure out the fucking Dewey decimal system."

"I'm surprised you know about the Dewey decimal system."

He snorts. Then after a minute he adds, "I can read."

"And write."

His sideways look threatens punishment if I continue. So of course I do.

"I mean that in the best way. You can really write. The way you threaded that story with your ideas for the escape. The way you knew exactly what to write so I'd feature it. Just enough truth to make it real. Just enough fiction to get a message to your friends."

He gives me a wary look. "Are you mocking me?"

I roll my eyes. "I'm being serious. You made me so

angry I couldn't see straight. That project meant a lot to me. But what you wrote was really good."

He looks away. He doesn't seem to want to talk about it.

"I don't understand—you guys were so young when you ended up in that basement. I saw the milk carton. You were five. And it sounds like you were all in there together. You were in there six years, and they weren't sending you to school, so…"

"Perverts who keep boys in basements aren't real likely to send them to school."

"And then when you got out of there, you were eleven?"

He runs his finger over a leather-bound ledger. "And the other guys were fourteen or fifteen by then."

"And you ended up at the Bradford."

"Yup. Checked into the Bradford Hotel," he says sarcastically. Because there'd be no checking in. I imagine them prying up the boards. Just kids. And that's when they started their life of crime.

"So how did you learn to read?"

"Nate taught me," he says. "Most of the guys were seven or eight when we went in. They mostly knew how to read by then. Nate is brilliant, though. He taught me, and he made the rest of us keep it up. It was a basement, you know? There were musty boxes of books down there. Some encyclopedias from 1920. That's what I learned on."

"Oh," I say. It explains a lot. The holes in his under-standing of things.

"Nate made up a lot of guessing games out of reading that stuff. Not exactly an education, but it felt like fighting back. Like saying, you can't take everything from us. Not much of an education, but—"

"It's amazing," I say. "Because you fought for it and it's yours. And it's amazing how you guys got each other through."

He slides his finger along a metal shelf.

"Why didn't you go back to your foster family?"

"They never felt like mine the way the guys did. When you're in something like that for so long, you can't get a bond fiercer. It was us against them, against everyone in the world."

His pain pierces me.

"That's a gift that those perverts gave you. Brothers who are more than brothers. More than a family."

"Don't candy coat it. Those animals that took us, Abby…they took a lot."

"No," I say.

He looks away, and this image comes into my mind of a time I was up north with my mom. We were in this slummy neighborhood and all night the sirens were going—from a house burning down, we learned the next morning. We walked over to look and it was this massive blackened shell, hung with icicles like diamonds against the blue, blue sky. The most beautiful thing I'd ever seen.

Grayson is like that house. Stunning in his destruction.

He studies me with haunted eyes. "Maybe they took too much, you know?"

I put my hand on his arm, over the battle-axe scar. "They didn't, Grayson. Don't say that."

"Why shouldn't I say that? Sometimes I look at other people, like the guys I met in prison, and they're different. They have something I don't have—I don't know what it is; I just know…" He shakes his head.

Did they take what makes him human? What makes him civilized? That's the question he's trying to articulate.

The library twists in front of me like the mirrored walls of a fun house, reflecting fucked-up versions of Grayson back at me. Reflections of myself, because I'm here with him. Everybody would say we're wrong in everything we're doing. But we don't feel wrong to me.

Did they take what makes him human? What makes him civilized?

Grayson looks at me with one part hope, one part dread. He wants my answer. He really wants to know. I pull him closer and shove my hand into his dark hair. "They didn't take anything important, baby. They didn't take what's important."

A strange expression passes over his face, one I haven't seen before. "Let's get those floor plans."

Chapter Thirty-Three

~Grayson~

ABBY LEADS ME through the library. First we look behind the front desk to find out where things are stored. This is a large city library with enough desks and stations for an army of librarians. I try to imagine it bustling with people, but all I can see are orange jumpsuits shuffling in formation.

They didn't take what's important. I keep going over and over that in my head. Like what? I want to ask. What did they take? What did they leave?

Is it enough?

It's times like these that I get how much distance is between us. A caveman—that's how she sees me. Barely human, she said to me once. I guess that's my answer right there. The answer of why she's dangerous, why I should cut her loose.

I never felt like I wasn't enough before Abby showed up. Pissed off, yeah. A fucked-up stranger in the world, yeah. But never like I wasn't enough.

That's part of why Stone wants her dead. *If we get the*

blueprints, he said before we left. *We don't need her anymore.*

But I need her. I won't tell Stone that because he'll see it as a weakness. And maybe it is, but I'm beyond caring. They don't get that she's the missing part of me.

The best part of me.

Nate doesn't like her around either. It's not about protecting me with him; it's more about not bringing more people into the madness. And then there's Calder. The Saint, which is a fucked-up name considering he's more lethal than anyone. He got the name because he doesn't fuck anyone. Or hasn't, since our milk-carton-kid days. He definitely doesn't like Abby around. None of the other guys do, either.

But I'm back in action, almost one-hundred percent, and anybody going for Abby goes through me. I'll always come for her and I'll always protect her and she knows it.

We bypass the elevator and go down the stairwell to the basement where she thinks the historical documents are kept. I angle my flashlight, helping her find her way through the stacks until she pulls out an old thick binder and holds it up to the beam. "Found it."

I raise my eyebrows. "That was fast."

"Well, it's *one* of these sheets. I don't know which one, and it will take time to find it. So I figured we can just take them all now and look for it back at the Bradford."

"Take them all." That makes me laugh. "I think I've had a bad influence on you."

She shrugs. Maybe she thinks so too. That shouldn't bother me. I grab the binder and study the numbers and letters.

She turns back, humor lighting her eyes. "They don't use the Dewey decimal system to store these."

She thinks it's funny that I know what the Dewey decimal system is. Yeah, I never went to school. The first and last grade I took was kindergarten, but I used the prison library.

I play along. "What system do they use then?"

"The Library of Congress," she says matter-of-factly. "It's better for physical items of varying shapes and sizes. Things with artifacts—or even instruments. Music libraries often—"

"Hang on." Shit, she's so earnest about this. It makes me hot. I glance around, but of course we're alone. Maybe I'm not good enough—not like one of her college boys. It doesn't stop me.

I put down the binder and back her up against the wall. Her eyes widen.

She knows what's coming.

She wasn't expecting this, and her shock just feeds my lust. My dick is pressing against my jeans. My dick has a lot of ego. It thinks it can burst through denim and shove up into her skirt and thrust right into her slick, warm cunt. It has the right idea.

I run my finger along her cheek. "I like it when you talk classification," I murmur.

She laughs, a little self-conscious. I like that too. I'm so fucking hard I'm hurting. I've always had a thing for smart chicks. Forbidden, somehow. But Abby is mine.

"Keep going," I say. "What's another kind?"

And then I lick her neck, from the base of her jaw down to her collarbone. She tastes like salt and outdoors and arousal. She sucks in a breath and tries to talk. "The United Nations…"

I bite down on the curve where her neck meets her shoulder. "Keep going," I murmur.

"The United Nations symbols are printed on the upper right-hand corner. Not the spine—" Her words cut off on a gasp. Probably because I cup her breast through her shirt. I love the weight of it, the feminine softness as I caress her. But it's not enough.

So I unbutton her shirt, baring her breasts to the cool, dusty air. "Tell me more."

She lets out a little sob, and even that turns me on. I want to hear her talk about systems and symbols. I want to hear her cry and moan and beg for me. I want to hear every sound she can make, and I'm going to help her get there.

Fuck it. I don't need to be a better man. I don't need to be more. I'm in charge here.

I find her nipple through the lace of her bra and pinch. A sharp noise this time. I rub my groin along her hip, needing friction.

"More."

A breath shudders out of her, but she's a good girl. She's obedient. That's why she works so well for me. She's spent her whole life teaching herself to obey. "The first segment…and sometimes the second…identifies the issuing body."

I laugh under my breath. "You're making that up."

"I'm not!" She sounds a little breathless. "I wouldn't joke about—about—"

But then she shuts up because I've found her nipple with my tongue. There's still lace between us, but it's damp now with my saliva. I could just as easily push the fabric aside, or rip it apart, but I like this roughness. That's the thing about lace. It looks so pretty and delicate—like Abby. But the way it feels? It's rough. I use it like sandpaper, running it over her nipple, listening to her suck in a breath.

"I've got your issuing body right here," I say, even though it's cheesy. I'm too worked up to give a crap. Plus I still think she might have been fucking with me. Issuing body? It's like she fucking wants to suck my dick. And she goes willingly enough when I grab her hair and shove her to the floor.

Her eyes are dark mysteries, staring up at me.

I let go and run my thumb along her lip. "You want this, baby?"

I tense up. Why did I ask that? It shouldn't matter to me what she wants, but it does. I want her to need us the way I do.

She looks up at me, and I have no idea what her answer will be. The scary part is, I don't know what I'll do if she says no. Let her go? I can't—she's mine.

But there's this new thing going on in my head where I'm not sure I can fuck her mouth if she doesn't want it. I'm not sure I can use the soft palate of her mouth to jerk off. Not sure I can come all over her face unless she tells me it's okay.

A little fucked up, but there it is.

She licks her lips, and I realize she's not going to answer at all. Instead her hands go to my jeans, unzipping and pulling me out. I shudder at the feel of her soft, small hands. God, those hands. I could come just like this. A few solid strokes.

She leans forward, and I hold my breath. Her lips press together. She kisses the tip of my cock. Kisses it. Like she's fucking courting it or something. I almost come.

"The issuing bodies can be the general assembly," she says in her prim teacher tone. Then she licks the slit of my cock.

"*Shit.*" I jerk my hips forward. The only way I keep

from coming is by grabbing her head. I fist her hair in my hands until she winces.

"Or the economic and social council." She takes my cock in her mouth this time, pushing it deep before releasing me again. She thrusts on my dick a few times before I take over. I grab hold of her hair and fuck her face, going deeper than she let me on her own.

When she pulls away, I let her. It feels like my balls are about to explode, but I fucking let her back away.

"The trusteeship council." Her voice wavers, and I know she's nervous now. She should be.

I lift her by her hair, giving her enough time to support herself. I'm not trying to rip her hair out. But I do want to scare her. She should have that much, at least. A little warning for what's about to come.

When she's standing, I drag her over to the nearest desk and push her on it, facedown. Her skirt is up, panties down, in two seconds flat. The curve of her ass looks fucking gorgeous in the dim light, milky white against the dark.

"Is that all?" My voice has gone completely hoarse. I'm one second from snapping.

"There's the...the secretariat." She stumbles over the word. And I think it must be the first time she's ever stumbled over the word, as big and awkward as it is. I did this to her, just like I made her thighs glisten. I push her ankles apart with my feet. My fingers slide home, and she's so wet.

It's an answer to the question I should never have asked. *You want this, baby?* And God, she does. She couldn't tell me in regular words. Not like *yes* or *please* or *fuck me.* Not my Abby. She has to speak in library words as she gives me the hottest, dirtiest, smartest blowjob on the planet.

I shove two fingers inside her, then three. I need her good and soft for what I have planned.

It takes me a second to slip a condom on. I'm a motherfucking Boy Scout, prepared for this even on a break-in. Maybe I always knew I'd fuck her in a library. Ever since the prison I've been dying to do it like this, with the smell of old books and ink in the air. She said once she likes a book smell.

I angle my dick at her cunt. But before I can press inside, she stutters. "Wait."

And for some reason, I do. For some reason that terrifies me. I think Stone may be right. I think I may have fallen for her.

"Security council," she says on an exhale, and I thrust inside her at the same time, forcing the words out. And I don't let up. I don't give her any time to adjust. All I have for her are bruising thrusts as I ride her from behind. I hold on to her hips, those lovely hips, and force my dick through her swollen flesh.

Her muscles clench around me. She cries out. God,

yes, she's coming in a wet, messy gush. I want her to make a mess all over the library, all over the pages and pages. I want her to smear the ink.

"Again," I demand, fucking her harder, faster.

She cries softly. "I can't."

"Don't fucking tell me that. Don't you fucking tell me that." I reach under her body and find the wet folds. And the hard little nub at the top. I twist it between my thumb and forefinger until she goes rigid and screams something I think Stone and Calder can probably hear.

Pride fills me, but I can't think about that for long. Because her inner muscles are squeezing me tighter than any fist. Her wetness is slicking and sliding over me wetter than any tongue. And all I can do is shout a useless denial before I'm coming too, spilling into her hot cunt, biting down on her neck so that neither of us can deny who owns who.

Chapter Thirty-Four

~ABIGAIL~

GRAYSON'S WEIGHT PINS me to the table, his heavy breaths pressing into me like an echo of his thrusts. His cock is still inside me, wet and hot. Without meaning to, my inner muscles squeeze. His cock flexes in response. There's a conversation happening between our bodies. A communion.

Maybe there always has been.

Even before he captured me, when I was teaching the class in prison and he was my student, my body responded to him. I pretend to be more than my mother. More than a junkie. More than an animal in heat. But the truth is, whenever I'm around him, I'm ready for him to use me and mount me and fuck me. I'm done fighting it. I want to lose to him. I want him to make me lose.

"Abby?" His voice is husky. With just one word, my softly spoken name, he asks a hundred questions. Am I okay? Do I hate him now? He's not just testing me—he's testing himself. If I'm not okay, will he care?

The answer comes to me when I struggle to find air, and he eases off. It comes to me when he sighs with resignation as his cock slips out of my damp body. Comes when I hear the snap of latex as he puts himself to rights. It comes to me when I turn back and find him watching me with something like softness.

It's strange to see on his face. Strange enough that I have to return the question. "Grayson?"

A rakish smile lifts his lips. "This is what I thought about, when I sat in your class."

My heart clenches. Because he didn't only think of this. He thought of his time in a different prison. He's still fighting to escape, but his chains aren't made of metal.

He needs to be free. Maybe going after the governor will help. Or will it? This is a crazy dangerous move.

"Are you sure about all this? What if it makes everything worse?"

"This is what we have to do," he says.

"You see him as the leader?" He nods grimly. "Why didn't you guys go after him before now?"

"We never found him before. We never even knew his name—we called him Blue Jacket. Until suddenly, there he was. After a decade of searching, he shows up on the TV, like a cockroach running into the light. The fucking governor. A respected husband and father. A pillar of society." His voice is mocking.

"He's the one who kidnapped you?" It's the obvious answer, but nothing about Grayson is obvious. He is all muscle and hardness—but I've peeled back the layers, and what I find inside is tender.

There is nothing tender in his expression when he answers. "No, that honor was reserved for a guy with a wad of cash and an ice cream truck. Did I want a Popsicle? Did I want some money too? I had fifty cents in my pocket, Abby. And I hadn't eaten lunch that day."

My stomach churns.

"The governor would never dirty his hands by doing actual work. There were men who kidnapped us and kept us. The governor just earned money from the films they made us do. And of course he visited us personally. Especially me." Grayson's laugh sends chills up my spine. "He can buy anything he wants. He can buy this whole state. He can buy little boys."

All I can do is go to him and put my hands on him. To speak to him in some twisted language of love that only we two speak, where we hurt each other just to soothe the wounds that follow.

Grayson's voice is raw now. Just like his words, his vignette. "I was his favorite. That's why the guys didn't try to kill him while I was locked up. It's because I was...I was his favorite."

His voice cracks.

The word *favorite* tastes like bile, burning me from the inside out. *Favorite.* And all the horrible things that would mean for a boy held captive by men.

There is sympathy I could give him. A normal person would say those things. *I'm so sorry. What he did was wrong. You didn't deserve it. I hate him.*

I love you.

Saying that would only mess him up worse, because he won't believe me. He can't believe me. So instead I say the one thing I know will help. The one thing that really matters. And by doing so, I bind myself to him more firmly than if I used rope or handcuffs.

"Let me come with you." Getting the floor plans isn't enough. I need to be with him on this twisted quest, even if I think it's wrong.

Especially then.

He raises his eyebrows. His voice is mocking when he says, "You."

I narrow my eyes and step forward, invading his space. The way he taught me, by example. "I'm tougher than I look."

His expression sobers. "I know that, sweetheart. You'd have to be, to survive me."

My throat tightens. This is how he sees himself. As something to be endured. Inhuman.

Unlovable.

I'm afraid that killing the governor won't give him the peace he wants. I'm afraid he'll break then, when he realizes nothing will.

CHAPTER THIRTY-FIVE

~ABIGAIL~

W E'RE AT THE big table in the main room, the place where they first laid out Grayson when I brought him here. The guys are all here: Nate, Stone, Grayson, Calder, Cruz, Knox, and Ryland. The guys are splitting tools and guns. They're suiting up.

I don't get a gun. There's just me, wrapped in a sense of dread. I think this is a mistake. I think killing the governor is a mistake.

But I can't turn away from Grayson. I can't tell him no. Some people have a relationship that's sunshine and roses. Ours is darkness and vengeance.

It's time.

We pile into two vehicles. They're stowing the Hummer nearby in case things get hot. One of their fancy toys they rarely use, but apparently it's bulletproof. I'm in the town car with Grayson. We drive across empty streets, barren of cars at four in the morning, until we're winding down the streets of an exclusive community. We park in the shadow of an outbuilding, and the five of us move quickly through the dark to the next block.

One of the guys settles in next to a stone gate that shields him from the moonlight and gives him a clear view of the governor's driveway. He'll alert Grayson and Stone and the rest of them to any danger. Maybe even fend it off. I wouldn't want to fight him.

The governor's mansion is illuminated by spotlights that shine upward from the ground, making it look like a castle. The guard inside the little booth at the gate is slumped over, drugged. I can't help but feel guilty.

I don't know why, but my resolve firms when I look at Grayson, beautiful in his woundedness, like an avenging angel, taking justice for lost innocence. The mortal rules don't apply.

Down the street, somebody's sprinkler swishes back and forth.

We split and rush down the driveway, hugging the shadows, and rush across the lawn. We slip through the shadows to the back of the massive house and crouch in the grass on the dark side of the stone rail that's held up by carved stone balustrades; it stretches all around the edges of the red tile porch. The plan is that Nate and I keep watch in back. Grayson and Stone and the rest of the guys are going in—through the roof. The blueprints we stole showed the way. They'll clear the house and let us in.

Grayson touches my cheek, and then he's off in the night.

A soft *pop* sounds across the quiet. Then another. Disabling the guards. Nate's fixed a few of the guys up with safari tranquilizer guns. We have intel that the governor and his wife sleep in separate rooms and the wife takes heavy sleep meds, but Nate thinks we should tranquilize her anyway.

I sit in the dewy grass, barely breathing. Nate eyes me. "They'll be fine. They're the best."

CHAPTER THIRTY-SIX

~GRAYSON~

THE GUYS SCALE the four-story mansion with ropes. Stone puts a rope ladder down for me—I can't hack our usual break-and-enter activities with my shoulder like it is. Nate didn't want me doing this part at all, but he's never been able to stop me from shit like this.

I've never killed a man in cold blood before. In the heat of a fight, yeah. Guys trying to kill me, yeah. But not a man helpless. Except the governor can never seem helpless—not to us. And it's huge that they reserved killing him for me. I remember the dark day Stone promised it to me. I was pretty fucked up, and he grabbed my hair and looked me in the eyes and he said, *We'll hurt him bad, but you'll get to kill him, Grayson. You'll get to kill him, okay?*

A few minutes later we lay on the mansion roof, watching the stars and waiting for Calder to give the go signal. I look over at Stone, next to me in his ragged black hoodie, eyes dark with death. Even gazing up at the cool, crisp sky, he looks angry. Hard. Like he hates the stars.

But he has a good heart—a dangerous heart, but a good heart. I wonder if Abby can see that. I want her to understand him. I want him to understand her.

"Soon," Stone whispers.

I imagine wrapping my hands around the governor's throat. I play it in my mind like I have so many times, feeling him jerk and struggle as the life drains out of him. While that doesn't make me feel happy, it gives me a certain comfort. Maybe even some peace. Hurting and killing the governor has always been a substitute for happiness. Because I knew I'd never have the real thing.

It's huge that Abby wants to come with me. So huge I don't know what to do with it, and my pulse races into overdrive when I think of her out there. I don't like leaving her, but I don't want her in on the dangerous work of clearing.

I see people saying shit like their wedding day was the best moment of their lives, or having a baby or whatever, but I can't imagine anything better than when Abby said she wanted to be there for me killing that motherfucker. Like she's okay with reaching into the darkest part of me. Like she actually wants to go there. Having a baby or getting a wedding ring or whatever could never hold up to that.

The historical blueprints gave us gold—a set of vertical tunnels for the old-fashioned hot-blast heating system that stretches up to the roof. That old system was later replaced by a radiator system, but the empty tunnels are still there if you know where to look.

Which we do, now.

We did measurements and got the location of an empty tunnel, more like a chute, right under part of the HVAC exhaust array on the west side of the roof.

Stone's phone buzzes. Time.

Prying the motherfucker up without making noise is a little bit of a bitch—we muffle the sound with rubberized blankets and smash through the paper-thin veneer of asphalt topping. There's a subattic. We knew about that, and that it's wired up like crazy.

The beauty of the hot-blast chute is that it bypasses the wired-up subattic. We pop in handholds so we don't slide all the way to the basement, and go down to the Sheetrock area on the fourth floor. We make a little too much noise punching through, but suddenly we're in.

Stone, Cruz and I haul ass down the stairs, weapons at our sides. Cruz breaks off at the wife's room to hit her with the tranq gun, and Stone and I burst into the governor's bedroom.

He's clearly just woken up. He's cowering in his bed, wearing a motherfucking sleep cap over his gray hair, holding a .357 in his shaking hand. A bedside lamp casts a circle of light to his side. Enough to see the horror on his face when he recognizes me. He scuttles back to the headboard. "I'll shoot—I will."

I'm vibrating with wild energy—maybe it's rage, I don't know. I glance at Stone. We don't need words—we know how to work a man with a gun. He goes to one side of the room, and I go to another.

"Help!" the governor calls, pointing his piece at me, then swinging it wildly to the other side, to aim at Stone. But he can't shoot both of us.

"You don't get to call for help," I say. "That sound familiar? Who else didn't get to call for help, you remember?"

He turns his gun back at me, aiming at me. He won't do it. He's a coward, and he knows the second he hits one of us, the other will kill him. If he was smart, he'd know he's dead already.

"Put down the gun and get the fuck out of bed," Stone growls, standing there all in black down to his massive motorcycle boots. "And take that motherfucking cap off your head. I want it off *now*."

The governor watches him stupidly.

"Now!" Stone's fixating on the cap thing. You never know what Stone is going to fixate on.

"I have money," the governor says. "I owe you; I understand. I can set you for life."

Stone storms to a bookshelf that's full of framed pictures and fragile-looking things, and with an angry swipe he pushes it all off. Stuff crashes to the floor. He

does it to the other shelves, wild with anger. *This is what we're going to do to you.*

That's my cue to fly at the governor, at his shooting arm, forcing it up and to the side where a shot can't do damage. A shot goes off, but it's wild. I twist his gun from his hand and wing it at the wall so hard it cracks the plaster. I put him on his face on the bed and pull his arm behind his back, knee in his spine.

"You owe us more than money," I grit out. I grab his hair and jerk his head, jerk his arm.

He gasps in pain. Maybe I'm breaking something, but I can't let off, because deep down I think if I let off, he could hurt me.

How fucked up is that? I'm twice as big as him, and I have my guys here, but the governor still seems like a threat.

Stone comes up and drives a fist into the man's jaw with a deafening *thwack* and force that I feel clear through my body. Yeah, I was the governor's favorite, but he screwed every single one of us in every sense of the word.

Stone pulls off the man's cap. "I said the cap comes off!" He wraps it around his knuckles and brings his fist down on the man's ear, which blooms with blood.

I jerk the governor's head up. "Your ass is ours now, and we're *not* gonna make it nice."

Stone makes the call, getting our guys in here, and

then he puts aside his gun and pulls out a blade.

"Grayson," the governor says, craning his head, looking up at me like we're friends, the look he used to give me.

Affection.

This sick feeling comes over me, remembering all those times when I was helpless under him, and he'd give me this look of affection. The worst thing is that I know he really did feel some twisted affection. "Grayson."

"Shut up." I jerk his arm, make it hurt. "You don't get to say my name."

The rest of the guys have arrived and crowd around the bedroom, all scars and leather and hard edges, making the furniture look clean and toylike. They've got guns, blades. We all want a crack at him.

My heart pounds as Abby slips in next to Nate. Cruz flops onto the couch, one leg over the armrest. Calder pulls a vase off a podium in the corner and hurls it across the room.

"Looks like everyone's here," I say. "What are we in the mood for, Governor?"

This terrible hush comes over the room.

The governor's shaking his head. "No, no."

Yeah, he remembers.

That's something he'd ask me and the other boys. *What are we in the mood for, Grayson? What are we in the mood for, Stone?* Like we had some kind of choice.

I tighten my grip on his hair and arm, twisting harder. "What are we in the mood for? *What?* Answer!"

"I have a wife," he pants. "A daughter."

I catch the glint of metal from the corner of my eye. Nate flashes a scalpel and advances. "Are you trying to humanize yourself? Are you honestly trying to humanize yourself to us after what you did to us?" he asks.

"Her name is Alana."

Nate sighs and looks at the ceiling.

I wince. Nobody brings out Nate's dark side like the governor. And he's just done it. Things could get bloody. "Calder, hold open his mouth," Nate says. "I need to cut out this man's tongue."

The governor's whipping his head back and forth, best he can, anyway, being that I'm gripping his hair.

Calder shoves his nine into his waistband and grabs the guy's face, readying to force his mouth open.

The governor pleads, "It wasn't me. Wasn't me running that operation."

Anger surges through me. "You think we're stupid?"

"It's bigger than me. They have other boys," the governor mumbles. "Right now…"

I feel sick. It can't be true. But I have a bad feeling it's true. Something about the way he says it. I jerk him by the hair. "Answer me. You think we're stupid?"

"No. I think you care. I can help you find them," the governor pants. "I didn't want it to keep going—I swear it. I have a contact. William Fossey…"

My gut wrenches. He says it like we should know that name. I look around. Stone looks wary, but he might just believe it too.

"Federal Judge William Fossey?" Abby says.

"Under the pictures." Dorman points.

Nate is at one of the bookcases, picking up pictures in shiny frames. "What are you talking about?"

"In the drawer under there. Me and the judge. There's one…look at the backgrounds…"

Nate jerks open the drawer and roots around. Then he lifts something out. "Shit," he says.

"What?" I ask.

Nate brings a photo to Stone, who takes a look and swears.

"Where?" Nate asks the governor. "The other boys are where?" So Nate believes him too.

"Let me go, and I'll help you!"

Nate tosses the framed photo, stalks to the bed, and shoves a blade deep into the governor's thigh with a viciousness I haven't seen in him in years. Dorman cries out in pain.

Here it goes. Nate's gone dark.

"Where?" Nate asks calmly.

"Where are they?" I growl, jerking him hard. "You tell us now."

"I don't know!" he gasps. "I got orders. It wasn't all

me. You can use me to find them. I'll help you…I can help you…please!"

I exchange glances with Stone. Yeah, we both know when a guy's given us everything he's got.

"Take off his pants," Stone says to somebody. "Let's do this."

"Grayson," he begs. "Please, Grayson…" I catch that hint of affection again, and this hot rage surges up in me and I lose it, and all I can do is hit him again and again, knuckles cracking bone. I can't stop myself; it's like I won't survive if I don't feel him breaking apart under my fists.

"Kill him," Cruz shouts.

The governor shields his face, but my fist is as un-stoppable as a fucking freight train. I haul him off the bed and hold him against the wall with one hand and punch the fuck out of his face with the other. Over and over, my fist connects with his bloody jaw, his bloody lip. His head jerks.

I feel my stitches ripping open, wound on fire. I don't care.

I can hear my guys, encouraging me to kill him, and I hear the love in their voices as I hit him, fist on fire, knuckles slick and hungry.

But then I remember Abby, and my arm slows. What the fuck? I should've never brought her. She thinks I'm a caveman, less than human.

She's right.

I pause. Shaking.

The governor looks at me with those blue eyes, the bright squinch he used to get when his emotions were supposedly hurt, like when you didn't act right or seemed to be rejecting him.

The look is like a fucking bolt of chaos in me, and suddenly I'm back at it, hitting him, smashing out his teeth. I can never get enough of hurting him. He took everything good from us. Everything that could make us good men. Everything that could make me worthy of a girl like Abby.

The sounds change and evolve. I need to crush every bit of him with my fist. He took everything.

"Grayson!" Abby.

"Get her out of here!" I hit him again.

"No!" She grabs the back of my shirt. "Stop it. Don't let him win like this."

I stop moving. It's a fucking miracle that I can, but I'm a rabid animal, and I don't want her to get bit. "Go," I pant. "You can't be here."

"Grayson," she says. I can feel the guys waiting for my cue, waiting to see if I really want her gone after dragging her here. It feels like a test. Revenge or failure. Them or her.

I'm shaking, holding Dorman to the wall while he stares at me with those bright, hurt eyes, blood pouring from every hole in his face, including a few that I made.

"You're better than this," she says from behind me. "You're a good man, Grayson."

I turn toward her, hauling him around with me to face her, holding half-conscious Dorman up by his shirt between us. His head bobs forward, chin to his chest.

I let her look at me, knowing I'm covered with his blood. It won't be the first time I'm coated with his fluids, and it feels like a dark, desperate glory, like hate, like war paint. Like oblivion.

I don't know what anything is anymore, but I can tell from her eyes that she's frightened as fuck, and she should be.

"I'm *not* better than this," I growl. I drive my knee right up into his face. It's a fucking piston and there's a sickening crack. He lets out a guttural cry. That would be his nose.

"No!" Abby's sobbing.

"I'm not a good man. I'm not even human."

"You're wrong, Grayson. You can't kill him."

"You can't change your mind!" I say. "You said you were with me. You said you were strong enough."

"I *am* strong enough," she says. "Strong enough to tell you no. Strong enough to know you're better than this. Strong enough to motherfucking love you."

It's too much, that last, and too much that I can never have. I knee him in the chest and feel the crack of a rib. He coughs, and it doesn't sound normal. He's broken. Because I'm fucking breaking him. I'm tearing him apart with my bare hands. "Get her the hell out."

The guys spring into action as I fling him onto the bed and pound him some more. They're taking her out—I can hear her fight them. I used to love how strong she was, how much of a fighter she was, but she can't fight me. Can't fight me and win, anyway.

I can hear her voice down the hall. I hit him again, even more pissed now. He's moaning. He's really hurt, but I can't stop myself.

I don't know how many more times I hit him, but there's this one point where I'm changing angles and I catch him looking up at me with those fucking eyes, but they're different now.

I pause, fist cocked, with this weird feeling in my gut. They're not those fakey hurt-feelings eyes. They're not those *what are we in the mood for?* eyes.

They're human eyes. Half-dead, yeah, but human. Suffering.

And I'm fucking shaking.

Because for a wild second, I see through his eyes to a hurt little boy, and I don't know if the hurt little boy is me or if it's him.

I'm shaking. I might throw up. And just like that all the killing energy drains out of me.

I roll off him and lie on the bed, panting, listening to

Dorman's uneasy breath. Broken-nose breath. Maybe punctured-lung breath. Probably both.

Stone flops down on the other side of me and puts his hand on my heart like he always did.

Calder comes up, looming over me and the governor. "Want me to finish him?"

"We have an hour left at least." Stone says. "He's not going anywhere. It's Grayson's call. Whatever you say."

Meaning who kills him. It goes without saying he needs to die. The dragon needs to be slain.

But I'm not so sure now. I can't shake that look in his eyes. He'd never seen us as human; that was his crime. But I'd never seen him as human either. I'd never seen a lot of people as human. "Is Nate with her?" I ask.

"Yeah," Stone says. "He's taking her off the grounds."

Of course it would've been Nate who took her out. He'd want to get away—his dark side was emerging. The amount of darkness inside Nate is as stunning as the amount of goodness inside him.

I shake off the guys and sit at the side of the bed. Of all the times to see the governor's humanity. Of all the times to think there's some fucking good to come of any of this.

Fuck.

"Fucking hurting and killing him. What does that make us?"

Stone sits up and glares. "Fuck no." He points an accusing finger at me. "No way." He's pissed, and he's looking right through me at Abby, like she fucked me up.

I stand. "I'm saying let's look at this."

"We've looked at it our whole lives," Stone says. He directs Cruz and the other guys to tie Dorman to the bedposts.

I listen, disoriented, to the furious sound of ripping sheets. Part of me still wants him to pay. I want his pain. It's all I ever wanted, but when Abby talked to me that way, when she told me I was good—*that she loved me*—it changed something.

"Please, no," Dorman says. "Please."

"Shut up." Stone drives a fist into the man's belly, then he flicks out his blade. Will Stone really slice off his balls and shove them into his mouth? Will Calder rip his guts out?

"I'm sorry," Dorman rasps.

Sorry. And I feel this new kind of pain.

Stone's eyes meet mine. He never could stand to see me in pain. Not any of us.

He stalks over to the governor, and with a movement swift and sure, he shoves the blade in the man's throat. There's this gurgling sound. "One blade to protect my brothers, one blade for vengeance," Stone growls. With vicious force, he yanks the blade across the governor's throat. The gurgling stops. He pulls out the blade and looks up at me, face spattered with blood.

It's done. A gift.

"Let's get out of here," Stone says.

"Fuck me!" Calder has his phone out. "Somebody's coming. A team. Not the cops. Up the road. The front."

"Abby," I breathe.

"They're safe by now," Stone says. He's right. Nate would've pulled her out the back the easy way.

"The team's up on the road, coming in the drive."

"Take the back stairs." Calder grabs the pack. We follow him down the hall and down a narrow staircase, careful not to make a sound.

We move out through the dark spaces on the first floor. Just as we clear the study, something crashes. Loud.

Calder speeds up, leading the way out over the veranda, and we all follow. A gun blast rips the cool night air.

Cruz disappears from my periphery. I look back. He's down.

"Fuck!" I shoot wildly into the house as the guys pull him over the stone rail. He's hit in the thigh.

"I'll cover," Stone shouts. "Get him the fuck up to that ridge. We'll crash out with the Hummer. I'll find Nate and Abby."

Stone is already in position, shooting from between

the stone balustrades. It should be me going after Nate and Abby, but there's no time to argue. Calder and Knox have Cruz between them. They need me taking rear or none of them will make it out alive.

Every part of me screams to find Abby, to be the one to make sure she's safe, but I can't abandon my crew. We rush across the dark, grassy lawn and out the back gate, which we'd unlocked.

"You keeping pressure okay?" Calder pants.

"Yeah," Cruz says. "I don't think it's an artery." We carry him up the hill, helping each other. It's slow going.

Finally we arrive up top, up to the Hummer. We lay him out on the ground. Calder's talking to Cruz, about where the pain is, how he feels, in case Cruz's passed out by the time Nate comes.

I go to the edge of the hill, wounded shoulder screaming in pain and wet with blood. Nate'll have to stitch me back up, but I don't care.

You can see everything from up top. The place is lit with flashing red, and all I can think about is Abby. Out there with Nate. Freaked out of her mind. And what if the cops get her? Even worse, what if the governor's men get her?

There's a rustling from the bushes to the side. I lift my piece.

"It's me." *Nate.*

"Where's Abby?" I say.

"Stone's getting her out the access alley."

"Fuck!"

"She's slow." Nate kneels at Cruz's side. Calder trains a flashlight on the wound as Nate cuts away the bloody fabric. "They'll circle back."

The guys have been casing this place and preparing forever, and there are endless escape ideas and contingency plans. This one's the obvious choice, and easier on Abby too, but I still don't like it.

Nate's asking Cruz questions, hands all over the wound. "You're okay," he's saying. "This isn't a bad one." I hear the rip of medical tape.

I look out over the sea of flashing red. Calder comes to my side and hands me the binoculars.

I lift them to my eyes and try to find where Stone and Abby could be, but it's too dark, and the side escape route has a wall blocking most of the way. I give them back to Calder and call Stone. It goes to voicemail. I don't like the feeling I get.

"Stone's got her," Calder says.

And Stone wants her dead. "I'm going down there."

"Don't be an idiot. You'll get picked up," Calder says.

"I have to."

The next thing I know, there's a gun shoved in my gut. Calder. "You think we can come after you out there? You're not going."

"Fuck you." I pull out my piece and jab it in his gut. We wouldn't pull the trigger. We're brothers.

Except if Stone hurts Abby. Then I'd have to kill him.

Chapter Thirty-Seven

~Abigail~

EVERYTHING HAPPENED LIKE a dream—too surreal, too fast. Grayson going wild on the governor. Nate forcing me back into the service alley, a walled alley that runs up the side of the mansion's grounds. I tried to get back to the house, back to Grayson, but Nate had my arm, and he wouldn't let me go.

People came, and there was shooting. Nate said it was the governor's guys. I don't know how he knew. Then the sirens sounded.

When Stone arrived, I knew things would go bad. He sent Nate up to the ridge that overlooks the river. He said Cruz was shot.

I want to go, to follow Nate and make sure Grayson's okay, but Stone has my upper arm in what feels like a vise. "I have to see him," I say. "I have to tell him it's okay."

Stone jerks me by the arm—hard—as soon as Nate's out of sight. "You think Grayson wants to see you after what you did? Grayson trusted you to be with him in the most important moment of his life, and you wrecked it. You made him feel like shit for what he had to do."

I try to pull away from Stone, heart racing. "I couldn't let him—"

He tightens his grip. "Do you know what it's like to go through what we went through?" Stone snarls. "No. And you never can. You can never be like us. You can never be with him."

"Did he—" I'm afraid to finish the sentence.

"What do you think he did?" Stone snarls. "The man took everything from us."

"Not everything." If he really took everything, then there's nothing left. If he took everything, there's no hope for Grayson—and I can't believe that.

A car approaches, and Stone yanks me between two dumpsters, gun at my temple. I can feel the rage seething from him. I don't move; I know he's looking for an excuse to open fire—on me, on the cops.

The car passes, but he keeps me down there on the coarse gravel, fingers digging into my flesh. This cold feeling comes over me as he turns to me and presses the gun to my neck.

I can feel his anger through his grip, his breath on the side of my head. I try to pull away, but his hand is steel. This is it. He finally has me alone, without Nate or Grayson to stop him.

He's going to kill me now.

"Let me go," I beg. "Please—I won't say anything, I promise. I'll say he kept me drugged the whole time. I don't remember anything."

"You won't pull it off."

"I will." My heart pounds. "I swear it!"

"You think I can trust my guys' lives to you? No fucking way."

"He knows secrets about me too. This one 9-1-1 call—it's a horrible secret. He has stuff on me too."

There's a pause where all I hear is my own panicked pulse. Then he says, "I'm sorry."

At that moment, everything comes crystal clear. This man will shoot me. There were enough shots being fired that he could blame it on somebody else. Or maybe Grayson wouldn't care, if he's really furious with me for trying to hold him back.

"You ready?" he asks softly as if he's read my mind, his eyes almost soft, almost kind, as he prepares to kill me.

My heart lurches. I try to pull away, but he's expecting it. He has me.

"You want me to count?" he asks.

"Count?" It seems crazy—who counts when they're going to shoot somebody? "*Count?*" Tears stream down my cheeks. I take a shuddery breath. "Wait. Tell him…tell him I think he's a good person—I still do," I say. "Tell him I know what's inside of him now. Tell him he's a good man," I whisper. "Those monsters never touched what was important in him."

Stone glares at me.

"Fuck you," I say. "Those monsters never took what was important in him. Tell him I love him."

There's this silence, and he presses the gun harder into my neck, angry. "You hurt him."

"I know," I gasp.

"You fucked him up."

"I love him."

"That didn't do him much good, did it?"

I freeze, waiting for him to shoot. My eyes squeeze shut. Does Grayson hate me now?

"I can't help that I love him," I say in a small voice.

There's this long silence.

He lowers his weapon then, and I finally suck in a breath. "Go. But if you say one thing about us, one fucking police sketch, one fucking peep about the Bradford, you are dead."

"Okay."

"You try to make contact, any contact with him, and you are dead. He doesn't want to see you. Go before I change my mind." He shoves me and points. "All the way to the cop car at the end. Turn yourself in like you got away. Go back home."

I take off running, face wet, knees shaking. I desperately want to see Grayson. Even if he hates me, I have to see that he's okay. But I don't know where he is, and Stone is still behind me, waiting to shoot.

As soon as I get onto the street, a spotlight gloms onto me. Somebody says to put my hands up. I slow, hands raised. I'm led up the driveway. I end up sitting on the back of an ambulance.

They're saying I'm traumatized. I guess it's true. I give somebody my name. Everyone wants to know where Grayson is. I say I don't know. It's the truth.

CHAPTER THIRTY-EIGHT

~GRAYSON~

STONE BURSTS THROUGH the bush line, panting. "Let's go."

No one shows up behind him. "Where the fuck is Abby?"

"She ran to the cops. She turned herself in. I'm sorry, man."

Denial slams in my gut. "What? No."

"Did you not hear me? She *ran* to the *cops.*"

I stomp over and grab his collar. "What the fuck did you do?"

He shoves me off. Pain like lightning sails through my shoulder. "She's gone. She left."

"Fuck you! She wouldn't do that." I start down the hill, but Calder's got me from behind, arms around my chest.

"She wouldn't just leave!"

Stone grabs me by the hair. "She said she won't give anything up," Stone says. "That you both have secrets, and she's staying quiet about our secret like you'll stay quiet about her 9-1-1 call. That mean anything to you? A 9-1-1 call?"

I try to rip out of Calder's grip. "It's not right. You're lying!" Even as I say it, some little voice wonders how he'd know about the 9-1-1 call if she didn't tell him. As a message to me. Like maybe this is real and she wanted to be done with me. "Don't come after me!"

I break free, and I run down there blind. Something hits me from behind. Stone, tackling me to the ground. We roll. My shoulder screams in pain.

"Let me go."

Stone's on top of me. "She made her choice!" he growls. "After what she saw in that bedroom? She watched you beating the bloody hell out of a man. You destroyed his face after she begged you to stop. Think what she saw, Grayson!"

My strength drains from me as his words seep in. What I did in front of her. The crunch of his face on my knee still lives in my muscle memory. Like a fucking animal. "I need to get to her. I need to explain." I'm ripping the hell out of my shoulder, trying to get away.

"She saw her one chance to be free, and she took it," Stone bites out. "She can still sell that she's a hostage who got away. It's not too late for her, like it was for us."

"Fuck you," I say.

"She was hysterical, Grayson." Nate's there, kneeling next to me, hand on my arm. "If you care about that girl at all, you'll let her go. Give her this one kindness."

I'm panting, struggling. This can't be how it ends.

"You know what she said?" Stone says. "She said, *I know what's inside of him now.* That's what she said, Grayson. *I know what's inside of him now.*"

It's then that all the fight goes out of me. It has the ring of truth. The ring of her words. She knows what's inside of me. Vengeance. Death. Ugliness.

I collapse and stare up at the dawn sky, lighter on one side than the other.

Barely human. Fucking caveman. How many times did she call me that?

"She was never yours," Stone says.

Because she knows *what's inside of me now.* It even sounds like something she'd say. I could convince her that I didn't kill him and it still wouldn't matter, because she saw enough of what was inside me. The thought of capturing her again moves through my mind, but Nate's right—I need to do her this kindness.

And there's the bit about the 9-1-1 call. That's a secret only she and I know. She told him so I would know her message was genuine. To be free from me.

"She knows where you live," Nate says. "If she wants to see you, all she has to do is to show up."

"We can't stay at the Bradford," Stone says. "Just in case."

"She won't talk," I snap.

ANNIKA MARTIN & SKYE WARREN

"We've got the feed from the camera at the entrance," Nate says. "We'll see if she comes."

"Get up." It's Calder. He's got binoculars. "You need to see this."

Stone helps me up. Nate and Knox are helping Cruz into the vehicle. Calder directs me to look at the driveway. All I can find is lights and confusion. He directs my gaze, and suddenly I see it—an ambulance, and she's sitting in the back. She's alone, but her chin is held high, shoulders back. She seems calm almost. Calm in a way I've never seen her.

"Let's go," Nate says.

A cop comes over, carrying a bottle of water. Her face lights up when she takes it, so grateful for one small favor. He wraps a blanket around her, and I grit my teeth as I watch him touch her shoulders. She's just been fucking traumatized, and this guy thinks he's Romeo. A tear glistens as it rolls down her face, reflecting the red-blue light from the sirens.

Why is she crying? I want to bash the cop's face in for making her cry even though I know…it's not sadness. She's relieved. Happy. Happy enough to cry.

I gave her water and blankets, and she never felt relieved. Never got so happy she cried with it. God, was she just surviving me? She liked me enough not to let me die, but she didn't want to stay.

My chest feels like it's caving in.

A hand on my shoulder. Nate. "Let's go, brother."

CHAPTER THIRTY-NINE

~ABIGAIL~

A LAWYER MEETS me at the police station and offers to represent me. I get the feeling my case is somewhat famous. She tells me not to answer questions. And she tells me something else too. She tells me the governor is dead. I'd expected that, but it stills hit me like a blow to the chest.

Stupid as it is, there was some part of me hoping that Grayson hadn't killed the governor after I left. As if maybe I'd been enough to save him.

But I failed.

Somebody has hot chocolate for me. I sip it, feeling calm in a way I never have before. Maybe because I have nothing left to lose. The prison journal is a distant memory. Class schedules and final exams feel like a world apart. And Grayson, I've lost him too.

You said you were strong enough. That's what he told me in the governor's mansion. I guess I'm not, because I couldn't stand to watch him kill like that. Couldn't stand to watch Grayson kill the last spark of humanity inside himself. So he pushed me out and did it without me watching.

I'm grateful when Esther arrives. I wrap myself around her and hold on for dear life.

My new lawyer thinks that if I tell where Grayson might be, I'll do no time. I tell her I don't know. I give a version of the truth over the next day—roughly what happened, without the sex.

I say I was drugged. In fear. I leave out the part about his guys and about the Bradford Hotel. I wouldn't have told, even without the promise to Stone to play dumb. I wouldn't do anything to hurt Grayson, even if he doesn't want me anymore.

I say we spent the night in a car and he brought me to the governor's home. No, I couldn't get away. Yes, I was scared for my life. The guy from the gas station has never come forward, and it's unlikely he will now. I'm guessing the guy has something to hide, and I really didn't take that much, anyway.

The governor's murder is national news, of course, and he's made out to be a hero. It makes me sick, knowing what I know, but I stick with my role of the barely conscious hostage with no useful information. I was with Grayson only a few days. The manhunt that's on is intense.

My lawyer has short brown hair and minty breath, and she convinces the powers that be not to file charges.

They stop asking me to tell where Grayson is—they're believing my story. I just have to sign a paper that says I won't sue the prison or the university.

It's that easy—except I can't go home yet. They say I have to stay in town, so Esther gets us two motel rooms. She stays near me and asks no questions.

She does give me advice, though. "They'll be watching you. Not just the media, but the cops. The Feds. Wherever you go, whoever you call. You understand?"

Maybe that's why they let me go—to see if I lead them to the guys.

There's a part of me hoping for that. Maybe Grayson will decide to forgive me for trying to stop him from killing the governor. Maybe, now that he's had his revenge, he'll want to be with me. But I don't get any calls. I think about finding him myself, just to see. To state my case or maybe beg him to take me back. It sounds kind of desperate, but that's how I feel. Even if he turns me away, I want to try. Except I can't go back to the Bradford Hotel if the Feds might be watching me.

I had worried he'd feel broken once he killed the governor, but I'm the one who broke.

My lawyer stands next to me at the press conference, which she suggested to quell the media attention. There's a book offer that I refuse, much to my lawyer's disappointment, but Esther understands.

We celebrate afterward. We go to a restaurant before

returning to the motel, but I feel like I'm in a world where I don't belong—everything is fake, like living inside plastic wrap.

I want to run to Grayson, to tell him I'm sorry and that I'm still with him, that I haven't told anybody anything. But I'm being followed. I won't be the weak link.

You said you were strong enough. Even if I couldn't be strong before, I'll be strong for him now. So I act normal and happy when all I want to do is curl up back in Grayson's shabby room and feel his stubble on my skin.

Sometimes when I see light fixtures I think, *That would be nice in the Bradford Hotel.* But I can't go back there, and I understand now that he won't come for me. There was a time when it seemed as sure as the sunrise that he'd come for me, but I guess even the sunrise has to stop sometime.

CHAPTER FORTY

~GRAYSON~

ANYTIME I'M OUT, my eyes are scanning faces, searching for her, and I know that's how it will always be, because she changed me. Made me into something new. Made me hers.

It's national news. The trumped-up BS that the small-town cop said to her, about her being an accessory, was thrown out the window. They've figured out she's the victim, which is true. They're saying my guys and I killed the governor. They're calling him a hero. Flags fly at half-mast. I want to rip every last one of them down off the poles.

But even more than that, I want to let her know it wasn't me, that I understood what she said to me. But Stone's right—for all the beating I did on the man, I may as well have killed him in front of her.

She's better off without me. Better off free.

Sometimes I follow her, just to make sure she seems okay. Out to eat with that lawyer. Going to the corner market by her motel. Walking at the park with her friend, the blind woman. She never even told me about her, which just shows I was deluded to think we had something. She's being followed by Feds, but I don't know if she knows that. I thought about getting a message to her, to tell her to be careful, but what does it matter? Abby doesn't do anything illegal. She doesn't need to be careful around the Feds.

She had a shitty childhood and turned out good. I went the other direction.

She hasn't said anything about us, but just to be safe, we've temporarily moved out of the Bradford into the old mill where we sometimes stay.

But if she went to the Bradford, I'd know she was looking for me. She never does.

Hey, I'm happy for her. She's going to be okay. Soon she'll move back to her home near the Kingman, and I'll never see her again. Back with her kind.

She even looks happy. Why not? She's not my prisoner anymore. Not getting shoved around by some lowlife who can't keep his hands off her, whose idea of protection is terrifying her and drugging her and fucking her. Sometimes I wonder how much of what she said in the library was real, and how much was just Stockholm Syndrome. Temporary insanity. And that bit in the governor's bedroom—I haven't forgotten that, of course. *I am strong enough. Strong enough to tell you no. Strong enough to know you're better than this. Strong enough to motherfucking love you.*

Did she mean it? Or was she just trying to keep me from killing the man? I guess it worked.

I'll be honest: I think about taking her captive again. All the time.

I think about the way she felt, struggling under my power out in the woods that day, and the way she collapsed underneath me in pleasure. I think about her in the library, the way she looked at me, rattling off those library terms. I think I could make her warm up to me again, just like she warmed up to me the first time, but I wouldn't do it to her.

She had that press conference where she said she was frightened for her life the whole time. Maybe she was.

Either way, Stone was right. She was dangerous, because right now, I'm worse off than dead, and it's all because of her—I miss her so much it makes me want to die. Stone promises I'll feel better, but he doesn't get it. There's a hole in me, and wishing I could see her and touch her is all I have left to fill it.

Rescuing those boys who are still captive out there, held by the ring that held us, is driving everything with us now, and it takes my mind off her sometimes. Because every day is about planning how to find them, working connections. We're all freaking out that there are more boys. We know better than anyone what they're going through. We have to get to them.

I shadow her to a bookstore during a free afternoon—I'm wearing this stupid hat and glasses, but I'm a fugitive, and the disguise works. I browse right on the other side of the shelves from her. I'm so close I can hear her breathe, I can smell her honeysuckle scent, and my chest aches. The urge to shove through to the other side and grab her and take her away with me is so strong, I'm shaking.

She buys a book of memoirs. Some painter from fifty years ago, and then she goes out and gets into a rental car and drives away. Passing the time. She's stuck here for the duration of the trial. She can't even return to college because of me.

I go back into the store and get the same book. Stone asks about it when I get back to the mill. I shrug and say it looked interesting. I don't tell him how the book connects me to her. It's a little psycho; let's face it. Maybe deep down I still have this hope she'll come back, and poof, we'll have something to talk about.

But that won't happen.

It makes more and more sense that she was terrified the whole time. Maybe every time she looked at me like she wanted me, like she got hot for me, like she *motherfucking loved* me, it was coming from the fear.

And so I do the only thing for her I can: I force myself to stop following her. I do what I promised I never would: I let her go.

CHAPTER FORTY-ONE

~ABIGAIL~

TWO WEEKS LATER, plainclothes Feds show up at my motel room door.

They bring me to a different jail, a federal holding center, for questioning. It's not as nice, and I don't get to make any calls for forty-eight hours—not even to my lawyer. They grill me—hard. I'm an accessory to the murder of the governor. They say they've got a witness whose identity is sealed. I need to tell what I know.

I stick to my story. Finally I get to have my lawyer. She says the interrogation is bullshit, but she can't make it go away. I can see in her eyes that she suspects I know more than I'm telling. I guess everybody thinks so. Maybe it was too much to expect them to believe Grayson dragged me across the nation and all over without my consent.

I'll never tell. I can't stop thinking about young eyes staring out from the back of a milk carton, and nobody ever came for them, and nobody ever saved them.

"You'll do time," my lawyer says. "Accessory to murder."

I don't feel any pain, though. Just cold. I *am* an accessory to murder, just not the murder they think. In a way, it feels right to finally pay for letting my stepdad die. Killing him, really. I'm tired of carrying around the guilt of it. I deserve this. My lawyer promises to get me out, but I'm not scared of prison. I've seen what it's like inside. There are worse things.

Worse prisons.

"They're trying to use this as leverage. So you'll tell them what you know." My lawyer pauses. "Can you give them something?"

You said you were strong enough.

I am strong enough. Strong enough to motherfucking love you.

"No," I tell her because I do love him. And I'm strong enough for this. "Nothing."

The days drag on.

Esther begs me to reconsider, but I have to do this. A trial would only increase the chance of Grayson getting found out. So I take a plea bargain. A week later it's settled: three years with good behavior.

I'm almost relieved when they tell me the transport to the federal penitentiary will be arriving the next night. It's been four weeks since I've seen Grayson, but it seems like four years. I'd give anything to talk with him again.

To touch him.

But I know that's what the Feds want—for me to contact Grayson and lead them to him. They can rot in hell waiting.

Chapter Forty-Two

~Grayson~

In the days that pass, my guys and I plan and carry out a massive robbery in the northern suburbs—a gold bug hoarding gold. One of these end-of-worlders. It goes great, and gold is easy as shit to sell. Just melt it down and no one can tell the difference. We're going after that judge, and those boys, but we need more money, equipment, time for planning smart. The gold will help, but I just can't feel happy.

I break down one day and go by her motel. The lights in her room are off. I go to the office and ask to rent the room. He hands me the key, and I go inside, even knowing what I'll find of her. Nothing.

I lie down on the bed she slept in, trying to feel her. How pathetic is that? Rent her old motel room just to…what?

She's moved back home, and that's probably for the best.

I return to my cave-like room, one of the offices at the old mill. I pour the Macallan down my throat at night trying to blot out the images of her.

There's a calendar from June of 1971 that's still on the wall. I feel like that calendar, except my world stopped the last time I saw her.

I hear a sound—the guys are back, way earlier than planned. They'd been celebrating after the recent heist. I should be worried, I guess, because that usually means somebody got into a fight or something, but I don't have a lot of energy for emotion. They'll tell me if they need me to help crack some skulls.

"Hey."

I look up. Stone's standing in the doorway. He has two sawed-off shotguns, one over each shoulder. He puts them down and comes in and takes the bottle from my hand. It's a nightly ritual, him taking the bottle from me. It's even kind of comforting.

I flop on my back. "What's up?"

"We can't come by for our little brother?"

I roll my eyes. *Little brother.* I can see the worry in his eyes.

"How fucked up are you right now?" he asks.

I know what the question means. It means they need me for action. They've pulled together some last-minute caper. "I can shoot straight," I tell him. "Run faster than you."

He gets this strange look.

I sit up. "What?"

He goes over to the crate in the corner and grabs my holster with my nine and tosses it to me. "We're grabbing her up."

"Who?"

"Abby. Is there another *her* you know?"

Shock bolts me upright. "What?"

"We're grabbing her."

"What? No. She's gone. We can't."

He sighs. "She's in a transport tonight. She's been inside, Grayson. Inside a federal holding facility."

I stiffen. "What the *fuck* are you talking about? They didn't press charges. I saw that with my own eyes."

"They didn't press charges for the breakout," Stone clarifies. "But they brought her up on accessory. For Dorman."

"What the hell? How do you know?"

"I know."

And then I realize. He's been keeping tabs on her. I made myself stop, but he'd kept going. "How long have they had her?"

He sighs. "Two weeks."

Fury slices through me, along with pain. "She's been inside two weeks, and you didn't tell me?"

"I wanted to be sure," he says. "See what she was made of."

He wanted to see if she'd rat us out. My heart pounds. She's inside because of what I did. Abby, locked up. "Fuck."

"There's more," he says. "The night at the governor's mansion…"

I stand, not liking the sound of that.

He sucks in a breath. "She didn't want to leave that night. She wanted to come back with us, but I told her you didn't want to see her again."

I'm on him in a flash, grabbing his collar. "What the fuck did you do?"

"I let her think you killed him, and that you don't want her anymore."

My fist connects with his face, and suddenly I'm on top of him, hitting him.

"I'm sorry, man," he gasps out, trying to shield himself. He can't—I'm too full of rage and pain. And he won't hit back. He knows he's done wrong. It's Calder who pulls me off and pins me to the wall.

"He's sorry!" Calder says.

"You're my fucking brother!" I say as Stone pulls himself up, spitting blood.

"I'm sorry," he says. "That's all I've got." He wipes his mouth with his arm. "That, and a truly badass plan to take down a transport."

"Fuck." I pull on my holster and grab a sawed-off. "She doesn't like closed spaces. She'll be scared. She'll hate to be locked up. What's the time?"

"Transport leaves in thirty," Calder says.

I get up nose to nose with Stone. I want to smash his face in some more, and I want to kiss him for pulling the gang into this. Getting us on board. He probably orchestrated it all with the guys. "Nobody touches her except me."

Stone nods.

I get down to the main floor, and the guys are there, six of us, suited up—all except Nate; he's back at his farm. "Could be a trick," Calder says. "Wanting to smoke us out."

"Probably is a trick," Stone says.

"We'll make them sorry they played it," I say.

Calder laughs. Then a couple of the other guys laugh. Yeah, it probably is a trick.

THE HIGHWAY IS dark and not hugely busy. The transport is a modified van. Black. Tinted windows up front, none in back. They chose an eight p.m. transport, hoping to avoid rush hour. I sit in the passenger seat next to Stone, who drives the stolen Jeep Cherokee with determination. We're in four vehicles.

The wind through the open windows whips my hair. Can she feel me out here? Does she know I'm coming for her?

Compared to taking down an armored car, taking down a prison transport is a piece of cake. We get a

stolen car in front of them with a scrambler to block
their radio. It's a big fucking machine in the trunk and it
only works at a range of twenty feet, but it blots out all
communication.

We spot the unmarked cars right away, and the guys
go to work.

A few shots. A few tires out. They drop back.

After that, the transport is a sitting duck, there to be
picked off, but we have to be fast to avoid a chase.

Stone forces it off the road. The key is to get the
vehicle disabled right away. He and Cruz jump out and
run around to the sides, shooting wild for shock value,
pulling the guards out and roughing them up. But all I
can think about is Abby, frightened, not knowing what's
going on.

Once the drivers are handled, Stone torches the rear
door and I sledgehammer it open. And there she is.
Alone. Hands cuffed. Prison orange.

I get in. "Baby."

She stands. "Grayson," she says, a sob in her voice.
"You came."

"Of course I came." I grab her face and kiss her wild,
like the starving man that I am. "I didn't know you were
here. I thought you were home."

"No time," Stone says.

"Abby," I say. "Do you want this? Do you want to
come with me?"

She raises her eyebrows. "Look where I am."

"No, I don't want to be a better choice than prison. We can find a way to get you out, baby—I'll go down for Dorman before I let you serve. What I'm asking is, do you want to come with me? Be with me? Like we were."

"Yes," she says, sounding happy, almost laughing. "Yes!"

Sirens in the distance. Cruz jingles a fistful of keys. I pull her into my arms and jump down. Stone has the door open. I carry her into the backseat and belt us in, with her on my lap still, because I'm not letting her go. Stone's driving, and Cruz's riding shotgun.

"Shit's gonna get rough," I say.

She looks into my eyes. She trusts me to protect her, and I will. She clings to my shirt with her cuffed hands as Stone peels out, fast as fuck.

"Three minutes," Cruz says. "We might be good." Meaning, we might have avoided a chase.

"That's called motherfucking planning, brother," Stone says.

Abby's not listening. "I couldn't call you," she says. She's babbling, crying.

"I know, baby." I brush aside her hair.

"They were tapping my phone, following me. But I knew you didn't do it."

I set my forehead against hers, feeling like shit for not trusting her. "I gotcha now," I say.

Chapter Forty-Three

~Abigail~

I'M SITTING IN the turret room. Grayson pulled down the boards and put in a screen window so that the summer breeze can blow through.

From here, I can see blocks and blocks of boarded-up ruins across the neighborhood, some looking decayed, others like an angry god smashed a fist through them. Greenery pokes out in unexpected places, nature trying to reclaim this space but turning it into something else instead. The beauty here is wild and dark. And it's ours.

At first it seemed so strange that such an outwardly ruined place as the Bradford could feel cozy inside, but after four months, it no longer seems strange at all. It just feels like home.

I've put pillows along the edge of one side of this circular room, and I can curl up here for hours, pausing from the pages of my book to watch squirrels dart between the scrub trees. I also set up a desk and chair so I can work.

Back in my old dorm room, the only green I ever saw

was the little patch of scrubby grass in the courtyard. Here, vines have grown up the walls of the buildings all around, thick like a blanket. Even the Bradford Hotel is covered with them. This place is overrun by nature—including the wild men who live here.

They're beautiful too, with the same primal strength as these stone walls.

Nate goes back and forth between here and his farm. He's tried to build a whole life there, but he can't quite leave the crew behind. I like to talk to him when he's here. I think he is relieved when I chat with him. He's still not comfortable with Grayson keeping me captive.

What I don't tell him is that I don't want to escape.

Stone still gives me this look sometimes, like he wants me gone. But we've formed a kind of truce. I think the murderous look in his eyes isn't really about me, anyway. Nowadays he's obsessed with finding the other boys. We all are, but it's a long road, full of dead ends.

Grayson and I have a nice, big private bedroom of our own on the fourth floor, and now there's this turret room, my library.

Well, I had to keep the books somewhere.

I hear footsteps behind me, and a smile tugs at my lips. A book lands on the nearby cushion. Pleasure fills me at the sight of the old, loose binding. One shelf is already full of the books Grayson has brought me.

"What's this one?" I ask.

"Open it," he says with a new kind of tension in his voice. I glance at him curiously. He stares down at me, brown eyes wary.

So far he's brought me Hemingway and Steinbeck—the classics. He's brought my childhood favorites by Madeline L'Engle and Cynthia Voigt. He brought me new paperback thrillers and murder mysteries, hundreds upon hundreds of pages flush with ink. I've loved every single one, so I don't know why he's nervous now. I pick up the book and look at the cover. Nothing but faded cloth. No title. No author. That isn't too surprising. Sometimes with old books, the ink will fade.

I open the cover. There's nothing inside. No title page.

Turn the page. Still nothing.

It's blank.

I look up at him, the question in my eyes. "What's it for?"

"It's yours." He clears his throat. He looks down, and when his gaze meets mine again, his eyes pierce me. I remember the way he looked at me that first day, in the hallway of the prison, as if he could see inside me, straight to the heart. He terrified me then. He still scares me, but in a different way.

"I don't…"

He shakes his head, gaze locked on mine. "It's your book, Abby. Your story to tell."

He wants me to write down my story. And he won't settle for anything fake, just like I wouldn't for him. He wants it real. Raw.

He always does.

✧　✧　✧

I STARE AT the empty book, lying on the floor. Days pass before I pick it up and move it to my desk. Another week passes by before I open it and look at the first blank page. Two more weeks pass before I manage to write a paragraph.

Then the floodgates open.

I have too much to say, about my mother. About all the times I waited for her and she never came for me. About the forgotten birthdays, but there was also the soggy mush of a birthday cake she made me when I was six. Or the five-dollar bill she would leave on the counter every time she left for a bender because, even when she abandoned me for the drugs, she wanted me to eat. About the way she looked when my stepfather lay dying on the floor, both pleading and resigned.

My hand can hardly keep up with demand, and soon enough, half the book is full. I read a few snippets to Grayson one day in bed. It feels weird but kind of good too.

"These are amazing," he says.

"You're an easy audience."

He grabs my hair and makes me look him in the eye. "They're fucking amazing."

I smile.

"Remember that intro story you wrote for the journal?" he asks.

I nod.

"It was such bullshit," he says.

"What?" I give him a punch in his non-wounded shoulder, and he grabs my wrist and flips me over, pinning me under him.

"Total bullshit. Some shit about college class."

I look up at him, feeling so perfectly helpless and enclosed. I think I'll never get sick of him. "The journal was for the prisoners."

A smile quirks his lips. "What do you think you are? I'm keeping you here. You can't leave."

He's just smug enough to make me hate him sometimes. But he's right about one thing. I'm one of them. Not only because I'm here, with Grayson. I was in jail too, even if Grayson busted me out on transport.

"It was a bullshit vignette," he continues, goading me. "You make all of us spill our guts, and you write about not being able to decide what to wear to class?"

"Excuse me," I say. I'm annoyed because I know he's right.

"You should change it."

"What? It's already published. It's on the site. I can't

just go in and change it. Even if I wanted to, I don't have the passwords."

"Knox could crack into it."

"You're serious?"

"It's a rush to have a piece up there—a real piece, I mean," he says, "I think it's always been leading to this. You teaching that memoir class. You didn't just show up to teach us. You needed to learn how to do it, from us."

Smug.

I don't hate him though. I love him. And I kind of love the idea.

"You want to do it," he says. "I can tell."

It's more than wanting to. It's like I've always needed to tell my story, just like those inmates needed to. But I could never open up to anyone. Only when I got taken hostage at gunpoint did the story start to spill out.

But that was only Grayson. This would be public. I pick up the book he gave me. "I'd have to choose one of the things I wrote in here. And make it nice."

"So do it."

The idea grows on me over the following days. Knox even gets me the password—he can do things like that. Right after they grabbed me from the transport, he made it so I could email Esther to let her know I was okay without it being traceable. Maybe if I change my story in the journal to be an honest and raw one like the guys, I'll have him help me email her again. Anonymously, so no one can track me.

The problem is my piece, finding just the right nugget to polish. One seems too rambly, another is just wrong. One feels too painful, another not true enough. None are right. I don't know why I can't find one. Maybe I'm scared.

Weeks go by, and I'm at my desk in front of the window, having put aside another vignette, when Grayson comes in. There's this look in his eye, and I know I'm in for it. He's a force of nature, a tornado, and I'm about to get swept away.

"It's been six weeks," he says, his voice deceptively calm.

"I know; I know." I've been stalling.

With rough, possessive movements, he takes my hair out of its bun. My heart races as he pushes it over my shoulder. I close my eyes and let him arrange me how he likes. He gets horny when I do anything that looks academic.

I have new glasses on. I should've taken them off when I heard him coming. I'm trying to work.

"I don't understand how you can be taking so long," he growls.

I swallow. I don't either.

"You filled all those pages, and you can't use anything?"

"None of it seems right."

He twists his hand in my hair.

"Don't," I say.

"Don't what?" With an evil gleam in his eye, he hauls me up from my keyboard. It hurts.

"I need to work on it," I whisper, knowing that's exactly the wrong thing to say. I've been working on it, but I'm not finishing it.

He pushes me into the wall. The air thumps out of me. He watches my eyes as he trails his fingers down my neck, my throat, controlling even my gaze.

"Please," I say as he nuzzles my neck with his stubbly chin, hard enough to leave marks.

"I think you're hiding up here. You don't get to hide with me," he rasps, pulling up my shirt.

"I'm not hiding," I say, trying to wriggle out of his grip, knowing I sort of am. I can't let him take me over. I'm pleading now. "I have to do this. I have to work."

"If you were working, you'd be done. Why is it taking you forever for something us guys did in a few weeks?"

"I don't know!" I wouldn't have let them get away with excuses—and he's not letting me either.

He pulls away and eyes me suspiciously. Then he pins my wrists above my head with one hand and just rips off my shirt, baring my breasts to the cool breeze. I feel way too exposed, way too vulnerable.

I close my eyes, heart pounding. "Grayson."

He palms my breast, moving against me, hot breath on my neck. I stay stiff, but he doesn't care. He presses his fingers down into my waistband, finding my clit. Forcing me to feel his finger, rubbing relentlessly.

"Grayson," I plead, starting to melt into him.

"I have to fuck you," he grates.

Yes.

I pant as he turns me around. I cling to the corner table just to keep myself up. He shoves his hand under my skirt.

My panties are satin and lace, a sugary confection from the large drawer. The panties and bras and lingerie arrive in hordes to our anonymous post office box. Grayson and his tribe are very inventive criminals and never seem to want for money, though I don't know where he gets the time to order it all. There's almost been something new to wear each day. I guess when I said he should have nice things, he took it to heart.

I'm his nice thing, his possession, and he dresses me up in every color and style and fabric he can find.

He pulls my panties down my legs and tosses the expensive scrap of fabric onto the bare wooden floor and slides his fingers along the wetness waiting for him.

Chapter Forty-Four
~Grayson~

I KNOW SHE'S working on changing her piece in the journal. I know I should leave her alone, but I can't. I have to fuck her. This is how it is between us. She's mine to do what I want with, and I can't leave her alone.

Can't stop fucking her.

But it's more than that—seeing her in her library room so worried and wound up, she reminded me of the girl I saw in the prison waiting room that day, and it felt all wrong in my gut. Not beautiful and smart like I know she is, but timid. Too composed. Hiding from everything like she isn't worth anything. Like she can't let people see her.

If I was a good man, I'd let her hide. I'd let her look out the window while I fucked her, the view pretty and vacant. Her skirt is flipped up, exposing her bare ass. I could jack myself off inside her cunt and then let her get back to her journal. But I'm not a good man, and I'm not going to let her hide.

It doesn't matter that she'd rather look at the sky so

she wouldn't have to face me. I flip her over against the desk—I want to see her eyes when I take her. She's my sky, and I'll watch her as I come.

She fights against me a little, and I grip her hard. I touch her the way that makes her boneless.

"Grayson…" Her breath speeds up, and her eyes fill with desire behind her glasses.

That look brings me to my knees. I kneel and press a kiss in the center of her cunt, right where it's open and wet. She sucks in a breath. I know she wants more, but she won't ask for it. I slide my tongue through her folds, learning the shape of her like I do every time. She shudders beneath me, quivering on the tip of my tongue.

Until I lick her clit. Then her whole body goes rigid. She moans something like my name. So I lick her again, and again, until I hear her clearly. *Grayson, please. Grayson, please.*

"What do you need, baby?"

She makes a sound like a tortured animal. I nip at her clit with the front edge of my teeth. She had to know this was coming, but she still cries out in surprise.

She likes me to nip her, to bite her, to hurt her a little—to make her feel. Her mom ignored and neglected her, but I'm the opposite; I can never get enough of her, and she knows it. Her cries echo through the room, through the open window, through the neighborhood of wrecked, unruly buildings.

My dick is hard, punching through denim. I pull myself free and clamp down on her thighs, positioning her, controlling her. I always move her body just how I want it, so I can fuck her how I want to. I used to hate when she called me a caveman, but not anymore. Yeah, I dragged her by her hair into my cave, and I'm not letting her go. I plunge inside—and fuck, yeah, it's sweet relief.

She pulses around me, reeling from the intensity.

She whimpers. "Grayson…"

Blood thunders in my ears as I suck air through my nostrils. It's all too much, and the only way I can bring myself back down is to lick and suck and bite at her breasts, leaving them pink.

"More," she grates out.

I shake my head with her nipple still caught lightly between my teeth. I'm holding on like an animal with its prey. She can never get free from me. And she can never hide from me, not in her journal or her books. Not anywhere.

My balls draw up. I'm seconds away from coming. I won't be able to hold back, so I make the most of it. I grasp her hips and she wraps her legs around me. Then I lift and rock her hips in both my hands, jacking myself off with her cunt in the coldest, rudest way possible.

She's spasming around me. Her cunt is milking my dick. Her arms are clawing me, holding me tight. Even her mouth has latched on to the skin at my neck, sucking me—and I'm not even sure she knows it. She's a feral thing in my arms, drawing me into her pleasure, drowning me in it. I shout as my cock releases into her, mixing with her wetness. I grasp her ass even tighter and use her body to wring the last drops of come and pleasure from my body.

I collapse over her, planting sloppy kisses on her neck, her ear. Then I pull myself up and look down at her.

She hated me once, but it's not hate I see in her eyes now. Not even fear.

It's love.

I don't deserve her love, but I have it anyway. I don't deserve her at all, but she's mine. Beautiful, smart. And so fucking strong.

It's like the universe gave her to me to make up for all the other shit. And I think if I had to go through it again, knowing she'd be there at the end, she'd be my prize, I'd do it. I'd do anything to have her look at me that way.

My breathing slows. "I know you're trying to figure out your piece for the journal. But I had to fuck you." The simple truth.

She sits up and shoves her hand in my hair, looking at me with those brown eyes. "I know."

"I don't want to stop you from finishing."

Her gaze softens. "It's okay. I know the piece I'll put

in now."

"You were thinking about the journal while I was fucking you?"

Her smile is a little wicked. Full of fire. My favorite kind of smile on her. "Just a tiny bit."

Her glasses are still on. Sometimes I like to take them away. Sometimes I like to break them, and we have to get new ones. But other times I like her to wear them. They're tilted after what we just did. I straighten them, the same way I arrange her hair and her body. I like moving her around. I like touching her. "Which piece?"

"This part I wrote of us in the car, right after the break out, when you touched my cheek. You touched me because you wanted to. Because you could."

"Always," I say.

"That's the one I'll put in. The day you escaped."

I feel her words on my skin, touching every nerve ending, lighting me up. "The day I made you mine."

"I escaped that day too. I just didn't know it yet." She smiles. "Look at you all hot on the journal."

I trace the line of her jaw with my knuckle. I've never let a person this close before, where what they want and need is more important than anything. It's scary sometimes, how deep I feel that. "Remember what you said? When a person tells their story, it helps to heal them. To make them whole."

She raises her eyebrows. "And right after, you said

that some people can never be healed," she teases. "Can never be whole."

"Maybe I was wrong. Not about the healing part, but a person can always be made whole. I know that for a fact. I know it personally."

She looks up at me now, caught by the seriousness of my tone. She knows I'm not talking about stories anymore, just like she knows she's mine. Just like she knows I'll always protect her, even as we move to take down bigger assholes than the governor.

She shifts around and snuggles against my chest. I wrap my arms around her like a wall against the world.

~THE END~

THANK YOU for reading PRISONER! We hope you love Abby and Grayson's story. If you haven't read Stone and Brooke's book yet, read *HOSTAGE* now, available at *Amazon.com, BarnesAndNoble.com, iBooks, and other book retailers.*

Want more dangerous romance from Skye Warren? SIGN UP for her newsletter at www.skyewarren.com/newsletter

Want more sexy romance from Annika Martin? SIGN UP for her newsletter at www.annikamartinbooks.com/newsletter

The price of survival... Don't miss Skye Warren's bestselling Endgame series, starting with the critically acclaimed THE PAWN. Gabriel Miller swept into my life like a storm.

> *"Edgy, provocative and deeply erotic, The Pawn is one of my top reads of the year! Skye Warren brings you a sensual battle of wills guaranteed to leave you gasping by the end."*

– New York Times bestselling author
Elle Kennedy

He's a devil in Armani...and he'll do what it takes to reunite his long-lost brothers—even kidnap his enemy's daughter. Grab DARK MAFIA PRINCE.

> *"Twisted, sexy and dark—Dark Mafia Prince is everything I love in a stay-up-all-night-can't-put-it-down read!"*
>
> ~author M. O'Keefe

❖ ❖ ❖

You are warmly invited to join our Facebook groups, Skye Warren's Dark Room and the Annika Martin Fabulous Gang, for exclusive giveaways and sneak peeks of future books.

❖ ❖ ❖

Turn the page for a sneak peek of HOSTAGE, Stone & Brooke's story....

Sneak peek of Hostage
by Skye Warren & Annika Martin
~Stone~

"YOU NEED SOMETHING to eat," I say. "That's your problem."

She gives me this incredulous look. "That's my problem? Really?"

"It sucks to be hungry. That's all I'm saying."

"It does," she says.

"You should eat."

"Got any fries?" And then she laughs. It's the way you laugh when things are fucked up beyond belief.

There's this buzzing in my head. I'm staring at her like an idiot because she's beautiful when she laughs. Her laugh, her smile, it all gets me by the throat. And the exit to Big Moosehorn River is up ahead, but I pass it by.

Her laughter turns into sniffles and sobs. She leans her head against the passenger-side window. Hopeless.

"We're gonna get you something to eat," I say. "There's a Burger Benny up at the next exit. Okay?"

"Okay," she whispers, trancelike.

I'll feed her before I kill her. It's the most messed-up thing I've done in a long time.

I shove a caterer's cap low over my head as I pull up behind the truck in the drive-through line. "I don't have to tell you to act right when we go through here, do I? Do I need to remind you how many people will die if you don't act right?"

She just watches me with this wounded, piercing look that's a little bit hot. Her light brown eyes shine with tears.

Doesn't matter how wide and brown her fucking eyes are, though. "Tell me you get it."

"I get it."

I stare at the lit-up menu. You'd think I've never ordered a fucking hamburger before. There was a time I hadn't. I didn't grow up with goddamn Happy Meals. The first time I experienced a drive-through, I was fifteen and fresh out of the basement after six years. Fresh from our violent escape.

I mostly remember the strangeness of it. How tinny and mechanical the voice on the other end of the machine sounded. Like a robot or something, rushing me to pick. Like a fist around my throat.

"Burger combo," I say because the fist never really eased up. Because she should know how it feels, taking what you can get. That's all she's doing now—taking what she gets.

"Would you like a drink with that?" the voice asks.

I consider asking what she wants, but that feels too personal. What kind of soda does she drink? Or maybe she's too rich and fancy to drink soda.

"Two colas. Anything," I say into the speaker, and then I drive forward before I get the total.

"Don't I get to pick my last meal?" she asks, real quiet. She's looking straight ahead, her face in profile.

I study her nose and her chin, the slope of her neck. I suddenly want to know what she smells like up close. I want to press my face into the vulnerable skin of her neck and breathe deep.

My body gets hot just thinking about it, and I hate that. I hate that feeling that rushes through me, that thickness in my dick. I hate that she makes me feel this way.

There's a part of me that wants to tell her this isn't her last meal, but I won't do that. And anyway, she should find out what it's like to scarf down what's in front of you, knowing there might not be more. Knowing you might not be alive even if there is. I want her to understand where I'm coming from.

"You want to die hungry, die hungry," I say.

The window slides open, and some punk kid reads the total without even looking up. I dig the cash out of my wallet and hand it over.

It's when he's passing back the change that he sees

her. His eyes fasten on her tits, pushed together by that fussy dress.

"Ketchup?" he asks, voice pitched high.

"Yeah," I growl because I don't like the way this horndog's looking at her. She's just a fucking kid. And she's in the passenger seat of my van. Mine.

Mine. The word comes out of nowhere, but it's true.

She stays quiet, staring ahead. She might as well be a mannequin in a store window. All except for the tear tracks shining in the moonlight.

I grab the food and drinks when the punk hands them out, shove the stuff into her hands, and pull away. No one else gets to see her. It was stupid letting anyone see her, linking us together—a fucking witness. She knows I killed Madsen, and now that punk saw me with her, a daisy chain that leads to me in jail.

Even so, even knowing how dangerous she is, I'm mostly mad that another guy checked her out.

The van bounces on the speed bump, and she lets out a small sound of alarm, clutching the bag like it's a damn roller-coaster bar. And then we're on the freeway, heading back to the Big Moosehorn Park exit.

The ride smoothes out. "Open it," I tell her.

Paper crinkles as she unpacks the food and holds it out like I might take it from her. Her hand looks small, especially holding the big wrapped burger. And she's trembling.

Fuck. What am I doing with her? Why isn't she dead?

"Eat it," I tell her. I'm ruining her. That's what I'm doing with her.

Her life was charmed—a pretty little rich girl at her sweet-sixteen party. Then she got a glimpse of me. Now she's facing death or whatever the fuck I want to do to her. Which is a lot.

She's this pure thing in my control, and I want to devour her. I want to press my face to those pushed-up tits above the edge of that dress and fuck her hard and fast.

Skin smooth and pretty like an egg.

But here's the thing about an egg: when you break it, you get everything you want, but then it's not smooth or perfect anymore. It's just this dead thing.

This is something I know a fuck of a lot about, let's just say.

And yeah, you can put yourself back together, but you're never right afterward, not really. You're cracked and misshapen and definitely not smooth and nice like this girl.

There should be some smooth and nice things left in this world.

"I'm not—" Her voice cracks. "—hungry."

I know she's thinking about what I said, about her dying hungry. Maybe she'd rather go that way, all focused on it. People like to think they'd be prepared for death. They don't want to be caught off guard. Me, I've always been the opposite. There's no honor in death, no clean way to go. It's always messy. Always painful.

Catch me by fucking surprise. Fight me.

I think it at her, as if she can hear. As if she'll suddenly learn how to use my gun, to take it from me. But she can't. She's completely defenseless.

"Did I ask what you want to do?" I say, nice and soft. "Open the wrapper and eat."

I only get to see the flash of her eyes, the light of anger, before she looks down. She puts the burger in her lap—I imagine it warming the tops of her thighs. She unfolds the paper slow—a small act of defiance.

It gets me hard, the way she's fighting with the only weapons she has. The way her small hands fold around the messy burger and pick it up.

The way her mouth opens wide.

Want to read more? HOSTAGE is available at Amazon.com, BarnesAndNoble.com, iBooks, and other book retailers.

Turn the page for a sneak peek of THE PAWN, the USA Today bestselling full-length dark contemporary novel about revenge and seduction in the game of love...

SNEAK PEEK OF THE PAWN
BY SKYE WARREN...

WIND WHIPS AROUND my ankles, flapping the bottom of my black trench coat. Beads of moisture form on my eyelashes. In the short walk from the cab to the stoop, my skin has slicked with humidity left by the rain.

Carved vines and ivy leaves decorate the ornate wooden door.

I have some knowledge of antique pieces, but I can't imagine the price tag on this one—especially exposed to the elements and the whims of vandals. I suppose even criminals know enough to leave the Den alone.

Officially the Den is a gentlemen's club, the old-world kind with cigars and private invitations. Unofficially it's a collection of the most powerful men in Tanglewood. Dangerous men. Criminals, even if they wear a suit while breaking the law.

A heavy brass knocker in the shape of a fierce lion warns away any visitors. I'm desperate enough to ignore that warning. My heart thuds in my chest and expands out, pulsing in my fingers, my toes. Blood rushes through my ears, drowning out the whoosh of traffic behind me.

I grasp the thick ring and knock—once, twice.

Part of me fears what will happen to me behind that door. A bigger part of me is afraid the door won't open at all. I can't see any cameras set into the concrete enclave, but they have to be watching. Will they recognize me? I'm not sure it would help if they did. Probably best that they see only a desperate girl, because that's all I am now.

The softest scrape comes from the door. Then it opens.

I'm struck by his eyes, a deep amber color—like expensive brandy and almost translucent. My breath catches in my throat, lips frozen against words like *please* and *help*. Instinctively I know they won't work; this isn't a man given to mercy. The tailored cut of his shirt, its sleeves carelessly rolled up, tells me he'll extract a price. One I can't afford to pay.

There should have been a servant, I thought. A butler. Isn't that what fancy gentlemen's clubs have? Or maybe some kind of a security guard. Even our house had a housekeeper answer the door—at least, before. Before we fell from grace.

Before my world fell apart.

The man makes no move to speak, to invite me in or

turn me away. Instead he stares at me with vague curiosity, with a trace of pity, the way one might watch an animal in the zoo. That might be how the whole world looks to these men, who have more money than God, more power than the president.

That might be how I looked at the world, before.

My throat feels tight, as if my body fights this move, even while my mind knows it's the only option. "I need to speak with Damon Scott."

Scott is the most notorious loan shark in the city. He deals with large sums of money, and nothing less will get me through this. We have been introduced, and he left polite society by the time I was old enough to attend events regularly. There were whispers, even then, about the young man with ambition. Back then he had ties to the underworld—and now he's its king.

One thick eyebrow rises. "What do you want with him?"

A sense of familiarity fills the space between us even though I know we haven't met. This man is a stranger, but he looks at me as if he wants to know me. He looks at me as if he already does. There's an intensity to his eyes when they sweep over my face, as firm and as telling as a touch.

"I need…" My heart thuds as I think about all the things I need—a rewind button. One person in the city who doesn't hate me by name alone. "I need a loan."

He gives me a slow perusal, from the nervous slide of my tongue along my lips to the high neckline of my clothes. I tried to dress professionally—a black cowl-necked sweater and pencil skirt. His strange amber gaze unbuttons my coat, pulls away the expensive cotton, tears off the fabric of my bra and panties. He sees right through me, and I shiver as a ripple of awareness runs over my skin.

I've met a million men in my life. Shaken hands. Smiled. I've never felt as seen through as I do right now. Never felt like someone has turned me inside out, every dark secret exposed to the harsh light. He sees my weaknesses, and from the cruel set of his mouth, he likes them.

His lids lower. "And what do you have for collateral?"

Nothing except my word. That wouldn't be worth anything if he knew my name. I swallow past the lump in my throat. "I don't know."

Nothing.

He takes a step forward, and suddenly I'm crowded against the brick wall beside the door, his large body blocking out the warm light from inside. He feels like a furnace in front of me, the heat of him in sharp contrast to the cold brick at my back. "What's your name, girl?"

The word *girl* is a slap in the face. I force myself not to flinch, but it's hard. Everything about him overwhelms me—his size, his low voice. "I'll tell Mr. Scott my name."

In the shadowed space between us, his smile spreads, white and taunting. The pleasure that lights his strange yellow eyes is almost sensual, as if I caressed him. "You'll have to get past me."

My heart thuds. He likes that I'm challenging him, and God, that's even worse. What if I've already failed? I'm free-falling, tumbling, turning over without a single hope to anchor me. Where will I go if he turns me away? What will happen to my father?

"Let me go," I whisper, but my hope fades fast.

His eyes flash with warning. "Little Avery James, all grown up."

A small gasp resounds in the space between us. He already knows my name. That means he knows who my father is. He knows what he's done. Denials rush to my throat, pleas for understanding. The hard set of his eyes, the broad strength of his shoulders tells me I won't find any mercy here.

I square my shoulders. I'm desperate but not broken. "If you know my name, you know I have friends in high places. Connections. A history in this city. That has to be worth something. That's my collateral."

Those connections might not even take my call, but I have to try something. I don't know if it will be enough for a loan or even to get me through the door. Even so, a faint feeling of family pride rushes over my skin. Even if he turns me away, I'll hold my head high.

Golden eyes study me. Something about the way he said *little Avery James* felt familiar, but I've never seen this man. At least I don't think we've met. Something about the otherworldly glow of those eyes whispers to me, like a melody I've heard before.

On his driver's license it probably says something mundane, like brown. But that word can never encompass the way his eyes seem almost luminous, orbs of amber that hold the secrets of the universe. *Brown* can never describe the deep golden hue of them, the indelible opulence in his fierce gaze.

"Follow me," he says.

Relief courses through me, flooding numb limbs, waking me up enough that I wonder what I'm doing here. These aren't men, they're animals. They're predators, and I'm prey. Why would I willingly walk inside?

What other choice do I have?

I step over the veined marble threshold.

The man closes the door behind me, shutting out the rain and the traffic, the entire city disappeared in one soft turn of the lock. Without another word he walks down the hall, deeper into the shadows. I hurry to follow him, my chin held high, shoulders back, for all the world as if I were an invited guest. Is this how the gazelle feels when she runs over the plains, a study in grace, poised for her slaughter?

The entire world goes black behind the staircase, only breath, only bodies in the dark. Then he opens another thick wooden door, revealing a dimly lit room of cherrywood and cut crystal, of leather and smoke. Barely I see dark eyes, dark suits. Dark men.

I have the sudden urge to hide behind the man with the golden eyes. He's wide and tall, with hands that could wrap around my waist. He's a giant of a man, rough-hewn and hard as stone.

Except he's not here to protect me.

He could be the most dangerous of all.

Want to read more? THE PAWN is available at Amazon.com, BarnesAndNoble.com, iBooks, and other book retailers.

And turn the page for a sneak peek of Dark Mafia Prince...

SNEAK PEEK OF
DARK MAFIA PRINCE
BY ANNIKA MARTIN

I PLEAD REPEATEDLY for news of my father, if only to know he's still alive. My captor just texts.

A crash from inside our mansion. They're wrecking the place.

"This is pointless." When he doesn't acknowledge me, I grab his wrist. "What does this get you? Come on!"

He looks at my hand and then looks up at me. For a moment I think he, too, senses the weird familiarity between us. Like we know each other from another life. He drops his phone in his pocket and takes my wrists. "You need to stop focusing on your beautiful life in there and start praying that Daddy decides to come through."

"Ow," I breathe.

"Good. That's you getting with the program. I'll do whatever I have to do to get my brother back. Do I want to hurt you? No. I don't. Will I?"

My heart races.

"Will I?"

"I get it," I whisper.

His grip is too tight, his gaze too intense, like he sees everything inside me. People rarely look too hard at me. When they look at me at all, they accept the version of me I serve up to them. The shopaholic Mafia princess. The dedicated lawyer in glasses.

"Dad's innocent. He'd tell you if he knew anything else."

"Wrong, Kitten. *Dad's* playing the odds."

A ping sounds. He lets me go and pulls his phone out of his pocket. A twenty-first century general waging battle.

Whatever the person on the other ends has texted him, it troubles him.

That's my chance—I take off running, tearing for the main road.

I get maybe ten feet when guys seem to materialize around me, taking me by the shoulders. I twist and fight. They lift me right off the ground, practically carry me back.

The strangely familiar intruder is still on the phone, eyeing me with that intensity, watching me struggle. A model between photo shoots if you didn't know any better.

They put me back in front of him. He lowers the phone and addresses me quietly. "Do it. Go ahead, Mimi, do it again. See what happens."

Mimi.

He blinks, waiting. "Do it, go for it."

Mimi. Only one person ever called me Mimi—Aleksio Dragusha. My childhood friend. But Aleksio and his family were slaughtered by a rival clan back when we were kids. I was wild with grief. They had to sedate me.

Five caskets lowered into the ground. Three small, two large.

I focus on the familiar freckle on his cheekbone. This man is so much bigger. So much harder and meaner. But his freckle...his eyes... "Aleksio?" I say in a small voice.

"Ding ding ding, we have a winner." He says it off-handedly, keeping his eyes fixed on the mansion with its majestic stone wings. The house where he once lived. Prince of a mafia empire.

"Oh my God. Aleksio!"

Still he won't look at me.

"We thought you were dead. We buried you."

"You buried a few rocks. Maybe some boiled cabbages, who knows."

I can't believe he's being so...flip. "Aleksio! We buried you." I'm repeating myself. "I thought they killed you..." If my life were postcards on a bulletin board, the image of Aleksio Dragusha's casket being covered up with dirt would be central, affecting everything around it. He was my best friend. I doubt I was his. Aleksio had lots of friends. Everybody loved Aleksio. Back when he was a boy, anyway.

He focuses on his phone, running his soldiers.

"We went to your funeral. It was so, so..." *Sad* isn't the word. *Sad* barely touches it. We were adventurers together, bonded together, carving out a sunny niche inside a world of darkness and secrets we sensed but didn't understand. I think that's what made us friends— the feeling of being refugees at the edges of something evil.

"Aleksio, you're being crazy!"

"You need to stop thinking you know me." He lowers his voice to a threatening tone. "You knew me once, but I promise, you don't know me anymore."

Want to read more? DARK MAFIA PRINCE is available at Amazon.com, BarnesAndNoble.com, iBooks, and other book retailers.

ALSO BY
SKYE WARREN

Endgame Trilogy & Masterpiece Duet
The Pawn
The Knight
The Castle
The King
The Queen

Underground Series
Rough Hard Fierce
Wild Dirty Secret
Sweet
Deep

Stripped Series
Tough Love
Love the Way You Lie
Better When It Hurts
Even Better
Pretty When You Cry
Caught for Christmas
Hold You Against Me
To the Ends of the Earth

Criminals and Captives standalones
Prisoner

Hostage

Standalone Dark Romance
Wanderlust
On the Way Home
His for Christmas
Hear Me
Take the Heat

Find a complete Skye Warren book list, along with
boxed sets, audiobooks, and print listings at
www.skyewarren.com/books

ALSO BY ANNIKA MARTIN (AKA CAROLYN CRANE)

Dangerous Royals
Dark Mafia Prince
Wicked Mafia Prince
Savage Mafia Prince

Criminals & Captives standalones
Prisoner
Hostage

Romantic Suspense
Against the Dark
Off the Edge
Into the Shadows
Behind the Mask

MM Spies
Enemies like You

Romantic Comedy
Most Eligible Bastard

About Skye Warren

Skye Warren is the New York Times bestselling author of contemporary romance such as the Chicago Underground and Stripped series. Her books have been featured in Jezebel, Buzzfeed, USA Today Happily Ever After, Glamour, and Elle Magazine. She makes her home in Texas with her loving family, two sweet dogs, and one evil cat.

Sign up for Skye's newsletter:
www.skyewarren.com/newsletter

Like Skye Warren on Facebook:
facebook.com/skyewarren

Join Skye Warren's Dark Room reader group:
skyewarren.com/darkroom

Follow Skye Warren on Instagram:
instagram.com/skyewarrenbooks

Visit Skye's website for her current booklist:
www.skyewarren.com

ABOUT ANNIKA MARTIN

Annika Martin (aka Carolyn Crane) loves dirty stories, hot heroes, and wild, dramatic everything. She enjoys hanging out in Minneapolis coffee shops with her writer husband and can sometimes be found birdwatching at her birdfeeder alongside her two stunningly photogenic cats. A NYT bestselling author, she has also written as RITA award-winning author Carolyn Crane.

Sign up for Annika's newsletter:
annikamartinbooks.com/newletter

Like Annika on Facebook:
www.facebook.com/AnnikaMartinBooks

Join the Annika Martin Fabulous Gang:
www.facebook.com/groups/AnnikaMartinFabulousGang
/

Follow Annika Martin on Instagram:
instagram.com/annikamartinauthor

Visit Annika's website:
www.annikamartinbooks.com